The Gnomes Grand Tour

By Mary Shay

Dedication

This book is dedicated to all the little adventurers, both big and small, who dare to dream big, explore the unknown, and find wonder in the most unexpected places. To those who believe in the magic of tiny things and the boundless possibilities of a world seen from a different perspective.

To every child who has ever felt lost, alone, or afraid but found the courage to step outside their comfort zone and embrace the unknown, this story is for you. May it remind you that even the smallest of creatures can embark on the greatest of adventures, and that the most thrilling journeys often begin with a simple step into the unknown.

This whimsical tale is a tribute to the spirit of exploration that burns bright within each of us. To the curiosity that drives us to discover new horizons, to the resilience that helps us overcome challenges, and to the unwavering belief in the magic that surrounds us, if only we take the time to notice it.

This book is for the dreamers, the wanderers, the curious souls who find joy in the unexpected turns of life's journey. May Barnaby Button's incredible adventures inspire you to find your path, to forge your own unique experiences, and to cherish the memories created along the way.

It is also dedicated to the unsung heroes of everyday life, the quiet souls who work behind the scenes, ensuring that the world continues to spin smoothly and beautifully. The unseen hands that craft intricate details, the hearts that nurture growth and encourage exploration, the minds that dream up new possibilities – this story is a tribute to their quiet dedication and enduring impact on the world.

This dedication is for those who believe in the power of stories to carry us away, to ignite our spirits, and to reveal the beauty woven into both the ordinary and the extraordinary. May the magic of Barnaby Button's travels ignite your imagination, encourage your creativity, and deepen your appreciation for the wonders that fill our world.

Finally, this book is dedicated to the enduring power of friendship, the bonds that connect us, the support that lifts us, and the shared adventures that create lasting memories. May the friendships Barnaby makes along his incredible journey remind us all of the importance of connection, empathy, and celebrating life's adventures together. For in the end, it is these connections that truly enrich our lives and make our adventures all the more meaningful.

Table of Contents

Chapter 1:

The Great Gnome Napping

Barnaby Button lived in a cozy gnome garden, a miniature Eden tucked away in the heart of a sprawling English meadow. Towering sunflowers, their faces turned perpetually towards the sun, cast long shadows over plump strawberries, their crimson jewels glistening with morning dew. Sweet peas, in a riot of pastel colors, tumbled over quaint little fences, weaving a fragrant tapestry around Barnaby's humble abode, a mushroom cap meticulously cleaned and decorated with tiny wildflowers. It was, to put it mildly, idyllic.

Barnaby himself was a gnome of impeccable taste and considerable charm. His beard, a wisp of spun gold, reached almost to his neatly-buttoned waistcoat, a miniature masterpiece stitched with threads of the finest dandelion fluff. His spectacles, perched precariously on his button nose (a truly remarkable resemblance to a button, hence his name), magnified the world around him, revealing the intricate beauty in a single dewdrop or the delicate veins of a butterfly's wing.

His days unfolded with the gentle rhythm of nature. He tended his miniature vegetable patch, carefully coaxing forth plump carrots and vibrant tomatoes from the rich earth. He collected dewdrops in tiny teacups, each one a miniature jewel reflecting the morning sun. He'd spend hours chatting with the bees, their fuzzy bodies dusted with golden pollen, listening to their industrious hum as they flitted from bloom to bloom. The rustling of leaves in the gentle breeze was a comforting lullaby, the soft chirping of crickets a soothing evening serenade. Life in Barnaby's tranquil garden was a symphony of soft sounds and vivid colors.

He knew every inch of his garden, every blade of grass, every pebble nestled amongst the roots of the ancient oak tree. He knew the secret hiding places of the ladybugs, the preferred sunbathing spots of the grasshoppers, and the best places to find the juiciest wild berries. His garden was his world, a perfect haven of tranquility and contentment. He felt utterly and completely at home, surrounded by the familiar comfort of his little patch of paradise. He often mused that even the most grandest castle couldn't offer the peace and joy that his little garden offered him. It was a magical place, full of secrets and wonders, known only to him and the creatures that shared his quiet world.

His evenings were particularly special. As the sun dipped below the horizon, painting the sky in hues of fiery orange and soft lavender, Barnaby would settle down amidst the sweet peas, a steaming cup of dandelion tea warming his tiny hands. He would watch the fireflies dance their nightly ballet, their tiny lights twinkling like stars fallen to earth. These were his moments of pure bliss, the culmination of a day spent in harmony with nature.

One such evening, as Barnaby savored a particularly sweet wild berry – a plump, juicy specimen that had ripened to perfection – he felt a strange sensation. It wasn't a jolt or a shock, but a gentle tug, a subtle shift in the very fabric of his being. It felt as if an invisible hand had reached out, not to grasp him forcefully, but to guide him with surprising delicacy. It was a sensation of being lifted, not against his will, but with a strange sense of inevitability, as if this was something that had been destined to happen.

The tug grew stronger, and Barnaby felt himself rising above his beloved garden. The sunflowers, once towering giants, shrank to the size of daisies. The strawberries, once plump and juicy, resembled tiny crimson beads. His little home, the mushroom cap, became a speck of white against the verdant expanse of the meadow. Everything was shrinking, receding, distancing itself from him with an ethereal lightness. It was a breathtaking, if rather disconcerting, experience.

Then, as suddenly as it had begun, the sensation ceased. The world around Barnaby was no longer shrinking, but had become pitch black. He felt himself falling, not with the plummeting terror of a great height, but with the slow, gentle descent of a feather on a silent night. His world had disappeared. His home, his familiar comforts, the sweet scent of the flowers and the hum of the bees - all were gone, swallowed by an enveloping darkness. Fear, sharp and icy, clawed at his tiny heart. He was alone, adrift in a darkness so profound it seemed to press upon him, suffocating him with its weight.

For a moment, utter terror threatened to overwhelm him, but then a strange calmness descended. Perhaps it was shock, or perhaps it was something else entirely, a quiet acceptance of the unknown. He squeezed his eyes shut, the darkness pressing in on him from all sides. He waited, uncertain of what would come next, but resolved to face whatever lay ahead with his usual gnome-like courage and quiet dignity. He held on to the memory of his sweet berry, its sweetness a fleeting reminder of the world he had left behind, a world he hoped, with a fragile flicker of hope, to return to one day. This strange, unexpected journey had just begun, and the fate of Barnaby Button hung suspended in the dark unknown, a speck of courage in the vast expanse of mystery. He waited, breathing slowly, a tiny gnome poised on the precipice of an incredible adventure.

The darkness wasn't a suffocating blackness, but rather a deep, velvety hue, like the inside of a perfectly polished black walnut. It wasn't cold, but strangely comforting, like sinking into a feather bed on a chilly night. He felt a gentle rocking motion, a subtle swaying that lulled him into a state of uneasy calm. There was no sense of falling, only a floating, weightless sensation. Then, as gently as it had arrived, the darkness began to lift, giving way to the faintest glimmer of light—a soft, ethereal glow that seemed to emanate from...somewhere.

The light grew stronger, and Barnaby opened his eyes, blinking in the sudden shift from absolute darkness to a muted luminescence. He found himself nestled within something soft and yielding, something that smelled faintly of pine needles and woodsmoke – a comforting, almost familiar scent. He was lying in a small, dark box, lined with a plush, velvet-like material, the texture surprisingly soft against his skin. The box itself seemed to be made of dark, polished wood, its surface smooth and cool to the touch. It was completely dark inside, except for the faint, diffused light that somehow managed to penetrate the wood.

Panic, sharp and sudden, threatened to overwhelm him. Where was he? How had he gotten here? The sweetness of the wild berry, the last taste of his familiar garden, seemed a lifetime ago, a distant dream. The feeling of being lifted, the strange, gentle tug, the unsettling shrinking of his world – it all felt surreal, like a bizarre, unsettling dream from which he couldn't wake. His heart hammered against his ribs, a frantic drumbeat in the otherwise silent darkness.

He tried to sit up, but his movements were clumsy, disoriented. He felt stiff and a little sore, as if he had been asleep for a very long time. He stretched out his tiny hands, feeling the soft velvet beneath his fingertips. He tentatively touched the sides of the box, its smooth, dark surface cool against his skin. The wood felt strangely polished, almost magical. It was as if it had been crafted by skilled hands, with meticulous care and attention to detail.

He took a deep breath, trying to calm his racing heart. He listened intently, straining his ears to catch any sound. The only sound was his breathing, a rapid, shallow rhythm that mirrored the frantic pounding of his heart. The silence was nearly suffocating, broken only by the faintest whisper of breath as he inhaled and exhaled. The silence made the darkness feel even more profound, an isolating, enveloping blanket that seemed to press in on him from all sides.

He felt utterly and completely alone. The familiar comfort of his garden, the cheerful hum of the bees, the gentle rustling of leaves – all were gone, replaced by a suffocating silence and an all-encompassing darkness. A wave of loneliness washed over him, a cold, chilling feeling that seeped into the very marrow of his bones. He longed for the warmth of his mushroom cap home, for the comforting smell of damp earth and the gentle sway of the sweet peas. He missed the familiar sounds of his garden, the comforting rhythm of nature.

He pressed his face against the soft velvet lining of the box, his eyes closed, trying to conjure up images of his home. He saw the plump strawberries, glistening with dew, the towering sunflowers, their faces turned towards the sun, and the vibrant colors of his little vegetable patch. He smelled the sweet scent of the peas, the earthy fragrance of the soil. He heard the gentle hum of the bees, the rustling of the leaves. These images, these scents, these sounds, were anchors in the storm of his fear and loneliness, tethers connecting him to the life he had left behind.

He opened his eyes again, the faint glimmer of light still illuminating the inside of the box. He felt around the inside of the box once more, his tiny fingers tracing the smooth, dark wood. There was nothing else inside the box with him, just the soft velvet, the polished wood, and the faint, diffused light. He was completely alone, completely isolated, and the weight of this isolation pressed heavily upon him.

Suddenly, he noticed something small and unusual. It was a tiny latch, almost invisible in the darkness, tucked away in the corner of the box. He reached for it, his fingers finding the small metal catch. It was surprisingly intricate, delicately crafted, as if made by a master artisan. With a gentle tug, the latch gave way, and the box lid began to open, revealing a sliver of the outside world.

The sight that greeted him was startling, unexpected. He wasn't in his garden, nor in any place he recognized. He stood in a dimly lit room, its walls lined with shelves holding curious objects, so small and delicate, they seemed almost magical. The air smelled of old books and dried herbs, a pungent yet strangely comforting aroma.

The air seemed to hum with a strange energy, a vibrant, pulsing force that was both thrilling and faintly unsettling. He felt a sense of wonder, of curiosity, but also a deep, gnawing uncertainty about his situation. He was clearly somewhere strange, somewhere extraordinary, and he had no idea how he had gotten there or what awaited him. The adventure, which had begun with a gentle tug and a fall into darkness, was now unfolding before him, a mystery waiting to be solved. The capture, though unexpected, felt less like a kidnapping and more like an invitation into an incredible and unknown world. The next chapter, he suspected, would be even more astounding.

The crack in the box lid was barely wider than a hair, yet it offered a tantalizing glimpse into the world beyond. Barnaby's heart, still a frantic drum against his ribs, thumped a little louder. He peered through the narrow opening, his breath catching in his throat.

What he saw was not what he expected. Gone was the oppressive darkness, the suffocating silence. Instead, there was a room bathed in a soft, diffused light, the kind that seems to emanate from glowing crystals or fireflies trapped in a jar. The walls, he could see, were lined with shelves, not just any shelves, but shelves overflowing with tiny, exquisitely crafted objects. Miniature teacups, so delicate they seemed to tremble in the air, sat nestled next to intricately carved furniture that was no bigger than his hand. Small, leather-bound books with gilded edges lined other shelves, their tiny pages whispering untold stories.

And then he saw them.

Two spirits. Not the kind of spirits you'd see flitting through a summer meadow, these spirits were something else entirely. Their wings were the most captivating thing he'd ever witnessed, shimmering like stained-glass windows, each facet a kaleidoscope of color. One pair shone with the ruby reds and sapphire blues of a sunset, while the other boasted the emerald greens and amethyst purples of a twilight forest. They were perched on a miniature stool, their laughter a delicate chime, a tinkling symphony of bells.

Their movements were quick, their gestures graceful, like tiny dancers in an unseen ballet.

He couldn't quite make out their faces – the crack was too narrow, and the light too dim – but he could sense them. He felt their energy, a playful, almost mischievous current that buzzed in the air. It was unsettling, certainly, to be observed by such creatures, creatures who clearly held him captive. Yet, there was something else too, something…intriguing. Their laughter wasn't cruel; it held a certain lightheartedness, a hint of amusement that didn't quite translate into malice.

They were giggling. Soft, musical giggles that seemed to vibrate the very air around him. As they chattered to each other in a language Barnaby didn't understand, a language that sounded like the rustling of leaves in a gentle breeze, they moved the box. The movement was smooth, almost effortless, as if they were carrying something weightless, a feather drifting on the wind. The box tilted slightly, making Barnaby's stomach lurch.

His first instinct was to shout, to scream for help. To let his voice echo through the miniature world, to alert anyone who might be within earshot. But a wave of fear, cold and paralyzing, washed over him. The spirits were small, yes, but their ethereal beauty held a power that was both captivating and intimidating. Their wings, with their vibrant colors and intricate patterns, seemed to possess an almost otherworldly quality. They seemed powerful, magical, capable of things far beyond Barnaby's comprehension.

He swallowed, his throat dry, his tiny voice caught in his chest. The fear was real, tangible, pressing against him like a physical weight. But alongside the fear, a strange curiosity began to bloom. These spirits, these magical creatures, were undeniably odd, undeniably unexpected. They were certainly not the kind of beings he would have expected to find himself in the company of, particularly under such unsettling circumstances. Yet, despite the fear, he found himself strangely fascinated by them.

He watched, mesmerized, as they continued to move the box, their delicate wings catching the light, painting shimmering rainbows across the miniature room. The room itself was a marvel, a testament to their skill and artistry. Every object, from the tiniest teacup to the smallest book, was crafted with incredible precision, with a level of detail that was breathtaking. It was as if the entire room was a meticulously constructed diorama, a miniature world brimming with detail and charm.

The spirits, oblivious to his silent observation, continued their conversation, their voices still that delightful chime of bells. They hummed a tune, a simple melody that was both haunting and strangely beautiful. Barnaby tried to memorize the tune, hoping it would somehow provide a clue, a key to understanding this bizarre situation. But the melody was as elusive as the spirits themselves, vanishing as quickly as it appeared.

As they carried the box, Barnaby noticed details he'd missed before. The shelves held not only miniature objects but also tiny, exquisitely painted portraits. He caught a glimpse of one – a miniature landscape, vividly rendered, depicting a rolling green hill dotted with tiny sheep. Another seemed to show a bustling market scene, teeming with miniature people going about their daily lives. The details were staggering, the artistry breathtaking.

The box stopped. The spirits set it down gently on a small, intricately carved table. Barnaby held his breath, his eyes fixed on the gap in the lid, his mind racing with a thousand questions. Who were these spirits? What did they want with him? Where had they taken him? And more importantly, what would happen next?

The spirits seemed to be preparing something. He saw them moving small, shimmering vials, their movements precise and deliberate. He caught a glimpse of colorful powders, their hues as vibrant as the jewels in a king's crown. He wondered if they were preparing a potion, a spell, some sort of magical concoction. The thought sent a shiver down his spine.

Suddenly, one of the spirits turned towards the box. Their eyes, now visible through the crack, shone with an unnerving light, a mixture of mischief and something else…something Barnaby couldn't quite decipher. Their gaze seemed to pierce the darkness, finding him in the box. For a moment, their eyes met, and Barnaby felt a jolt, an electric charge that seemed to connect them across the divide.

The spirit smiled, a tiny, almost imperceptible smile. Then, with a graceful wave of their hand, they slipped a small, exquisitely crafted silver key into the lock. The key turned, a delicate click echoing in the silent room. The box lid opened wider, revealing a full view of the magical room and its captivating inhabitants. Barnaby knew, with a sudden certainty, that his unexpected adventure was only just beginning. The next moments, he felt, would hold even more wonder, more mystery, and perhaps, even more danger than he could have ever imagined. The feeling of being kidnapped, replaced by a growing sense of curious anticipation. He braced himself for whatever lay ahead, preparing for whatever the whimsical world of these miniature spirits might bring. The journey had begun, and whether it was orchestrated or not, Barnaby Button was ready to embrace the unknown.

The box lurched and swayed, a dizzying dance that sent Barnaby's stomach into a series of somersaults. It wasn't a smooth ride. The journey felt like a rollercoaster winding through a miniature landscape, a bumpy and unpredictable trek across unfamiliar terrain. He could feel the movement, a constant rocking and tilting, as if the spirits were navigating a winding path, their tiny feet carrying an unexpectedly heavy burden. He tried to peer through the widening crack in the lid, but the darkness beyond was frustratingly opaque, offering only fleeting glimpses of blurred colors and shapes.

He strained his ears, attempting to decipher the snippets of conversation carried on the gentle breeze that seemed to filter through the cracks. It was a high-pitched, melodic language, a symphony of chirps and whistles, punctuated by occasional bursts of laughter that sounded like tiny bells tinkling in the wind. He caught fragments of words, like shimmering jewels plucked from a hidden treasure trove: "miniature," a word that echoed the size of his surroundings, and "photography," a word that conjured images of cameras and lenses much smaller than even his thumb. And then, a word that sparked a flicker of hope in his chest: "adventure."

The word hung in the air, a single, luminous star in the inky blackness of his uncertainty. Adventure. It wasn't the word he would have chosen to describe his current predicament – kidnapped and confined to a tiny box – but it was a word that hinted at possibilities, a word that implied a journey, a quest, maybe even a happy ending. The thought, fragile as a butterfly's wing, fluttered in his heart, gently nudging aside the cold grip of fear.

The box dipped and rose, the movement growing more erratic. Barnaby braced himself, his small hands gripping the sides, his knuckles white. He imagined the spirits navigating a treacherous path, their tiny wings beating furiously, their delicate bodies struggling against some unseen force. He pictured miniature mountains and valleys, miniature forests and rivers, a miniature world teeming with unseen dangers and hidden wonders.

He listened more intently, focusing on the sounds, trying to glean any information he could from the melodic conversation. He caught another word, this one more familiar: "museum." A museum? Could it be? Was this a museum of miniature things? Was he being taken to some sort of secret exhibition, some hidden trove of tiny treasures? The possibility, however unlikely, offered a tantalizing sliver of relief. Perhaps this wasn't a kidnapping after all, but a strange, unexpected invitation to a world he never knew existed.

The swaying continued, relentless and rhythmic, like a lullaby that masked a deeper, more unsettling rhythm. He felt a pang of loneliness, a sharp ache in his chest. He was alone, completely alone, in a tiny box, hurtling through an unknown world. But even in his isolation, the word "adventure" pulsed like a heartbeat, a persistent reminder that this journey, however unsettling, might lead to something unexpected, something extraordinary.

He tried to focus on the positive, on the possibility that this might not be as dire as it seemed. He conjured images of miniature landscapes, of tiny forests bathed in sunlight, of miniature rivers sparkling under a miniature moon. He imagined a world of minuscule creatures, bustling cities constructed from grains of sand, and towering trees carved from acorns. He allowed himself to dream, to escape the confines of the box, to imagine a world of boundless possibility.

The box tilted sharply, throwing him against the wooden sides. He gasped, his breath catching in his throat. He heard a sharp cry, a high-pitched squeak from one of the spirits. Then, silence, a heavy, pregnant silence that stretched on, adding another layer of uncertainty to the already bewildering journey.

The rocking subsided, the box settling into a more even rhythm. The sounds of the spirits' conversation returned, softer now, more subdued. He heard fragments of words, fleeting glimpses into their world: "exposition," "artifact," "exhibition." The words were like pieces of a puzzle, each one offering a small clue, a hint of understanding in this strange, miniature realm. A wave of dizzying nausea passed, replaced by a renewed sense of determination. He would persevere. He would endure. He would discover the truth behind this bewildering adventure.

The journey continued, seemingly endless. The box became a tiny vessel, carrying him through an unseen landscape, a silent ship sailing through a sea of mystery. He closed his eyes, letting the rhythm of the box lull him into a state of uneasy calm. He imagined the spirits, their delicate wings beating tirelessly, guiding him through this unknown world, their purpose still unclear, their motives still veiled in the shadows of mystery.

But even in the depths of his uncertainty, a tiny seed of hope took root. This kidnapping, if it even was a kidnapping, felt different. It lacked the cold, calculated malice he'd expected. There was a whimsical, almost playful quality to it, a strange sense of lightheartedness that hinted at a different kind of story. This was not a tale of terror, but a tale of enchantment, a journey into the heart of a miniature world.

He clung to this thought, letting it sustain him through the endless rocking and swaying. He pictured the tiny spirits, their delicate wings shimmering, their laughter echoing in his ears, like a constant, gentle reassurance that everything would somehow, eventually, turn out alright. He imagined their faces, their eyes twinkling with mischief and wonder, and he felt a surge of strange, unexpected excitement. He was on an adventure, a real adventure, and despite the uncertainty and fear, he was strangely, undeniably, ready for whatever came next. The world beyond the box, no matter how small, beckoned with a promise of magic, a promise of mystery, and a promise of something wonderful that lay just beyond the horizon of his miniature world. The anticipation was almost unbearable. The long journey, however unpredictable, was proving to be unexpectedly thrilling. Barnaby braced himself for the next chapter in this unexpected adventure, his heart filled with a strange mix of fear and exhilarating excitement. He was ready. He had to be.

The stillness was unsettling after the constant rocking. It was as if the world had held its breath, waiting. Barnaby, his senses sharpened by days of confinement, felt the absence of the rhythmic swaying more acutely than he had felt its presence. His stomach, which had performed a non-stop acrobatic routine for what felt like an eternity, finally settled, leaving behind a lingering queasiness. He cautiously shifted his weight, testing the stability of the box. It remained stubbornly still, a silent sentinel in an unseen world.

A strange calmness descended upon him, a counterpoint to the earlier panic. He had been so focused on the movement, on the unpredictable journey, that the sudden stillness had caught him off guard. Now, in this unexpected quiet, a different kind of anxiety took hold – the anxiety of anticipation.

He reached into his pocket, his fingers brushing against the smooth, cool surface of his miniature trowel. The trowel, a tiny replica of the gardening tool he used back in his gnome village, felt strangely comforting in his small hand. It was a connection to his former life, a reminder of home, of a world that now felt impossibly far away.

He felt a flicker of defiance. He wouldn't be a prisoner in this box forever. He would escape. He had to. The thought, once a fragile whisper, had grown into a strong, insistent voice within him.

He cautiously examined the lid of the box. The crack he'd noticed earlier had widened slightly, perhaps from the strain of the journey. It wasn't much, just a sliver of an opening, but it was enough. Enough to give him hope.

He pressed his tiny trowel against the crack, working it carefully, using the small wooden handle as leverage. The wood creaked softly, a sound that filled the silent box with an almost unbearable tension. He worked with quiet precision and patience, each delicate movement a step closer to freedom. He felt the wood give way, the crack widening ever so slightly. He could almost taste freedom.

He worked for what felt like hours, the tension in the box palpable, mirrored by the tension in his small body. His breath came in short, shallow gasps, each breath a testament to his determination. Finally, with one last, determined push, the wood splintered, and the crack expanded to a small but significant opening.

A shaft of sunlight, bright and warm, sliced through the darkness, illuminating the inside of the box. Barnaby squinted, his eyes adjusting to the sudden change in light. He could see, beyond the tiny gap, a sliver of daylight, a glimpse of the world beyond his prison.

He felt a surge of exhilaration, a rush of pure, unadulterated joy. He had done it. He had created an opening, a pathway to freedom. He breathed deeply, savoring the fresh air that filtered through the crack, a scent of earth and something else–something sweet and floral, a hint of wildflowers.

He peered through the widening gap, his heart pounding in his chest like a drum. He saw a patch of vibrant green grass, dotted with wildflowers of impossible colors. A small, winding path snaked its way through the grass, disappearing into a miniature forest of trees that seemed barely taller than himself.

The sight of the outside world, miniature as it was, ignited a fire in his tiny heart. This was it. His chance. He couldn't waste it.

He began to formulate his escape plan. It needed to be swift, efficient, and undetectable. He couldn't just climb out; the spirits might be watching. He needed a distraction, a way to divert their attention while he made his escape.

He studied the miniature landscape beyond the crack. He spotted a tiny, fluttering creature, a miniature butterfly with iridescent blue wings, dancing among the wildflowers. He thought for a moment, an idea beginning to take shape in his tiny gnome mind.

He carefully reached into his pocket again, pulling out a small, brightly colored bead – a treasure from his gnome village. It was a deep crimson, almost glowing in the sunlight. He carefully maneuvered the bead toward the gap in the lid, placing it just outside the opening.

The butterfly, drawn to the bright color, fluttered toward the bead, its delicate wings beating against the air. It gently landed, its slender legs clinging to its surface. Barnaby held his breath, watching.

The distraction was working. He quickly used his trowel to pry the lid open further, widening the gap enough to squeeze through. He felt a sudden tremor of fear – the butterflies fluttering might not keep the spirits away. But he had no time to hesitate; this was his only chance.

With a surge of adrenaline, he wriggled out of the box, landing softly on the grass. He quickly rolled under the nearest wildflower, keeping as low as he could, and he was thankful it was too small for any other creatures to notice him. He watched the butterfly, still captivated by the bead, its delicate wings fluttering rhythmically.

He was out. He was free. The small world around him, no longer confining, now pulsed with the excitement of discovery. The miniature landscape, previously a source of fear and uncertainty, now held the promise of adventure. He glanced back at the box, a tiny prison that had held him captive for what felt like an eternity. He was free, and the adventure had just begun.

He looked around, taking in the details of his miniature surroundings. The wildflowers, more vibrant than anything he'd ever seen, shimmered with an almost ethereal glow. The tiny trees, their leaves a kaleidoscope of greens and yellows, rustled gently in the breeze. A tiny stream, no wider than his thumb, gurgled merrily nearby, its water sparkling under the afternoon sun.

He saw signs of life beyond the butterfly. Tiny insects, so small he could barely see them, crawled along the blades of grass. A miniature ladybug, its shell a vibrant red, rested on a leaf, its tiny antennae twitching. He even saw, in the distance, what appeared to be a miniature village – houses built from acorns and pebbles, paths made of twigs and leaves. It was a world teeming with life, a world he never knew existed.

He felt a surge of wonder, a childlike curiosity pulling him forward. He was small, yes, but he was also free. He was a gnome in a miniature world, and the possibilities were limitless. He picked his way along the winding path, his tiny trowel clutched tightly in his hand, ready to face whatever adventures this strange, new world might throw his way. The escape had been successful, but his journey had only just begun. He smiled, a wide, delighted grin spreading across his gnome face. This was going to be an adventure for the ages.

He followed the path, his eyes scanning his surroundings, taking it all in. The path wound through a miniature forest, the trees dense and leafy, their branches intertwined, creating a canopy of shade. The air was filled with the scent of pine needles and damp earth. The path was uneven, sometimes rising to miniature hills, sometimes descending into tiny valleys. He encountered small creatures along the way – a tiny squirrel with a bushy tail, a miniature bird with feathers the color of amethyst. Each encounter filled him with wonder and excitement.

He was careful to remain hidden, moving quietly through the undergrowth, always alert to the possibility of the spirits finding him. He wasn't sure what their intentions were, but he didn't want to risk being captured again. He would make his way to that miniature village, and from there, he'd try to find a way home.

The journey was challenging, but the beauty of the miniature world made it worthwhile. He saw waterfalls cascading down miniature cliffs, their water sparkling like diamonds. He saw pools of water, crystal clear, reflecting the sky and the trees. He noticed tiny flowers, some familiar, others entirely new and unknown.`

The miniature village, when he finally reached it, was even more captivating than he had imagined. The houses, perfectly scaled, were built with remarkable craftsmanship. The paths were clean and well-maintained, and small gnome-sized tools were placed tidily near every doorway. There were tiny clotheslines strung between houses, with miniature clothing items drying in the sun.

He felt a pang of homesickness, a longing for his village, but also a sense of awe and wonder at this new miniature civilization. He knew he had to find a way back home, but he also knew that this miniature world held a thousand secrets yet to be discovered. He felt a thrill of exhilaration, a feeling that surpassed even the relief of his escape. He was free, yes, but he was also embarking on a journey that was already shaping up to be the most extraordinary adventure of his life. And he was ready. He was more than ready. The miniature world waited for him. He had many, many adventures to experience here.

Chapter 2:

Marrakech Mayhem

The world exploded into a kaleidoscope of sights and sounds. One moment, Barnaby was nestled amongst the wildflowers; the next, he was standing in the heart of a roaring marketplace, a vibrant tapestry woven from a thousand threads of human activity. The air, thick with the scent of exotic spices – cinnamon, cloves, saffron – hung heavy and sweet, a stark contrast to the crisp, clean scent of his gnome village. The sounds were equally overwhelming: a cacophony of bartering voices, bleating goats, the rhythmic clang of a blacksmith's hammer, and the insistent cries of street vendors hawking their wares.

He was overwhelmed by the sheer immensity of everything around him. The stalls, overflowing with goods, seemed to stretch endlessly, their vibrant colors a dazzling assault on his senses. Mountains of richly hued spices spilled from burlap sacks, their aromas mingling in a heady perfume. Rolls of silk, shimmering with an iridescent sheen, were piled high, their colors ranging from deepest indigo to the palest blush of rose. Intricately woven carpets, their patterns telling ancient stories, lay spread out on the dusty ground, their textures inviting to the touch. Everywhere he looked, there was something new to marvel at, something to capture his attention.

Barnaby felt a strange mixture of fear and exhilaration. The miniature world he'd escaped from felt distant now, a faded memory replaced by the overwhelming reality of this bustling marketplace. He was utterly alone, a tiny gnome lost in a sea of human activity, yet he felt a surge of excitement, a sense of adventure that propelled him forward.

He cautiously navigated the crowded pathways, his tiny trowel clutched tightly in his hand. He moved like a shadow, slipping between the legs of shoppers, dodging the hooves of stray goats, and squeezing past overflowing baskets of dates and figs. He marveled at the sheer diversity of the people. Men in flowing djellabas, their faces etched with the wisdom of generations, bartered fiercely over the price of rugs. Women in brightly colored caftans, their laughter echoing through the market, haggled over spices and silks. Children, their eyes bright with mischief, darted through the crowd, their hands clutching sweet treats.

The sheer scale of the market was breathtaking. He saw towering piles of oranges, their skins gleaming like polished jewels. He saw baskets overflowing with dates, their sweetness palpable even from a distance. He saw mounds of olives, their briny scent sharp and distinct. He saw sacks of nuts – almonds, walnuts, pistachios – their shells gleaming under the sun.

A vendor, his face framed by a riotous tangle of grey hair, caught Barnaby's eye. He was selling intricately carved wooden boxes, their surfaces adorned with geometric patterns and brilliant colors. Barnaby, drawn to the familiar shape, approached cautiously. The vendor, oblivious to the tiny gnome at his feet, continued to call out his wares in a loud, booming voice.

Barnaby peered into one of the boxes, its interior lined with soft velvet. He noticed a tiny, intricate carving on the inside of the lid, a miniature depiction of a gnome tending a garden. It was strangely familiar, an echo of his world, a comforting reminder of his home.

He felt a sudden urge to possess this box, a connection to a simpler, more familiar time. But he knew he couldn't afford it, not even if he had all the gold in his village. He sighed and turned away, his heart heavy with a longing for home. He continued to wander through the market, his senses overwhelmed by the sheer variety of sights, sounds, and smells.

He came across a stall laden with brightly colored textiles. Silks and velvets, satins and brocades, were draped and piled in a dazzling array of colors and textures. The vendor, a young woman with eyes as dark and deep as the night sky, smiled warmly at Barnaby, mistaking his fascination for genuine interest.

She picked up a length of silk, its color a vivid sapphire blue, and held it up to the light. The fabric shimmered and danced, its beauty breathtaking. Barnaby gasped in awe. It was unlike anything he had ever seen in his quiet gnome village.

The woman, seeing his fascination, carefully laid the silk down and showed him a range of other fabrics, each more exquisite than the last. She explained their origins, their methods of production, and their uses. Barnaby listened intently, mesmerized by her knowledge and passion. He learned about the rich history of Moroccan textiles, their intricate designs, and the traditions that lay behind them.

The woman then presented him with a small, intricately woven tapestry, a miniature masterpiece depicting a scene from Moroccan folklore. It was small enough for him to carry comfortably and perfect as a souvenir. Barnaby, overcome with gratitude, accepted the gift.

As he continued his exploration, he noticed a group of musicians playing traditional Moroccan music. Their instruments – oud, darbuka, and flute – created a mesmerizing melody that filled the air. Barnaby closed his eyes, letting the music wash over him, transporting him to another world. The music pulsed with energy, a vibrant celebration of life, reminding him once again of the vitality and beauty of the human world.

He spent hours wandering through the maze-like alleys of the market, his senses constantly bombarded with new and exciting experiences. The smells alone were a feast: the sharp tang of lemons, the sweetness of oranges, the earthy scent of spices, the musty aroma of old rugs. The sounds were a constant symphony: the chatter of vendors, the laughter of children, the rhythmic pounding of hammers, the braying of donkeys.

As the sun began to set, casting long shadows across the market, Barnaby felt a growing sense of weariness. He was tired, hungry, and a little bit overwhelmed. Yet, he couldn't deny the thrill of adventure that pulsed within him. He had travelled far, from a quiet gnome village to the vibrant heart of Marrakech, and the journey had only just begun. He knew, as he made his way out of the bustling marketplace, that he would carry the memories of this extraordinary day with him always. The memory of the vibrant colors, the exotic scents, and the lively sounds would forever be etched in his memory. He knew his journey was far from over. He was ready for what the world threw at him. He was more than ready.

Just as Barnaby was beginning to feel utterly lost in the swirling chaos of the Marrakech marketplace, a shadow fell across him, surprisingly large and comforting in its immensity. He looked up, his tiny neck craning, and saw two enormous, gentle eyes gazing down at him. They belonged to a camel, a magnificent creature with a coat the color of sun-baked sand and eyes that held a depth of kindness that was both startling and soothing.

The camel knelt gracefully, its legs bending with a surprising fluidity that defied its massive size. A low, rumbling sound emanated from its throat, a sound that Barnaby instinctively understood as a greeting. He felt no fear, only a sense of unexpected calm in the presence of this behemoth.

A voice, deep and resonant like the desert wind, spoke in surprisingly clear English. "Lost, little one?"

Barnaby, startled but not frightened, managed a tiny nod. He was so small, he could barely see over the camel's enormous, leathery knees.

"I am Omar," the camel rumbled, its voice like warm honey. "And I believe you need a helping hand."

Barnaby, surprised at the ability of a camel to speak English, felt a surge of relief wash over him. He hadn't encountered any creatures who spoke English in the human marketplace. It seemed unlikely for a camel to speak in English, either. Yet here was Omar, offering him help, a kindness so unexpected in this vast and bewildering place.

Omar gently lowered his head, offering Barnaby his broad, soft hump. It looked surprisingly comfortable. Hesitantly, Barnaby climbed onto the hump, feeling the surprisingly smooth, warm fur beneath his tiny hands. From his vantage point, the marketplace transformed. He could see over the heads of the crowds, the dizzying array of colors and wares unfolding before him like a vibrant, chaotic tapestry.

The ride was surprisingly smooth. Omar moved with a gentle sway, navigating the crowded paths with an ease that astonished Barnaby. He effortlessly sidestepped bustling shoppers, avoided the unpredictable movements of stray goats, and even managed to prevent Barnaby from being trampled by a heavily laden donkey. It was as if Omar possessed an uncanny awareness of the market's hidden currents, moving with a grace that belied his size.

As they journeyed through the maze-like alleys, Omar shared stories of the desert, tales filled with ancient wisdom and the magic of the natural world. He spoke of shimmering mirages, of hidden oases teeming with life, and of the silent majesty of the starlit night. Barnaby listened, captivated, his initial fear replaced by a sense of wonder and growing companionship.

Omar, it turned out, possessed a vast knowledge of the marketplace. He knew the best places to find the sweetest dates, the most fragrant spices, and the most skilled artisans. He even knew where to find the quietest corners, where Barnaby could rest and gather his strength. He pointed out hidden gems, things Barnaby would have never noticed on his own; intricate carvings on ancient buildings, stunning mosaics hidden in the shadows, and tiny details woven into the fabric of the market's daily life.

At one point, Omar stopped at a stall overflowing with golden dates. He gently plucked a handful, their skins glistening like polished amber, and offered them to Barnaby. The dates were incredibly sweet, their flavor a revelation. They were nothing like the ones Barnaby had seen before in his tiny gnome village.

Later, Omar led Barnaby to a shaded alleyway, where a friendly vendor offered them refreshing mint tea. The tea was served in tiny, intricately painted cups, and it was the most delicious drink Barnaby had ever tasted. The cool, refreshing liquid soothed his parched throat and calmed his racing heart.

As they sipped their tea, Omar chuckled, a deep, rumbling sound that vibrated through Barnaby's tiny body. He was surprisingly funny, his humor dry and gentle, peppered with ancient proverbs and whimsical observations about human behavior. Barnaby learned that Omar was a wise old camel who had seen countless travelers pass through the marketplace, each with their own stories and dreams.

Omar helped Barnaby avoid several potentially disastrous situations. He warned Barnaby about a particularly slippery cobblestone, preventing a potentially painful tumble. He also steered them away from a group of boisterous children who might have accidentally stepped on him. Omar's large size and calming presence seemed to have a pacifying effect on the surrounding crowd, creating a small bubble of tranquility in the otherwise frenetic marketplace.

As the sun began to dip below the horizon, casting long shadows across the bustling marketplace, Omar and Barnaby found themselves near the edge of the market's chaos, in a quieter, less crowded area. Omar brought Barnaby a little closer to the less chaotic alleyways.

As Omar continued his steady progress through the labyrinthine alleys, Barnaby, perched comfortably on his hump, felt a growing sense of wonder. The marketplace, initially a terrifying maelstrom of sights and sounds, was slowly revealing its hidden charms. With his uncanny knack for navigating the bustling streets, Omar was revealing a Marrakech Barnaby could never have imagined on his own. The air, thick with the aroma of exotic spices, fruits, and unfamiliar perfumes, was a constant sensory feast.

Suddenly, a dynamic splash of color caught Barnaby's eye. Tucked away in a narrow side alley, almost hidden from view, was a stall unlike any he had seen before. It wasn't large or particularly imposing, but it pulsed with a vibrant energy that drew Barnaby in.

The stall was overflowing with tiny, exquisitely crafted spices. Each tiny jar, no bigger than Barnaby's thumb, was filled to the brim with spices of every imaginable hue. There were shimmering golds, fiery reds, deep ambers, and luminous greens – a breathtaking rainbow of aromatic treasures. The spices themselves seemed almost impossibly perfect, each grain meticulously formed, as if crafted by a tiny, unseen artisan. The scent was intoxicating, a complex and alluring blend of sweet and pungent aromas that tickled Barnaby's nose and made his mouth water.

Omar, sensing Barnaby's fascination, gently stopped beside the stall. The stall keeper, a tiny, wizened woman with eyes that twinkled like distant stars, looked up from her meticulous work. Her face was a roadmap of wrinkles, etched by years of sun and laughter, but her smile was as bright as the spices before her. She wore a brightly colored headscarf that matched the vibrant hues of her wares, and her hands, gnarled with age, moved with surprising dexterity as she arranged the miniature jars.

"Welcome, little one," she chirped, her voice surprisingly melodious. She spoke in perfect English, just like Omar. Barnaby, no longer surprised by the ability of animals and people to communicate in his language, felt a warmth spread through him. It seemed that kindness and understanding were as abundant as the spices themselves.

She gestured towards the overflowing jars. "These are the secrets of the desert, little gnome," she whispered, her voice full of mystery and wonder. "Each spice holds a story, a journey, a whisper of the wind." She pointed to a jar filled with threads of luminous orange. "This is saffron, the most precious of spices. It holds the sun itself, the warmth of a thousand dawns."

She reached into a small, wooden box tucked beneath the counter and pulled out a tiny, intricately woven pouch. It was made of soft, supple leather, the color of rich, dark chocolate. Inside, nestled amongst folds of delicate silk, was a small amount of saffron. The threads shimmered like liquid gold in the afternoon sunlight.

"Take this, little one," she said, offering the pouch to Barnaby. "It's a gift. May it bring you warmth and joy on your journey."

Barnaby, overwhelmed by her generosity, took the pouch with trembling hands. The saffron smelled divine – a rich, earthy aroma with a hint of sweetness that was both intoxicating and comforting. It was a scent that promised warmth, adventure, and the promise of countless delicious culinary creations.

As Barnaby gratefully accepted the gift, the old woman launched into a series of enchanting tales. She spoke of her travels across the vast Sahara Desert, of encounters with nomadic tribes, and of the hidden oases where life thrived in the midst of seemingly endless sand. She described vibrant sunsets that painted the sky in hues of fiery orange and deep violet, and moonlit nights filled with the songs of the desert wind. She spoke of the magic of spices, not just as ingredients but as carriers of memories, emotions, and stories passed down through generations.

She spoke of her childhood in a small Berber village, nestled in a hidden valley, where she learned the secrets of spice cultivation from her grandmother, a legendary herbalist. She described the meticulous process of harvesting and preparing each spice, the ancient rituals and techniques passed down through centuries. She shared stories of her travels, selling her precious spices in far-off lands, encountering people from different cultures and backgrounds, and sharing her passion for spices with anyone who would listen.

Barnaby listened, captivated. He learned of the medicinal properties of various spices, of their ability to heal and soothe, to invigorate and uplift. He learned of the role spices played in religious ceremonies, in traditional medicine, and in everyday life. He learned that spices were not simply ingredients, but vessels of stories, carrying with them the echoes of ancient traditions, cultural heritage, and the rhythms of life in the desert.

The old woman's stories were peppered with humor and wisdom, her words weaving a tapestry of enchantment that enthralled Barnaby. He learned about the importance of sharing, of kindness, and of the unexpected connections that can be forged in the most unlikely of places. Her words resonated deeply with Barnaby, reminding him of Omar's gentle guidance and the unexpected kindness he had encountered thus far on his journey.

The sun dipped lower in the sky, casting long shadows across the alleyway. The old woman, sensing it was time for Barnaby to continue his journey, smiled warmly. "Go now, little one," she said, her voice gentle but firm. "May the saffron bring you warmth, and may your journey be filled with kindness and adventure."

Barnaby, clutching the precious pouch of saffron, waved goodbye to the kind old woman, his heart overflowing with gratitude. He felt a newfound confidence, a sense that even in the chaotic bustle of Marrakech, kindness and generosity could be found in the most unexpected places. He climbed back onto Omar's broad hump, feeling the warmth of the setting sun on his face and the intoxicating aroma of the saffron filling his senses. The journey ahead still held uncertainties, but with the memories of Omar's kindness and the old woman's generous gift, he felt ready to face whatever challenges lay ahead. He knew, deep in his heart, that the kindness he had found in Marrakech would stay with him always, a warm beacon illuminating his path through the adventures that lay ahead. The saffron, a tiny but potent reminder of the kindness and unexpected friendships encountered amidst the mayhem, would be a cherished keepsake from his Marrakech adventure. He rode away into the setting sun, leaving behind the chaotic but ultimately kind and generous marketplace, carrying the warmth of new memories and the potent fragrance of saffron. The journey had been long, the experiences intense, but the warmth of human kindness, encountered in the most surprising places, outweighed any hardship. He knew he'd never forget his time in Marrakech. It was, after all, a place where even the smallest gnome could find immense kindness and the most unlikely of friendships. He had faced the Marrakech mayhem and emerged, not only unscathed but enriched by the experience.

The sun, a molten orb sinking towards the horizon, cast long shadows that stretched and twisted like playful serpents through the Marrakech marketplace. The air, once vibrant with the intoxicating aroma of spices, now felt thick with a different kind of energy-a restless, almost palpable tension. The joyous cacophony of the earlier hours had morphed into a more ominous hum, a low thrum of voices and hurried footsteps that prickled Barnaby's sensitive ears. The crowds had thickened, pressing in on him from all sides, a swirling tide of brightly colored robes and anxious faces.

He noticed a shift in the atmosphere, a subtle change that sent a shiver down his tiny spine. The smiles seemed less genuine, the eyes less friendly. He saw several faces – men with shifty eyes and hands hidden deep within their voluminous robes – who seemed to be studying him with unsettling intensity. Their gazes felt like cold, probing fingers, making the hairs on his neck stand on end. He felt a growing unease, a prickling sensation that something wasn't quite right.

One man, in particular, caught Barnaby's attention. He was tall and gaunt, with a hooked nose and a perpetual frown etched deep into his weathered face. He wore a dark, hooded cloak that swallowed him whole, leaving only his sharp, glinting eyes visible. He seemed to drift through the crowds, his movements fluid and almost imperceptible, like a shadow cast by the setting sun. Barnaby felt a cold dread grip his tiny heart as he noticed the man's gaze lingering on him, assessing him, as if deciding whether to pounce.

The man's gaze unnerved him. The jovial atmosphere that had previously charmed him had vanished, replaced by a palpable sense of menace. He suddenly felt vulnerable, exposed in the chaotic swirl of the bustling marketplace. He imagined all sorts of nefarious plots – being stolen, perhaps used as bait in some cunning scheme, sold into some sort of bizarre gnome-slavery. His imagination, fueled by the growing fear, ran wild with the most improbable and unsettling scenarios.

He glanced down at the small pouch of saffron, nestled safely in his pocket, a tiny ember of warmth against the growing chill of apprehension. The gift from the old woman, once a symbol of kindness and hope, now felt like a precious talisman, a small comfort in the face of looming danger.

Barnaby, with a sudden surge of instinct, leaped onto Omar's broad hump. The camel, sensing his rider's sudden anxiety, let out a soft, rumbling sigh. He didn't need Barnaby to explain his fear; Omar understood. He had a keen awareness of the shifting moods of the marketplace, and the growing menace was unmistakable.

Omar's large, brown eyes seemed to assess the situation, the worry mirroring Barnaby's own.

With a gentle shift of his massive frame, Omar began to weave his way through the increasingly dense crowd. His movements were fluid and purposeful, a masterclass in navigating the chaotic labyrinth of the marketplace. He moved with a graceful strength that belied his size, expertly maneuvering around jostling shoppers, laden donkeys, and overflowing stalls, his large, padded feet making scarcely a sound on the cobblestones.

The shady characters, sensing that Omar was not an easy target, seemed to hesitate, their pursuit faltering slightly. Omar, seemingly aware of their presence, increased his pace subtly, his movements a dance of calculated precision through the swirling mass of humanity. He expertly used his broad body as a shield, creating a protective space for Barnaby while at the same time keeping a watchful eye on their pursuers.

The alleys grew narrower, the crowds denser. The scent of spices gave way to the musty aroma of damp earth and decaying fruit. The sun's rays, filtered through the narrow passages, cast long, dancing shadows that played tricks on the eyes, obscuring faces and intentions. The atmosphere became increasingly claustrophobic, heavy with tension. The fear, however, was palpable. Barnaby clung tightly to Omar's thick, woolly coat, his small body trembling slightly.

After what seemed like an eternity of navigating the maze-like streets, Omar suddenly turned a sharp corner, emerging into a narrow alley that was surprisingly quiet. It was a stark contrast to the chaotic marketplace they had just left behind. This narrow passage, almost hidden from sight, offered a reprieve from the oppressive atmosphere of the market. The alley opened into a hidden courtyard, a small oasis of calm amidst the city's frenzy.

The courtyard was a haven of tranquility, a secret garden tucked away from the bustling city. Lush, flowering plants climbed the weathered walls, their blossoms in a riotous explosion of color. A small, gurgling fountain in the center of the courtyard provided a soothing counterpoint to the city's clamor. Birds chirped softly from unseen branches, their songs a gentle melody that washed over Barnaby. The air, fragrant with the scent of jasmine and orange blossoms, was a balm to his troubled spirit.

Omar, with a low, contented sigh, stopped beneath the shade of a sprawling fig tree. Barnaby slid down from his hump and sank onto the soft earth, his small body finally relaxing. He took several deep breaths, allowing the peace of the courtyard to wash over him. The immediate danger had passed; for now, at least, he was safe.

The courtyard offered a much-needed respite. The transition from the chaotic marketplace to the serene courtyard felt almost surreal. It was like stepping from a turbulent storm into the gentle embrace of a sun-drenched meadow. The contrast was breathtaking, the peace almost too profound after the stress of the previous moments. Barnaby watched as Omar calmly grazed on some fallen leaves, the image reflecting his own need to recover and recharge. The camel's tranquility was almost contagious.

The quiet hum of the courtyard's fountain provided the perfect backdrop for Barnaby's contemplation. He sat quietly, letting the calmness seep into his tiny frame. The sounds of the city, just beyond the walls, seemed distant, muffled, almost unreal. It was as if he had crossed some unseen threshold, leaving the relentless chaos of the marketplace behind. He felt the weight of his fear begin to lift.

He reached into his pocket, clutching the small pouch of saffron. The scent, once a promise of warmth and joy, now felt like a tangible reminder of the kindness he had encountered. It served as a symbol of his resilience, a testament to his ability to navigate even the most daunting challenges. The saffron was more than just a spice; it was a memento of hope. He knew, with a growing certainty, that his adventures in Marrakech were far from over, but for the moment, the sanctuary of the courtyard offered him a moment of much-needed peace. The journey continued, but for now, he was safe, and that was enough. The tranquility of the courtyard garden allowed Barnaby the space and quiet to process the events of the past hour. The memory of the menacing figures, their unsettling stares still fresh in his mind, was a stark reminder of the potential dangers that lurked in the vibrant and unpredictable heart of Marrakech. But now, sheltered within the tranquil embrace of the hidden oasis, the fear began to recede, replaced by a quiet sense of gratitude for Omar and the unexpected haven they had found.

The scent of jasmine and orange blossoms hung heavy in the air, a fragrant counterpoint to the lingering unease that still clung to Barnaby. He sat nestled against Omar's broad flank, the camel's warmth a comforting presence against the cool earth of the courtyard. The quiet hum of the fountain, the soft chirping of birds, all contributed to a sense of fragile peace, a temporary respite from the whirlwind of events that had unfolded in the marketplace. He clutched the small pouch of saffron, the spice's aroma a comforting reminder of the kindness he had encountered earlier.

Omar, seemingly content with his leafy repast, let out a low, rumbling sigh. Barnaby watched him, a quiet understanding passing between them. The camel, with his intuitive understanding of Barnaby's fears, had been his silent protector, his steadfast companion in the face of danger. The bond between them, forged in the crucible of shared anxiety, felt stronger than ever.

Suddenly, Omar shifted his weight, a subtle movement that caught Barnaby's attention. He reached into a surprisingly capacious pouch slung across his hump, producing something that made Barnaby's eyes widen in astonishment. It was small, brass-colored, and oddly familiar – a camera.

Barnaby had seen pictures before, of course. Back in his village, his Uncle Silas, a renowned (though slightly eccentric) beekeeper, possessed a rather cumbersome contraption that produced images on special paper. But this was different. This was tiny, delicate, and held in Omar's surprisingly deft fingers.

Omar, with a knowing smile that crinkled the corners of his kind eyes, adjusted the focus with surprising precision. He held the camera, almost reverently, before slowly positioning it to frame Barnaby against the backdrop of the flowering vines and the gurgling fountain. Barnaby, initially surprised, found himself cooperating readily. The camera was so strange, so unexpected, that he felt a surge of curiosity overpower any remaining apprehension.

"Ready?" Omar rumbled, his voice a low, comforting drone. Barnaby, though unsure what was about to happen, simply nodded.

There was a faint click, almost inaudible amidst the gentle sounds of the courtyard. Then, Omar lowered the camera, a satisfied expression on his weathered face. He carefully extracted a small, rectangular piece of paper from a tiny compartment on the side of the device. The image was developing slowly, the latent details slowly appearing, like magic.

As the image materialized, Barnaby gasped. There he was – captured in a moment of stillness against the vibrant backdrop of the courtyard. He was seated beneath the sprawling fig tree, his small form outlined against the profusion of green leaves and blooming flowers. The light seemed to catch the gold in his hair, enhancing the richness of his color. Omar's skillful hand had captured the essence of the scene perfectly; the contrast between his serene expression and the wild, untamed beauty of the surroundings was striking.

He looked more carefully. He could see the intricate detail, the subtle textures. The individual petals of the flowers, the intricate pattern of the courtyard stones, even the tiny glint of sunlight on a dewdrop clinging to a leaf were all remarkably clear. This wasn't just a picture; it was a miniature window into a moment in time, a perfect encapsulation of the peace he had found in the hidden courtyard.

Omar handed the picture to Barnaby, the paper still slightly damp. Barnaby accepted it with reverence, the image a precious memento of his journey. It was more than just a photograph; it was a tangible representation of his resilience, his ability to navigate unexpected dangers and find sanctuary in the most unlikely places.

"A memory," Omar said softly, his voice filled with warmth. "To remember this place, this moment, forever."

Barnaby looked at the photograph again, tracing the outline of his small form with a finger. The image was a testament to his experience, a tangible piece of his adventure. It was a reminder of the kindness and unexpected discoveries that had marked his journey so far. Holding the picture, he felt a sense of quiet contentment wash over him. The photograph wasn't just a souvenir; it was a symbol of his growing confidence and the strength of the bond he shared with Omar.

He thought about the marketplace, the swirling crowds, the menacing figures, the overwhelming sense of unease. The memory was still fresh, sharp and vivid, but the fear, the anxiety, felt distant, softened by the calm of the courtyard, the warmth of the sun, and the comforting presence of Omar. The photograph was a tangible connection to that fear, a reminder of how far he had come.

He carefully folded the photograph, tucking it safely into his pocket, alongside the pouch of saffron. The two objects, seemingly disparate yet intrinsically linked, represented two contrasting aspects of his journey: the danger he had encountered and the unexpected peace he had found. Together, they represented the totality of his experience, the complex tapestry woven from fear, bravery, kindness, and discovery.

The sun began to dip lower in the sky, casting long, slanting shadows across the courtyard. The time for rest was over. The adventure was far from finished. But as Barnaby stood, preparing to rejoin the bustling world outside, he knew he would always cherish this small, precious photograph, a tangible link to the tranquility and unexpected friendship he had found in the heart of Marrakech. It was a reminder that even in the midst of chaos, moments of peace could be found, and even the most unlikely friendships could blossom in the most unexpected places.

The photograph also served as a potent symbol of his personal growth. He had faced fear, uncertainty, and even danger, but he had emerged stronger, more resilient, and with a newfound appreciation for the kindness and unexpected support that life could offer. The memory captured in the small picture wasn't just a record of a place and a moment, but also a representation of his transformation, a testament to his burgeoning courage and his developing ability to navigate the complexities of the world around him.

He felt Omar's gaze on him, a silent communication passing between them, a shared understanding of their adventures, their shared journey through the bustling maze of the Marrakech marketplace and the tranquil sanctuary of the hidden courtyard. They would journey onwards together, and Barnaby knew, with a deep certainty that transcended words, that whatever adventures lay ahead, they would face them together, their bond solidified not only by shared experiences but also by the small, carefully folded photograph in Barnaby's pocket—a reminder of a moment of quiet peace in a world of relentless change. The photograph would be a keepsake, a physical reminder of the unlikely friendship between a boy and a camel and the unexpected magic of Marrakech.

As they left the courtyard, stepping back into the familiar hum of the city, Barnaby felt a renewed sense of purpose, a quiet confidence settling over him. The memory of the photograph, a tiny square of time frozen forever, would serve as a constant reminder of the strength and resilience he had discovered within himself during his adventures in Marrakech. The journey continued, and as Barnaby looked towards the setting sun, casting a vibrant orange glow across the cityscape, he knew this was only the beginning of his incredible adventure. The camera, the photograph, the courtyard oasis, and the unwavering support of his camel companion Omar—these would all become interwoven into the rich tapestry of his memories, a testament to the unforgettable days spent in the multifarious, chaotic, and ultimately rewarding heart of Marrakech.

"You'll be alright now, little one," Omar said softly, his voice a warm comfort in the gathering dusk. "Remember the kindness you find in unexpected places. And always remember that even the smallest creature can have the biggest impact."

Barnaby, feeling a deep sense of gratitude, gave Omar a tiny hug, grateful for the kindness of this large and gentle being. He knew he would never forget his encounter with Omar, the kind camel who had guided him through the mayhem of Marrakech and shown him the true meaning of a helping hand. He smiled, his heart filled with warmth and the sweet taste of dates and mint tea. He knew his journey wasn't over, but with Omar's kindness and advice echoing in his ears, the uncertainties that lay ahead felt a little less daunting. He was ready. He was more than ready. He had found a friend in the most unlikely of places, and that was an adventure in itself. The memory of Omar's gentle presence and wise words would stay with him long after he left the bustling marketplace of Marrakech, a reminder of the unexpected kindness that can be found even in the most chaotic of places.

The sun had set, but the warmth of his new friend's kindness illuminated the path ahead. He had survived the mayhem and learned much about the surprising ways people and animals could help each other in an unfamiliar place. The experience had been challenging, yet ultimately enriching. He was ready for whatever else the world had in store for him, armed with a newfound confidence, a full belly, and the memory of a most unlikely friendship.

Chapter 3:

Scottish Highlands Adventure

The bustling marketplace of Marrakech faded into a distant memory as Barnaby, still clutching his precious photograph and the small pouch of saffron, found himself on a completely different kind of adventure. The scent of jasmine and orange blossoms was replaced by the crisp, clean air of the Scottish Highlands, a bracing change after the heat of the Moroccan sun. He was far from the familiar sights and sounds of his village, yet a strange sense of comfort settled over him. This new adventure felt both thrilling and strangely familiar.

His journey from Marrakech had been as unexpected as his encounter with Omar. He had found himself on a dock, bewildered, but with a renewed sense of purpose. A small, brightly painted ship, its sails billowing with the promise of faraway lands, had appeared as if by magic. The captain, a jovial woman with eyes that twinkled like the sea itself, had offered him passage–passage, she'd winked, "to a land of mist and magic." The voyage had been long, filled with the rhythmic creak of the ship's timbers and the cries of gulls wheeling overhead. He'd spent his days gazing at the endless horizon, imagining the wonders that lay ahead.

Finally, land had appeared on the horizon, a misty, green expanse punctuated by jagged peaks that clawed at the sky. The ship had docked at a small, secluded cove, the air thick with the scent of peat smoke and damp earth. As Barnaby stepped onto the shore, he was greeted not by the clamor of a bustling city but by the gentle bleating of sheep and the soft patter of rain on the mossy stones.

It was here, amidst the rolling hills, that Barnaby encountered Angus, a sheepdog unlike any he had ever seen. Angus was magnificent, a creature of pure, unadulterated fluffiness. His coat, a thick cloud of creamy white wool, seemed to absorb the mist itself. His eyes, intelligent and kind, held a spark of mischievous humor. Angus was, in Barnaby's estimation, the most charming sheepdog imaginable.

Barnaby, feeling a little lost, had approached Angus cautiously. To his utter surprise, the sheepdog had responded with an enthusiastic bark and a wagging tail that sent a flurry of woolly snow swirling around Barnaby's feet. Angus, it seemed, had a fondness for adventure, a shared characteristic with our intrepid young traveler.

The sheepdog, sensing Barnaby's need for direction (and perhaps a comfortable ride), had offered a solution as unexpected as it was delightful. With a low, rumbling woof and a playful nip at Barnaby's trousers, Angus indicated that Barnaby should climb onto his back. Surprisingly, Angus's back was as soft and springy as a giant, furry pillow. Barnaby, still somewhat bewildered but also inexplicably trusting, accepted the offer with a relieved laugh.

And so, Barnaby began his journey across the Scottish Highlands on the back of a friendly sheepdog. Angus's fleece was warm and insulating, a surprisingly comfortable mode of transport, even when the rain started to fall in earnest. The journey was far from easy. The terrain was rugged, and Angus had to navigate steep slopes and rocky paths with impressive skill and agility. But Barnaby hung on tight, enjoying the ride.

The Highlands unfolded before them like a breathtaking tapestry woven from emerald hills, sparkling lochs, and dramatic mountains that pierced the often-misty sky. The scenery was utterly captivating – a dramatic contrast to the arid beauty of Marrakech. Waterfalls cascaded down sheer cliffs, their roar echoing through the valleys. Tiny villages, their stone houses snuggled together like woolly sheep, dotted the landscape. Ancient castles, their stony ramparts weathered by centuries of wind and rain, stood sentinel over the land.

Angus, seemingly unfazed by the challenging terrain, would often pause to allow Barnaby to take in the view. He'd point his shaggy head toward a particularly stunning vista, his tail thumping a steady rhythm against Barnaby's side. Their journey was as much a visual feast as it was an adventure, each turn revealing new and breathtaking sights. The landscapes were so dramatic, so captivating, that even the persistent drizzle seemed to add to their magical quality.

They passed herds of sheep, their woolly coats the same soft white as Angus's. Barnaby noticed that Angus often exchanged friendly woofs with the other sheepdogs in the area, forming a sort of silent communication network that facilitated their journey through the often-isolated landscape. Barnaby learned to read Angus's subtle cues, understanding when a rest was needed, when a path was too dangerous, and when a detour was necessary.

The days flowed into weeks as they journeyed deeper into the Highlands. They shared meals of berries and wild herbs, Angus finding the juiciest morsels and sharing them generously with his passenger. Barnaby learned to appreciate the silence of the Highlands, the peace that came with being surrounded by nature's grandeur. He even learned a few words of sheepdog language, a series of woofs and barks that conveyed a surprising range of meaning.

Their journey wasn't without its challenges. They encountered sudden downpours that soaked them to the bone, slippery paths that tested Angus's agility, and moments of loneliness when they were far from any sign of human habitation. But Barnaby and Angus faced each challenge together, their bond strengthening with each passing day. Their shared adventures forged a friendship as strong and steadfast as the ancient mountains that surrounded them.

One evening, as the sun dipped below the horizon, painting the sky in hues of fiery orange and deep purple, Barnaby and Angus reached a small, isolated cottage. Smoke curled from its chimney, a welcoming sight against the darkening sky. A kind old woman, her face as weathered as the surrounding landscape, opened the door, welcoming them with warmth and hospitality. She offered them hot porridge and a warm bed, a much-needed respite after their long journey.

As Barnaby drifted off to sleep, nestled in a bed of soft wool blankets, he realized that his adventure wasn't just about reaching a destination. It was about the journey itself, the shared experiences, the unlikely friendship, and the breathtaking beauty of the Scottish Highlands. The memory of the photograph, tucked safely away in his pocket, served as a comforting reminder of his earlier adventures. He had come so far, seen so much, and encountered such unexpected kindness. And he knew, with a certainty that warmed him from the inside out, that this was merely one chapter in a wonderful adventure, a continuing journey of discovery and friendship. He had Marrakech and now the

Highlands, each with its unique treasure, both etched forever in his heart and forming a canvas for further adventures yet to come.

The next morning dawned crisp and clear, the mist clinging to the hills like a shy veil. Angus, his fluffy coat glistening with dew, nudged Barnaby awake with a gentle lick to his cheek. The old woman's porridge had given him the energy of a mountain goat, and he felt ready for whatever wonders the day might hold. Their journey continued, the landscape changing subtly with every passing mile. The rolling hills gave way to steeper, more dramatic peaks, the air growing colder with each upward climb.

As they crested a particularly high ridge, Barnaby gasped. Below them, nestled amongst the heather and bracken, lay a vast expanse of water, a shimmering, sapphire jewel set against the emerald tapestry of the Highlands. It was Loch Ness. A legend whispered on the wind, a mystery shrouded in mist and folklore. Barnaby had heard tales of Nessie, the legendary Loch Ness Monster, a creature both feared and revered by the locals. He had dismissed them as fanciful stories, charming myths to entertain weary travelers. But standing here, overlooking the immense loch, a shiver of anticipation ran down his spine.

Angus, sensing Barnaby's excitement, let out a low, rumbling woof, his tail thumping rhythmically against the ground. He seemed to share Barnaby's anticipation, his usually playful demeanor replaced by a quiet, almost reverent stillness. They descended the ridge, the path winding downwards towards the loch's edge. The closer they got, the more palpable the sense of mystery became. A thick fog, like a ghostly shroud, hung low over the water, obscuring the far shore. The air was still and silent, broken only by the occasional cry of a distant gull.

As they reached the water's edge, Barnaby paused, mesmerized by the loch's stillness. The surface of the water was as smooth as glass, reflecting the surrounding mountains like a perfect mirror. Then, a ripple. A small ripple that spread outwards, disturbing the perfect reflection. Another ripple followed, then another, growing larger and more distinct. Barnaby's heart pounded in his chest. He could feel the ancient magic of the place, the weight of centuries of legend pressing down on him.

Slowly, majestically, a creature emerged from the depths of the loch. It was enormous, its long, serpentine neck rising gracefully from the water. Its skin was a deep, mottled grey, almost the color of the loch itself, making it nearly invisible against the misty backdrop. Its eyes, large and intelligent, regarded Barnaby with an air of gentle curiosity. Barnaby knew, instinctively, that this was Nessie.

Nessie's head emerged fully, her eyes twinkling with an ancient wisdom that seemed to encompass centuries of untold stories. She was even more magnificent than Barnaby could have ever imagined. She had a kind face, with a long, graceful neck that moved with surprising fluidity. She didn't seem monstrous at all, but rather serene and majestic, a creature of myth made real.

Nessie let out a sound, a low, melodic hum that resonated deep within Barnaby's chest. It wasn't a roar or a growl, but a gentle, almost musical sound, like the whispering of the wind through the ancient pines that lined the loch's shore. Angus responded with a soft, respectful woof, his tail wagging gently. A sense of peace settled over Barnaby, a profound connection to this ancient creature and the land itself.

Nessie remained submerged for a moment, then spoke, her voice like the murmuring of a stream, soft and resonant. "You have traveled far, little one," she said, her words echoing the ancient lore of the Highlands. "Your journey is more than an escape; it is a quest for understanding."

Barnaby, completely speechless, could only nod. He'd been so focused on fleeing his pursuers, on finding a haven, that he hadn't considered the deeper meaning behind his journey. Nessie's words resonated with him, stirring something deep within his soul.

Nessie continued, her voice weaving tales of ancient battles, of powerful kings and forgotten queens, of druids and fairies, of the land's rich history and mystical past. She spoke of the Highlands' hidden magic, of the spirits that dwelt within the mountains and lochs, of the interconnectedness of all living things. She told stories of bravery and resilience, of friendship and loyalty, of the importance of protecting the land and its creatures. Her stories were captivating, each word painted with the vivid colors of the Highlands, filled with the scents of heather and peat smoke, the sounds of rushing waterfalls and the wind whistling through the mountains.

As Nessie spoke, Barnaby felt a growing understanding. His journey wasn't just about escaping the clutches of those who sought to harm him; it was about discovering himself, about connecting with the natural world and its ancient magic. He saw the Highlands not just as a landscape, but as a living, breathing entity, filled with history, secrets, and an immense sense of wonder.

Angus, perched patiently at Barnaby's side, seemed to understand too. He would occasionally nudge Barnaby with his head, as if emphasizing the importance of Nessie's words. The two creatures seemed to share a profound bond, an ancient understanding that transcended the boundaries of species.

As the sun began its descent, casting long shadows across the loch, Nessie's voice grew softer, her stories winding down. She shared with Barnaby a prophecy, a whisper of a future where humanity and nature could co-exist in harmony. A future where the magic of the Highlands would flourish once more.

"Your journey," Nessie murmured, her eyes holding Barnaby's gaze, "is not yet over. You have much to learn, much to do. But remember always the wisdom of the ancient land, the strength of friendship, and the beauty of the world around you."

With a final, gentle sigh, Nessie slipped back into the depths of Loch Ness, disappearing as silently as she had appeared. The ripples she left behind danced on the surface of the loch, like fleeting memories of a magical encounter.

Barnaby and Angus sat in silence for a long time, absorbing the wonder and the weight of Nessie's words. Barnaby knew, with absolute certainty, that his life had changed forever. He had found more than just a haven in the Scottish Highlands; he had discovered a deeper purpose, a connection to something ancient and elemental. The photograph remained tucked safely in his pocket, but its significance was overshadowed by the newfound meaning of his journey, a journey guided not only by his own will but by the wisdom of a creature of legend, and the loyalty of a most magnificent sheepdog. He knew his adventure was far from over, that his journey was only just beginning. He looked towards the horizon, towards the uncertain future, filled with a sense of purpose and a newfound hope, ready to face whatever challenges lay ahead, with the warmth of Nessie's words echoing in his heart. The misty hills seemed to whisper their agreement, a silent promise of further wonders yet to come.

The path leading away from Loch Ness wound upwards, eventually emerging onto a sun-drenched plateau. The air hummed with a different kind of energy now, a lively, joyful buzz that contrasted sharply with the quiet reverence of the loch. As Barnaby and Angus crested the rise, a vibrant scene unfolded before them, a kaleidoscope of color and sound.

It was a Highland Games, but not the grand, sprawling events he'd seen pictures of. This was a smaller, more intimate affair, a celebration held in a sun-dappled meadow nestled amongst the rolling hills. Tiny tartan flags fluttered in the gentle breeze, their colors mirroring the bright kilts worn by the merrymakers. The air throbbed with the surprisingly loud, yet charmingly off-key, notes of miniature bagpipes, played with gusto by a group of children whose cheeks puffed out with each toot. Laughter spilled from the crowd like sparkling champagne.

Angus, his ears perked, let out a happy bark, his tail wagging furiously. He seemed as captivated by the scene as Barnaby. The atmosphere was infectious, a vibrant blend of excitement and camaraderie that swept Barnaby up in its tide. He found himself smiling, the weight of his recent ordeal lifting from his shoulders like a heavy cloak.

The Games were in full swing. Children, no bigger than Angus, were attempting to toss miniature cabers, their tiny arms straining with effort. Their laughter echoed across the meadow, a joyful soundtrack to the spirited competition. Older children were engaged in a spirited tug-of-war, their faces flushed with exertion and determination. The air was filled with the scent of woodsmoke, freshly baked oatcakes, and something sweet and subtly spiced – perhaps shortbread or gingerbread.

A group of women, their cheeks rosy with good health and laughter, were seated near a large cauldron bubbling merrily over an open fire. The aroma of something delicious wafted towards Barnaby, a savory blend of herbs and roasted meats. He could see hearty oatcakes, still warm from the fire, stacked high on a nearby table, alongside mugs of steaming liquid, presumably tea or perhaps something a little stronger.

As Barnaby and Angus approached, a woman with bright, welcoming eyes and a smile that could melt glaciers noticed them. She was dressed in a tartan skirt and a simple woolen sweater. Her hair, the color of burnished copper, was woven with ribbons that shimmered in the sunlight.

"Well now, what have we here?" she exclaimed, her voice warm and melodious. "A traveler and his fine companion. Welcome to our little Highland Games!"

Barnaby, still a little shy after his encounter with Nessie, offered a hesitant smile. "Hello," he murmured, feeling a sense of relief wash over him. He hadn't encountered such genuine kindness in a long time.

The woman chuckled, her eyes twinkling. "You look like you've had a bit of a journey. Come, join us! We've plenty of food and stories to share."

She beckoned him towards the cauldron, offering him a steaming mug of something fragrant and spicy. It was a warm, comforting drink, the perfect antidote to the chill of the highlands. He learned it was spiced heather tea. She then presented him with a freshly baked oatcake, its texture both crisp and chewy, its flavor earthy and satisfying.

Angus, meanwhile, had already made friends with a pack of similarly fluffy sheepdogs, engaging in a boisterous game of chase around the periphery of the games. Barnaby watched them, their playful energy a stark contrast to the grim determination that had driven him for so long. He felt a surge of gratitude for the simple pleasure of their company. For the first time since his escape, he felt safe, accepted, and genuinely happy.

The woman, whose name he learned was Morag, introduced him to other members of the community. Each person welcomed him with the same warm hospitality. They shared tales of their lives in the Highlands, stories of bravery and resilience, of community and loyalty. They spoke of their ancestors, of the land's history and the spirits that inhabited it.

He listened, captivated, as they recounted stories of legendary heroes, of ancient battles, and the enduring spirit of the Highlands. Each story was woven with the colors of the landscape, the scents of heather and peat smoke, the sounds of rushing waterfalls and the whistling wind. He learned of their customs and traditions, their deep connection to the land and its creatures. Their stories echoed Nessie's words, reinforcing the importance of protecting the land and its magic.

One old man, his craggy face etched by time and weather, told Barnaby a tale of a shepherd who had outsmarted a grumpy kelpie – a mischievous water spirit – by offering it a bag of oatcakes instead of his sheep. Another woman described a thrilling race between two rival clans, their competition fueled by fierce loyalty and friendly rivalry. The children chimed in with their fantastical tales, their voices filled with vibrant imagination.

As the sun began to dip below the horizon, casting long shadows across the meadow, Morag led Barnaby to a cozy cottage nestled on the edge of the glen. It was a small, welcoming space, filled with the warmth of a crackling fire and the comforting scent of home-baked bread. She offered him a warm bed and a hearty supper.

He ate his fill of delicious stew, its flavors a delightful symphony of earthy vegetables and tender meat. As he ate, he felt a profound sense of peace wash over him, a sense of belonging he hadn't felt before. The highlanders welcomed him with open arms and a full heart. He was no longer just a runaway; he was a welcomed guest, a part of this small, thriving community.

The day concluded with the community singing traditional Gaelic songs, their voices blending harmoniously under the vast, star-studded sky. Angus slept soundly at his feet, his dreams undoubtedly filled with images of chasing playful sheepdogs across sun-drenched meadows. Barnaby, his own heart full of gratitude and newfound hope, drifted off to sleep. For the first time in a long time, he felt he was exactly where he should be. The Highlands, once a place of desperate refuge, now felt like home. He had found not only shelter, but a community, and a warmth that penetrated the deepest parts of his soul. The kindness and acceptance of these highlanders filled a deep void that no amount of fleeing could ever solve. He was ready to face the unknown future, strengthened by the warmth of newfound friendship and comforted by the ancient magic of the Highlands.

The sun-drenched plateau, with its joyful Highland Games, faded behind Barnaby as he began the ascent into the Misty Mountains. The jovial atmosphere gave way to a hushed reverence as the path snaked upwards, disappearing into a swirling veil of mist that clung to the rugged slopes like a spectral shroud. The vibrant colors of the kilts and fluttering flags were replaced by the muted greens and greys of the mountainside, punctuated only by the occasional splash of purple heather. The cheerful sound of bagpipes was swallowed by the wind's mournful whisper through the crags. Angus, usually so boisterous, trotted quietly at Barnaby's heels, his keen senses alert to the changing environment.

The climb was arduous. The path, barely more than a goat track in places, wound its way through a labyrinth of rocky outcrops and treacherous ravines. The mist, thick and clinging, reduced visibility to mere yards, making every step a calculated risk. Barnaby, initially relying on his instincts and the faint scent of pine clinging to the damp air, soon found himself relying more on his wits. The terrain demanded ingenuity, a quality he hadn't known he possessed until this moment.

He encountered a sheer drop, the misty abyss yawning before him like a hungry beast. Below, he could just make out the blurry outline of a rocky stream far below, its white water a tiny, insignificant ribbon in the vastness of the landscape. There was no way to circumnavigate this precipice; the sheer rock face rose on either side. Panic threatened to overwhelm him, but he pushed it back, remembering the resilience he'd witnessed in the Highlanders. He needed a solution, and he needed it quickly.

His eyes scanned the surroundings, taking in every detail. He noticed a cluster of tall thistles, their spiny leaves reaching towards the sky. An idea sparked in his mind, a faint flicker of hope in the grey gloom. He carefully approached the thistles, their prickles scratching against his skin. With painstaking care, he began to strip the long, tough stalks, separating the fibrous inner core from the spiny outer layer. He worked methodically, his fingers numb from the cold, his breath fogging in the misty air.

It took considerable time and effort, but eventually, he had gathered a substantial collection of thistle stalks. He bound them together, using smaller pieces as binding, creating a makeshift rope, surprisingly strong and resilient. The process was slow and tedious, but the thought of overcoming this obstacle spurred him onward. The rope wasn't perfect; it lacked the smoothness and consistency of proper rope, but it was enough. He secured one end to a sturdy rock, testing its strength before carefully making his way down the precipice, using the thistle rope as a lifeline. The descent was slow and cautious, each movement measured and deliberate. The mist swirled around him, obscuring his vision, but he clung to the rope with unwavering determination. Angus stayed patiently at the top, his watchful eyes never leaving Barnaby.

The misty mountains presented a series of such challenges. Sometimes it was a narrow ledge clinging to a near-vertical cliff face, other times a treacherous bog that threatened to swallow him whole. He used the same ingenuity repeatedly, fashioning makeshift bridges from fallen logs and creating handholds from the sturdy roots of ancient trees. Each obstacle overcome fueled his resolve, building his confidence and resilience. The journey was shaping him, molding him into someone tougher, more resourceful, more capable than he ever imagined. He was learning to rely not only on his physical strength but also on his mental agility and his capacity for problem-solving.

He encountered various animals during his travels. Agile mountain goats, seemingly unconcerned by the precipitous terrain, would scamper effortlessly over rocks that Barnaby would have to carefully navigate. He saw shy deer, their coats blending seamlessly with the heather-covered hills. Once, he even glimpsed a majestic golden eagle soaring effortlessly in the swirling mists, its keen eyes scanning the landscape below. These encounters, however fleeting, filled him with a sense of awe and wonder.

The misty mountains weren't just a physical challenge; they also tested his mental fortitude. The isolation, the constant damp chill, the ever-present threat of the unknown – all these factors chipped away at his resolve. There were moments of doubt, moments when he questioned his ability to continue. But then he would remember the kindness of the Highlanders, their warmth and hospitality, and their stories of resilience and courage. These memories spurred him on, giving him strength when he was weak and hope when he felt despair.

He learned to read the signs of the mountains: the subtle shifts in the wind, the change in the scent of the air, the way the mist would cling to certain areas and dissipate in others. He began to recognize the language of the mountain itself – its moods, its rhythms, its hidden pathways. He discovered hidden streams, their waters crystal clear and sweet, offering him much-needed sustenance. He found patches of edible berries, their tart sweetness a welcome relief from the monotony of his rations.

One evening, he found a small, sheltered cave, hidden amongst the rocks. Exhausted and chilled to the bone, he crawled inside, grateful for the protection from the wind and rain. He built a small fire, using the dry branches he had gathered along the way. The warmth of the flames chased away the cold, and as he watched the flickering light dance on the cave walls, he felt a sense of peace settle over him. He was alone, yet he felt connected to the mountains, to the land, to something far greater than himself.

As days turned into nights, he traversed deep gorges where the mist seemed to become a living entity, obscuring his path and blurring the edges of reality. It coiled around him like an ethereal serpent, whispering secrets only the mountains could understand. The silence was piercing, broken only by the occasional screech of a hawk or the gurgle of a hidden stream. Yet, the silence wasn't empty; it was filled with the presence of the mountains themselves, a powerful, ancient energy that filled Barnaby with a sense of awe.

The landscape changed as he climbed higher. The heather gave way to bare rock, and the mist thinned, revealing breathtaking vistas stretching as far as the eye could see. He glimpsed distant valleys, their green carpets dotted with small farmsteads, and towering peaks that pierced the sky. The mountains, once daunting and intimidating, began to reveal their beauty, their wild majesty. He felt a growing respect for their power, for their enduring strength. He began to understand the connection that the Highlanders felt to this land – a deep, abiding bond forged over centuries of shared history and mutual respect.

His journey through the Misty Mountains was a crucible. It tested his limits, physically and mentally. But it also transformed him, revealing hidden strengths and resilience he never knew he possessed. He emerged from the mountains a changed person – stronger, wiser, and more connected to the natural world than he had ever been. The mountains had been a challenge, but they had also been a teacher, a guide, a transformative force in his life. He was ready for whatever lay ahead, confident in his abilities and grateful for the lessons learned in the heart of the Scottish Highlands. Angus, his faithful companion, remained at his side, their bond strengthened by the shared hardships and triumphs of their journey. They continued their journey, ever onward, their hearts filled with anticipation for what lay beyond the mountains.

The wind whipped Barnaby's hair across his face, stinging his eyes with icy droplets. He paused, breathing heavily, his lungs burning with the exertion of the climb. The path, or rather, the lack of one, wound precariously along a narrow ridge, the drop on either side a dizzying expanse of mist-shrouded nothingness. Angus, ever vigilant, whined softly, his nose twitching as he sniffed the air, a silent guardian against the unseen dangers lurking in the swirling grey.

A prickle of fear stirred in Barnaby, swiftly overtaken by a rush of exhilaration. He was high above the world, a speck against the vast backdrop of the Misty Mountains. The view, though obscured by the mist, was awe-inspiring, a landscape of rugged peaks and hidden valleys stretching as far as the eye could see. He felt a deep connection to this wild, untamed land, a sense of belonging he hadn't experienced before.

He reached into his backpack, pulling out a half-eaten oatcake and a flask of water. The oatcake, now slightly softened by the damp air, was surprisingly satisfying, the simple sustenance a welcome reward for his efforts. He drank deeply from the flask, the cold water invigorating and refreshing. As he ate, he looked out at the panoramic view before him, the vastness of the landscape dwarfing him into insignificance.

Suddenly, a hearty laugh startled him. He spun around, expecting to find some mischievous mountain spirit, but instead, he saw a figure emerging from the mist, a silhouette against the grey canvas. As the figure drew closer, Barnaby recognized the familiar sight of a kilt and the distinctive glint of a silver sporran. It was an old shepherd, his face weathered and wrinkled like the bark of an ancient oak, his eyes twinkling with mischief and kindness. He carried a long shepherd's crook and, surprisingly, a rather modern-looking camera.

"Well now, lad," the shepherd boomed, his voice surprisingly strong for a man of his apparent age. "You've made it further than most. Not many venture this high." He smiled, a network of fine lines crinkling around his eyes. "Mind telling me your name?"

Barnaby introduced himself, explaining his journey and his quest. The shepherd listened patiently, nodding his head occasionally, his gaze fixed on Barnaby with a keen, perceptive look. When Barnaby had finished, the shepherd chuckled. "A brave lad, you are," he said. "I've seen many a traveler come this way, but few with your spirit. Tell me, have you seen the golden eagle yet? They nest somewhere up higher, amongst the peaks."

He then produced his camera, a sleek, black device that seemed out of place in this rugged, ancient landscape. "Hold still now," he said, raising the camera to his eye. "Let me capture this moment. It's not every day I see such a determined young man amongst the heather."

Barnaby, slightly embarrassed but also feeling a surge of pride, obliged. He sat down amidst the vibrant purple heather, the wind ruffling his hair, the vast expanse of the mountains forming a stunning backdrop. The shepherd snapped several pictures, his movements surprisingly deft and experienced for someone seemingly so unassuming.

After the photographs were taken, the shepherd handed Barnaby a small, flat object wrapped in a piece of cloth. Unwrapping it carefully, Barnaby discovered a smooth, grey stone, etched with strange symbols. "Keep this," the shepherd said. "It's a little something to remember your journey by. It's said to bring good luck to those who find their way through the Misty Mountains."

Barnaby thanked him profusely, feeling a warmth spread through his heart. The shepherd's kindness and the unexpected gift were a welcome respite from the solitude and challenges of the climb. He felt a renewed sense of purpose, a strengthening of his resolve. He tucked the stone safely into his pocket, a concrete reminder of his adventure.

The shepherd continued his work, his silhouette disappearing slowly into the mist as he made his way across the hillside. Barnaby watched him go, feeling a deep sense of gratitude. The encounter had been a surprising yet welcome interruption to his arduous journey. He felt an innermost sense of connection to the old shepherd, a link to the ancient traditions and resilience of the Highland people. He reflected on the kindness shown to him and the unwavering support he had found throughout his adventures thus far.

He continued his ascent, the shepherd's words echoing in his mind. He thought of the golden eagle, its majesty and freedom mirroring his spirit. The stone, now nestled safely in his pocket, felt warm and comforting, a symbol of the unexpected kindness he had encountered along his path. The challenges ahead were still daunting, but his spirit remained unbroken. The view, though shrouded in mist, had opened to reveal not only magnificent landscapes but the beauty of human interaction and the enduring warmth of human kindness. The combination of the vastness of the Highland landscape and the unexpected generosity of its inhabitants had further fueled his resolve to press on, to reach his goal, and to experience all that the Highlands had to offer.

As the day wore on, the mist began to thin, revealing glimpses of breathtaking vistas. He saw distant glens bathed in sunlight, the green valleys dotted with sheep grazing peacefully. He saw waterfalls cascading down rocky cliffs, their roar a symphony of nature's power. The mountains themselves seemed to be unveiling their beauty, their wild majesty, slowly revealing their many hidden secrets. Each vista was more breathtaking than the last.

He realized that his journey wasn't just about reaching a destination; it was about the journey itself, the lessons learned, the challenges overcome, and the unexpected connections made. He felt an overwhelming sense of peace, a deep contentment that surpassed any physical discomfort. The mountains, once a daunting obstacle, had become his teacher, his guide, his confidante.

He pressed on, his pace steady and deliberate, guided by the sun, the wind, and the echoes of the shepherd's laugh. He carried with him not just the physical weight of his pack, but also the weight of his experiences, his memories, and the unwavering spirit of the Scottish Highlands. The path was not always easy; there would be more obstacles and challenges, but now, he walked not with fear but with anticipation, with a heart full of hope and a spirit emboldened by the beauty and resilience of the land and its people. The old shepherd's image and the gift of the stone became symbolic of his journey, a reminder of the kindness and unexpected joys that could be found even in the wildest, most challenging terrains. He looked forward to seeing more of what these mountains had to offer. Angus, ever by his side, seemed to share in his renewed determination, his tail wagging with quiet enthusiasm as they continued their journey out of the heart of the Scottish Highlands. The adventure was far from over, but Barnaby felt ready for whatever came next. The mountains had tested him, but they had also revealed a strength and resilience he never knew he possessed. He was ready. He was, indeed, ready for anything.

Angus and Barnaby descended the ragged crags together, marveling at the ever-changing beautiful scenery. He was happy and sad at the same time as he realized their odyssey together was coming to an end. They arrived at a bus stop at the foot of the highlands where Barnaby said his goodbyes to his faithful companion and boarded a bus to Edinburgh - wedged between a bagpipe and a disgruntled cat. He was content and excited about his next adventure.

Chapter 4:

Himalayan Heights

The Scottish Highlands, with their rugged beauty and unexpected kindness, had prepared Barnaby well. Yet, nothing could have truly prepared him for the Himalayas. The sheer scale of the mountains dwarfed even his most ambitious expectations. After weeks spent traversing the gentler slopes of the Scottish hills, he found himself at the foot of the colossal Himalayan range, a wall of snow-capped peaks piercing the sky. The air was crisp and thin, carrying the scent of pine and snow, a stark contrast to the damp, earthy aroma of the Highlands. His sense of adventure had never been so thick.

He had journeyed for weeks, making his way through bustling markets and quiet villages, always keeping his eyes fixed on the towering peaks in the distance. The journey itself was an adventure, a tapestry woven with the threads of vibrant cultures and breathtaking landscapes. He'd learned to haggle in Nepali, tasted exotic fruits he'd never even heard of before, and slept under a sky bursting with stars, brighter and more numerous than he'd ever imagined. Each sunrise painted a new masterpiece across the canvas of the mountains, the colors shifting from deep purples and fiery oranges to soft pinks and gentle blues.

He'd heard tales of the yaks, magnificent creatures perfectly adapted to the harsh mountain environment. These weren't the gentle sheep he'd seen in the Scottish glens; these were powerful, majestic beasts, their long, shaggy coats protecting against the biting winds and icy temperatures. Finding a yak to carry him higher into the mountains proved to be both a challenge and an unexpected delight.

It wasn't a simple matter of finding a yak and hopping on; it required a level of understanding and respect for these animals and their herders. He spent several days in a small village nestled at the base of the mountains, observing the yak herders, learning their ways, and earning their trust. He learned how to approach the yaks calmly, how to read their moods, and how to communicate with them through gentle touch and soothing words. The villagers, with their kind smiles and generous hospitality, quickly became his friends. They shared their stories, their songs, and their wisdom, imparting knowledge about the mountains, their dangers, and their beauty. They shared food around crackling fires, the warmth of the flames combating the chill of the night. The nights were filled with laughter, stories, and the hypnotic rhythm of Nepali lullabies.

Finally, after much patience and a healthy dose of luck, he found himself facing a magnificent yak, its eyes as deep and dark as the mountain shadows. Its fur was the color of dark chocolate, thick and long, protecting it from the harsh elements. Its horns, curved and powerful, seemed to reach towards the sky itself. The herder, a wizened old man named Tenzin, spoke to the yak in a low, soothing voice, his words gentle and respectful. Tenzin then introduced Barnaby, highlighting his respect for the mountains and his determination to reach the higher peaks.

Barnaby, armed with the knowledge gained from Tenzin and the villagers, approached the yak slowly and calmly. He reached out a hand, gently stroking the yak's thick fur. The yak responded with a low rumble, a sound that seemed to vibrate through the very ground beneath Barnaby's feet. He felt a strange connection with the creature, a silent understanding that transcended language. It felt like a partnership, a mutual respect forming between man and beast.

With Tenzin's help, Barnaby secured his supplies on the yak's back, his backpack strapped carefully to its sturdy frame. He climbed onto the yak's broad back, feeling the rhythmic sway of its powerful strides. It was an exhilarating experience, a harmonious partnership between man and beast, ascending the unforgiving slopes of the Himalayas. The air grew thinner with each step upward, the landscape slowly transforming from lush green valleys to a stark, breathtaking world of snow and ice.

The climb was arduous. The path, if it could even be called a path, was nothing more than a narrow, winding track carved into the mountainside. Sometimes, it was barely visible, disappearing entirely at times under a fresh blanket of snow. The yak's surefootedness was his salvation, its massive hooves finding purchase on the icy slopes with remarkable ease. Barnaby clung to the yak's back, his grip tightening as they navigated treacherous turns and sharp inclines.

The air grew colder, thinner, drier. Barnaby's lungs burned with each breath, the exertion pushing his body to its limits. He drank deeply from his water flask, the icy water a welcome relief. He ate sparingly from his rations, conserving his energy for the ascent. Despite the challenges, a sense of wonder and exhilaration filled him. The views were breathtaking, panoramic expanses unfolding before him with each upward step. Glaciers snaked their way down mountain slopes, their icy tongues glistening in the sun. Distant peaks loomed, their snow-covered summits disappearing into the clouds.

The silence of the high altitudes was profound, broken only by the rhythmic breathing of the yak and the occasional crunch of snow underfoot. The world seemed to shrink, his focus entirely on the climb, on the steady rhythm of the yak's steps, on the beauty of the landscape unfolding around him.

One evening, they paused to rest at a small, sheltered area. Barnaby dismounted, his legs stiff and aching, his body weary but his spirit soaring. He looked out across the vast landscape, the sun dipping below the horizon, painting the snow-capped peaks in hues of orange, pink, and gold. The view was breathtaking, a panorama of unparalleled majesty. He felt an inherent connection to the mountains, to the earth, to the very essence of nature. He felt small, insignificant, yet simultaneously powerful, filled with a sense of wonder and awe.

As the days turned into weeks, the landscape continued to transform, the vegetation growing sparser, the air colder and thinner. Barnaby, his body acclimatized, found a rhythm to the climb, his movements synchronized with those of the yak. Tenzin, his silent companion, had become a true friend, sharing his knowledge of the mountains and his respect for their power. They shared stories, the murmurs exchanging unspoken understandings.

The higher they climbed, the more difficult it became, the terrain growing increasingly treacherous. They encountered icefalls, crevasses, and steep slopes of loose scree. Yet, with each challenge overcome, a sense of accomplishment and confidence grew within Barnaby. He learned to trust both his instincts and the yak, his faithful companion, a symbol of strength and resilience in the face of nature's formidable challenges. His journey, he realized, was not just a physical ascent, but also a journey of self-discovery, a test of endurance and perseverance. He was reaching for the Himalayan heights, not just in physical distance, but also in spiritual attainment. The majestic peaks, once daunting symbols of his ambitious quest, now felt as much a part of him as the very air he breathed. The next stage of his journey was still far ahead, but now, propelled by determination and the memory of shared kindness, he felt a quiet, unwavering certainty he would succeed. The Himalayas, in all their formidable glory, had become his teacher, guiding him towards the ultimate summit, both physical and spiritual.

The air thinned further, becoming a fragile, almost invisible veil between Barnaby and the vast, unforgiving expanse of the sky. The landscape, once a vibrant tapestry of greens and browns, had transformed into a stark, monochrome world of snow and ice. The sun, a distant, pale disc in the immense blue sky, offered little warmth, its rays diffused by the altitude and the ever-present clouds. The silence was profound, broken only by the rhythmic thud of the yak's hooves and Barnaby's ragged breathing.

He felt an acute sense of isolation, a feeling not entirely unpleasant. It was a solitude that fostered introspection, a space where the clamor of the world faded, leaving behind only the raw, elemental beauty of the mountains. He was, in a sense, alone with nature, a humbling experience that stripped away the layers of societal conditioning, revealing a primal connection to the earth.

One afternoon, while traversing a particularly treacherous icy slope, the yak suddenly stopped, its ears pricked, its body tense. Barnaby, startled by the unexpected halt, looked around, his eyes scanning the icy landscape. There was nothing visible, no obvious obstacle, no sign of danger. Then, from behind a curtain of shimmering ice crystals, a figure emerged.

It wasn't a creature of flesh and blood, not as Barnaby understood such things. It was… different. Immensely tall, towering over even the massive yak, it was covered in thick, white fur, matted and shaggy, as if sculpted from the very snow and ice that surrounded them. Its eyes, dark and deep-set, held an ancient wisdom, a knowing that resonated deep within Barnaby's soul. This was no ordinary beast; this was a Yeti, a creature of legend, a being whispered about in hushed tones by the villagers in the valley below.

Fear, a primal instinct, flickered briefly within Barnaby, but was soon replaced by an unexpected sense of calm. The Yeti didn't radiate menace; rather, it emanated a quiet, powerful presence, a sense of age-old wisdom and serene acceptance. It stood motionless for a moment, its gaze fixed upon Barnaby, before emitting a low, rumbling sound, a sound that seemed to vibrate through the very bones of the mountains.

Then, to Barnaby's utter astonishment, the Yeti spoke. Its voice was not harsh or guttural, as he'd imagined, but surprisingly gentle, melodic even, like the wind whistling through a mountain pass. It spoke in a language Barnaby didn't understand, yet somehow, he understood its meaning. It was an ancient tongue, woven from the very fabric of the mountains themselves, a language spoken by the glaciers and the wind, by the stars and the snow.

The Yeti gestured towards a sheltered alcove in the ice, inviting Barnaby to approach. Hesitantly, yet with a growing sense of trust, Barnaby dismounted the yak, leading it to safety nearby before approaching the enormous creature. The Yeti remained still, its massive form seeming to blend seamlessly with the surrounding landscape.

Inside the ice alcove, which seemed to have been carved by the hand of nature itself, Barnaby found a surprisingly comfortable space. The ice walls radiated a gentle warmth, and the air within was surprisingly still and dry. The Yeti, settling down with a quiet sigh, began to share stories.

It spoke of the mountains, of their ancient history, of the creatures that lived within their icy embrace. It spoke of the stars, their distant light illuminating the endless night, each twinkling point a story unto itself. It spoke of the wind, its ceaseless journey across the peaks, carrying secrets and whispers on its breath. The stories flowed seamlessly, each one intertwining with the next, creating a tapestry of myth, legend, and profound wisdom.

The Yeti also spoke of the importance of protecting the environment, of respecting the delicate balance of nature. It lamented the changes it had witnessed over the centuries, the scars left upon the mountains by human encroachment. It spoke of the glaciers receding, the snow melting, and the delicate ecosystem of the high altitudes being threatened. Its words resonated deeply within Barnaby, stirring within him a sense of responsibility, a commitment to protecting the wild beauty of the world.

Barnaby, in turn, shared his own story, his journey from the Scottish Highlands to the Himalayas, his experiences with the kind villagers and the trust built with his magnificent yak. He spoke of his ambition to reach the summit, not for the glory or the recognition, but for the profound connection it would forge with the earth, with nature. The Yeti listened intently, its dark eyes reflecting Barnaby's passion and determination.

Their conversation continued long into the evening, illuminated only by the faint light of the stars. They talked not just with words, but with a silent understanding, a communication that transcended language and culture. It was a conversation between two souls, a sharing of experiences and perspectives, a bond forged in the heart of the Himalayas. The Yeti's wisdom was immense, its gentle nature both humbling and inspiring.

As dawn approached, casting a soft pink glow across the snow-covered peaks, the Yeti rose, its movements surprisingly fluid and graceful for such a massive creature. It looked at Barnaby, its eyes filled with a gentle sadness, a hint of farewell. It placed a hand, large and surprisingly warm, upon Barnaby's shoulder. Barnaby felt a surge of warmth flow through him, not of heat, but of energy, of understanding. It was a farewell, yet also a blessing, a silent promise of protection and guidance.

The Yeti then vanished as quickly as it appeared, melting back into the shimmering curtain of ice crystals, leaving Barnaby alone in the ice alcove. He sat there for a long time, the silence filled with the echo of the Yeti's stories, the weight of its wisdom settling upon his soul. He felt changed, forever marked by his encounter with the legendary creature. He knew, with a certainty that ran deeper than mere belief, that he would carry the Yeti's wisdom with him, not just to the summit, but for the rest of his life.

The experience reinforced his resolve. The summit wasn't just a geographical point; it was a symbol of his commitment to environmental conservation, a testament to the power of human-animal connection, and a profound reminder of the ancient wisdom held within the heart of nature. He felt a renewed sense of purpose, a determination not only to reach the highest point but also to honor the wisdom shared with him in the heart of the icy mountains. His journey had become something more, something far greater than simply climbing a mountain; it was a pilgrimage, a spiritual quest, guided by the memory of the Yeti and its gentle wisdom. He felt ready for whatever challenges lay ahead, knowing that he wasn't alone; the mountains, the yak, and the memory of the Yeti were with him, guiding him every step of the way. The air was crisp, the sky was bright, and in his heart, he carried the quiet hum of a mountain legend, a promise whispered on the wind, a testament to the magic hidden in the heart of the Himalayas. The climb ahead was daunting, yet filled with a renewed sense of purpose and an unwavering faith in the journey. He saddled his loyal yak and, with a deep breath, started upward once more, his heart filled with the quiet strength and gentle wisdom gifted to him by his extraordinary encounter. The majestic peaks, in all their formidable glory, had become not just a challenge, but a teacher, a guide on his extraordinary journey.

The wind, a sculptor of ice and snow, whipped around Barnaby as he ascended further. The landscape, though breathtaking in its stark beauty, was unforgiving. Each step required careful calculation, a delicate dance between his strength and the unpredictable nature of the icy terrain. His yak, a steadfast companion, plodded patiently beside him, its breath puffing out white clouds in the frigid air. Then, a splash of vibrant color pierced the monochrome world.

Far below, clinging to a rocky outcrop, he saw them: prayer flags. Not just a few, but hundreds, perhaps thousands, fluttering in the wind like a kaleidoscope of wishes caught in an icy breeze. They were a riot of color – deep blues, fiery reds, vibrant greens, and sunshine yellows – a stunning contrast to the stark white of the snow and ice. Each flag, rectangular and relatively small, snapped and flapped with a joyful energy that seemed to defy the harshness of the environment.

Intrigued, Barnaby urged his yak towards the outcrop. As he drew closer, the vibrant colors intensified, a living tapestry woven into the rugged landscape. The flags were attached to long lines strung between rocks, creating a kaleidoscopic curtain that swayed gently in the breeze. He noticed that many were tied in bundles, dozens or even hundreds together. Each flag was adorned with intricate designs, texts, and symbols, which Barnaby initially found inscrutable.

As he paused to admire the spectacle, a figure emerged from a nearby cave—an elderly woman with a weathered face and eyes that held the wisdom of ages. She carried a bundle of new prayer flags, their colors still rich and undimmed. Her presence was as comforting and reassuring as the warm glow of a hearth fire on a cold night. Her smile, though etched by time and the elements, radiated a quiet joy, a serene acceptance of the harsh beauty that surrounded her.

She greeted Barnaby with a gentle nod and a warm smile, her voice a soft melody against the wind's howl. She didn't speak English, but her gestures were welcoming and her eyes conveyed peace and acceptance. Barnaby, instinctively understanding her intent, offered her a small pouch of dried fruit and some herbal tea he'd been carrying. She accepted the gifts with grace and gratitude.

Through a series of gestures, pointing and simple drawings in the snow, she began to explain the significance of the prayer flags. Each flag, she conveyed, was a prayer, a wish, a blessing offered to the gods and the spirits of the mountains. The colors, she showed, represented different elements and aspects of life: blue for the sky and wisdom; white for purity and peace; red for energy and strength; green for nature and healing; and yellow for happiness and prosperity. The mantras and symbols inscribed on the flags, she explained, were potent invocations, carrying the wishes and prayers of the people to the heavens.

Barnaby learned that the placement of the flags wasn't random. They were deliberately placed in locations believed to be spiritually significant, where the wind would carry their prayers and blessings across the mountains and beyond. The flags were seen as a form of communication with the divine, a way to express gratitude, seek protection, and offer blessings to others.

The woman showed Barnaby how the flags were made, sharing the meticulous process with a quiet pride. It was a labor of love, she conveyed, involving the selection of specific fabrics, the precise inscription of mantras, and the careful sewing of each flag. Each flag was infused with the maker's intentions, their hopes, and their aspirations, imbued with a palpable spiritual energy.

She explained that the flags were not merely decorative; they were active participants in the spiritual life of the community. Their fluttering movement was viewed as a continuous offering, a constant stream of prayers ascending to the heavens. They served as a visual reminder of the interconnectedness of all things, a symbol of faith, hope, and perseverance. The worn and tattered flags, fading in color, were evidence of prayers carried far and wide, their message delivered on the winds.

As Barnaby spent more time with the woman, he began to appreciate the profound spiritual significance of these flags. They weren't simply colorful decorations; they were tangible expressions of faith, hope, and connection. They represented the indomitable spirit of the people who lived in harmony with the rugged mountain landscape.

He observed the woman's quiet reverence as she added new flags to the existing lines. She carefully unfurled each one, smoothing out the fabric, and then affixed it to the line with a gentle touch, her actions imbued with a deep sense of purpose and respect. The fluttering flags represented a silent conversation between the people and the mountains, a dialogue between human aspirations and the vastness of the natural world.

Barnaby felt a deep sense of peace and tranquility amidst the vibrant colors and the constant fluttering motion of the prayer flags. He understood the importance of community and faith within the harsh environment of the Himalayas. It was a feeling unlike anything he'd ever experienced before. The harshness of the mountains was softened, somehow, by the sheer vibrancy and optimistic spirit of the prayer flags. Their presence was a testament to the human ability to find beauty and meaning even in the most challenging circumstances.

The woman showed him how to write a simple prayer on a small piece of cloth, guiding his hand as he carefully traced symbols and words she dictated. It was a deeply moving experience, a feeling of connection and participation in something ancient and profound. Barnaby's prayer, written in clumsy but heartfelt script, was a simple expression of gratitude for the journey and a hope for the preservation of this fragile and beautiful world. He carefully attached it to the line of prayer flags, his small offering becoming part of the vibrant and flowing tapestry of wishes and blessings.

As the sun dipped below the horizon, casting long shadows across the snow-covered peaks, Barnaby bid farewell to the elderly woman. He felt entirely changed by his encounter, his heart filled with a newfound appreciation for the spiritual richness of the Himalayan culture. He carried with him not just the memory of the vibrant prayer flags but the essence of their message – a testament to the resilience of the human spirit, the power of faith, and the beauty of finding meaning in the face of adversity. The image of those fluttering flags, each carrying a prayer on the wind, became a symbol of hope and perseverance, a beacon guiding him on the rest of his journey to the summit. The air was crisp, his heart light, and the path ahead seemed less daunting, bathed in the warm glow of the Himalayan sunset and the enduring spirit of the prayer flags. He felt ready to face whatever challenges remained, knowing he carried with him not only the wisdom of the Yeti but the spirit and hope embodied in the vibrant prayer flags of the Himalayas. The mountains themselves seemed to offer a silent blessing, their silence now filled with the whispering prayers carried on the wind. He resumed his climb, his steps lighter, his spirit renewed, carrying with him the radiant colors and the hopeful message of the prayer flags – a constant reminder of the interconnectedness of humanity and nature, a testament to the human spirit's ability to find beauty and hope amidst the stark, breathtaking beauty of the Himalayas.

The sun, a pale disc in the vast expanse of the sky, offered little warmth. The air bit with a ferocity that threatened to steal the very breath from Barnaby's lungs. He pressed onward, his sturdy yak, a furry mountain sentinel, plodding faithfully beside him. The snow, a pristine white blanket, concealed treacherous pitfalls. Each step was a gamble, a calculated risk against the unforgiving landscape. One misstep, and the icy grip of the mountain could claim him.

Barnaby's small stature, usually a source of amusement, now proved surprisingly advantageous. His low center of gravity, a gift from his gnome heritage, helped him maintain his balance on the slippery slopes. He moved with a surprising agility, his movements fluid and precise, a testament to his years spent navigating the rocky terrains of his homeland. He had faced slippery stones before, but this was something else entirely - a realm of treacherous ice and bottomless crevasses. The air thinned with every upward step, making each breath a conscious effort.

He remembered the Yeti's words, a mix of warning and encouragement echoing in his memory: "The mountain tests the spirit. Only those who persevere, those who embrace the challenge, will reach the heights." The Yeti's wisdom was proving particularly helpful now, as Barnaby had to use both his physical prowess and his mental fortitude.

The path twisted and turned, a serpentine trail etched onto the face of the mountain. Sometimes, it was a narrow ledge clinging precariously to the cliff face, with a dizzying drop below. At other times, it was a steep incline, a seemingly endless slope of packed snow and ice, demanding all his strength and endurance. He used his ice axe with skill, its sharp point striking the frozen surface, his boots fitted with crampons that provided necessary grip.

He encountered crevasses, gaping fissures in the ice, lurking like hidden mouths ready to swallow him whole. These weren't just small cracks in the surface; these were enormous chasms, their depths shrouded in shadow. Barnaby would meticulously probe the snow ahead with his ice axe, testing the solidity of the ground before placing his weight. He spent several anxious moments testing the ice with his axe across a large expanse of what looked like solid snow, only to discover it was just a layer over a near-bottomless chasm. His heart hammered against his ribs, his breath catching in his throat.

He moved with a cautious precision, his eyes scanning the terrain ahead, constantly assessing the risks. He utilized every available handhold, every slight rise in the snow, every projecting rock to aid his ascent. His yak, a silent and unwavering companion, followed his every movement, its padded feet finding purchase in the snow, its surefootedness an emblem of quiet confidence and support.

The higher Barnaby climbed, the more intense the wind became. It howled around him, a deafening roar that seemed to challenge his very resolve. The snow whipped and stung his face, creating a blizzard of tiny, icy darts. He often had to shield his face and stop to regain his breath. Visibility often became quite poor, reducing the already difficult journey to one of pure trust and skill.

He navigated a series of icefalls, each one a breathtaking and terrifying spectacle. The ice, sculpted by wind and weather, formed a fantastical and dangerous landscape of towering spires and shimmering columns. He carefully picked his way through this frozen labyrinth, relying on his agility and his knowledge of ice formations.

He used his skills to create anchors in the ice, carefully testing them before trusting his weight to them. It was a slow, painstaking process, each step measured and deliberate, a dance between caution and determination. His small frame allowed him to squeeze through impossibly narrow crevices.

He discovered a small, sheltered alcove half-hidden behind a curtain of ice and used it as a brief respite from the harsh wind. There, nestled among the icy rocks, he shared his remaining supplies with his yak. He rested for a while, allowing the warmth of his meager rations to infuse his body with energy.

The journey was a test of endurance, not merely physical but also mental. Doubt gnawed at him at times, whispers of failure slithering into his thoughts. But then, he would remember the prayer flags, their vibrant colors a symbol of hope and perseverance. He remembered the elderly woman's quiet faith, her serene acceptance of the mountain's challenges. He remembered the weight of his prayer, a small but heartfelt offering fluttering among the others.

The thought of the summit, of the breathtaking view that awaited him, spurred him on. He envisioned himself standing on the highest point, a tiny figure against the vast backdrop of the Himalayas, his heart filled with a sense of accomplishment and triumph. This fueled him as he pressed on, using his agility, his resourcefulness, his determination, and the inner strength he had found in his encounters with the Yeti and the prayer flags.

The final ascent proved the most arduous. The slope was incredibly steep, and the ice particularly treacherous. Barnaby found it hard to stay focused, his fatigue mounting. Yet, he pushed himself to the limits of his strength, his will unbroken. He reminded himself of the prayer flag he had created, his prayer for the preservation of the beautiful world, and he continued his struggle, his every action infused with the meaning and purpose of the prayer.

Finally, after what seemed like an eternity, he reached the summit. Exhausted but triumphant, he stood on the highest point, the world stretching out before him in a panorama of breathtaking beauty. The snow-capped peaks extended in a seemingly endless chain across the horizon. He had done it. He had conquered the mountain, not by sheer brute force, but by a combination of skill, determination, and the unwavering support of his loyal yak. He had faced the mountain's dangers, and he had prevailed. His journey was a triumph of the human spirit over adversity.

The wind, a relentless sculptor, had carved the snow into fantastical shapes, creating a landscape both beautiful and treacherous. Barnaby, breathless but exhilarated, stood on the summit, his small frame dwarfed by the immensity of the scene before him. The air was thin, each breath a precious commodity, but the view… the view was beyond anything he could have ever imagined. A panorama of snow-capped peaks stretched to the horizon, an endless chain of jagged teeth against the pale blue sky. Glaciers, rivers of ice, snaked down the mountain slopes, their paths marked by the deep scars they had carved into the earth over millennia. Below, the world appeared miniature, a tapestry of valleys and forests painted in shades of white, green, and brown.

He looked down at his faithful yak, its breath puffing out in small white clouds against the crisp mountain air. The creature seemed to share in Barnaby's triumph, its dark eyes mirroring the vastness of the landscape. Barnaby knelt beside his companion, offering the last of his dried meat. The yak accepted it with a gentle nuzzle, its furry head resting on Barnaby's shoulder for a moment, a silent testament to their shared journey and their enduring bond.

Then, a figure emerged from behind a jagged rock formation. It was the Yeti, his fur the same color as the surrounding snow, making him almost invisible against the white expanse. He carried something in his hand – an object that looked oddly out of place in this pristine environment. As he approached, Barnaby recognized it: an antique camera, its polished brass gleaming faintly in the sunlight.

"Magnificent, is it not?" the Yeti rumbled, his voice a low growl that echoed slightly in the thin air. He gestured towards the panoramic view. "A view that has witnessed countless sunrises and sunsets, a scene that has inspired poets and painters for centuries."

The Yeti held up the camera. It wasn't a modern device, but an archaic piece of equipment that looked like it belonged in a museum. The lens was large and prominent, the body made of dark wood and polished brass, intricately engraved with swirling patterns. It seemed oddly incongruous against the stark simplicity of the snow-covered landscape, yet it fit perfectly in the Yeti's hands, as if it had always been meant to be there.

"I have captured many scenes like this," the Yeti continued, adjusting the camera's focus with a practiced hand. "But none quite like this. This is… special." He looked at Barnaby, a twinkle in his ice-blue eyes. "You, my young friend, are the perfect subject."

Barnaby felt a blush creep up his cheeks. He wasn't used to being the center of attention, especially not in such a dramatic setting. But there was something about the Yeti's sincerity, his genuine appreciation for the moment, that put him at ease.

The Yeti carefully composed the shot, positioning the camera to capture the breathtaking panorama. He skillfully arranged the vibrant prayer flags that fluttered in the wind, creating a colorful border around Barnaby's small figure. The flags, bearing messages of peace and hope, seemed to dance and sway, adding to the magical quality of the scene.

The Yeti took several pictures, each click of the shutter echoing in the stillness of the mountain air. With each photograph, he seemed to capture not just an image, but also the spirit of the moment, the essence of Barnaby's triumph, and the raw majesty of the Himalayas. He worked with meticulous care that went far beyond a simple snapshot; each image was a work of art in itself. He adjusted the camera's settings, meticulously checking the focus, the angle, and the lighting. He even repositioned some of the prayer flags to create a more aesthetically pleasing composition. It was clear he treated this as a truly important undertaking.

"Ready?" he finally asked, his voice soft and reverent. Barnaby nodded, feeling a mixture of excitement and apprehension. He stood tall, feeling the wind whip through his hair, the cold biting at his skin, but the sense of accomplishment warming his heart. The cold wind didn't bother him nearly as much as the incredible feeling of pride and achievement welling up in his chest.

The Yeti clicked the shutter. The sound was small, a gentle pop against the backdrop of the wind's roar, yet it captured a moment in time that would never be forgotten. The photograph, when developed, would show Barnaby silhouetted against the breathtaking backdrop of the Himalayas. The prayer flags, a kaleidoscope of vibrant colors, framed him, creating a living border around his small but heroic form. The image would be a testament to his courage, his perseverance, and the indomitable spirit that had carried him to the summit.

The Yeti handed Barnaby a small, beautifully carved wooden box. "This is for you," he said, his voice surprisingly gentle. "A memory of this day, a reminder of your journey, and the heights you have reached."

Inside the box, carefully nestled in soft cloth, was a print of the very photograph he had just taken. The image captured more than just a scene; it showed a triumph of the human spirit against the backdrop of nature's sublime power. It captured the essence of hope and perseverance, and the beauty of a journey well-traveled.

Barnaby carefully closed the box, clutching it to his chest. It was more than just a photograph; it was a tangible representation of his accomplishment, a keepsake he would cherish for the rest of his life. He carefully placed the box inside his backpack, ensuring its safety.

The Yeti turned to leave, melting back into the snowy landscape with an uncanny grace, his silhouette becoming almost indistinguishable from the towering peaks and vast expanse of snow.

The sun began to sink below the horizon, casting long shadows across the snow-covered peaks. The sky, once a pale blue, now blazed with a vibrant display of oranges, pinks, and reds. It was a breathtaking spectacle, a fitting end to Barnaby's incredible journey. He watched the sunset, the image of the photograph still fresh in his mind, the memory of his achievement warming his soul, even as the cold wind bit at his skin. He savored this moment, knowing he would never forget it. This was more than just climbing a mountain; it was an experience that had transformed him. He had faced adversity, he had overcome challenges, and he had learned valuable lessons about resilience, determination, and the unwavering support of friends, both human and yak-like.

As the first stars began to appear, Barnaby and his yak began their descent, the setting sun casting an ethereal glow on the snow-covered slopes. The journey down was easier than the climb up, but still treacherous and demanding. Barnaby's muscles ached, his breath came in ragged gasps, but his spirit was soaring. He had reached the summit; he had captured the majesty of the Himalayas in a photograph; he had a memory to last a lifetime; he had done what he set out to do. He had answered the call of the mountain, and the mountain had rewarded him with the most extraordinary of panoramas and a treasure to keep close to his heart. The journey, with all its challenges, had been transformative. He was no longer just Barnaby, the small, adventurous gnome; he was Barnaby, the mountain conqueror. He had stared into the face of the vastness and come away with a renewed understanding of his own courage and inner strength.

He had conquered not just the mountain, but his doubts and fears, leaving them far below on the snow-covered slopes. He had proven to himself that even the smallest among us can accomplish great things with courage, determination, and the help of friends. And as he descended, he knew he would carry this memory, this experience, and this newly discovered strength with him always. The memory of the vistas, the photograph, and the Yeti's quiet wisdom would serve as constant reminders of the incredible journey he had undertaken and the indomitable spirit that had brought him safely and triumphantly back down the mountain.

Chapter 5:

Rio's Radiant Beaches

The mountain air, crisp and biting just moments ago, was replaced by a warm, humid breeze carrying the scent of salt and something indescribably sweet – a fragrance Barnaby couldn't quite place, but found utterly captivating. He blinked, the lingering image of snow-capped peaks fading as he found himself perched precariously on the back of a remarkably large and surprisingly friendly seagull. The bird, whose name Barnaby later learned was "Rio" (a coincidence he found rather amusing), chuckled, a sound like pebbles tumbling down a hillside.

Below, a breathtaking spectacle unfolded. Gone were the icy glaciers and snow-covered peaks; instead, a vibrant city stretched out before him, a kaleidoscope of colors splashed across a landscape of turquoise ocean and lush, green hills. This was Rio de Janeiro, a world away from the frigid heights of the Himalayas. The transition was so abrupt, so utterly unexpected, that Barnaby felt a dizzying sense of unreality. One moment he was battling the elements, his breath frosting in the air, the next he was soaring through the sky, a gentle breeze ruffling his hair, the sun warming his face.

Rio, his feathered steed, dipped and soared, navigating the bustling cityscape with effortless grace. Buildings painted in every imaginable shade rose towards the sky, their colors radiant and bold, a stark contrast to the monochromatic world Barnaby had just left behind. He saw bustling markets overflowing with exotic fruits, their vibrant hues a symphony of colors; he saw narrow, winding streets filled with people, a luminous tapestry of humanity; and he saw the impossibly blue Atlantic Ocean stretching out to the horizon, its surface sparkling under the brilliant sun.

The seagull swooped low, allowing Barnaby to glimpse the intricate details of the city – the intricate carvings on colonial buildings, the multihued street art adorning the walls, and the lush greenery that seemed to spill out from every available space. He noticed small details, things he wouldn't have observed from the mountaintops: a woman selling brightly colored flowers, a group of children playing a game in the street, their laughter echoing through the air; a street musician strumming a guitar, his music a joyful melody that filled the air with an infectious energy. The sheer variety and energy of it were astounding.

Rio landed with a soft thud on a broad, sandy beach. The sand was warm beneath Barnaby's feet, a welcome change from the icy grip of the Himalayan snow. He hopped off the seagull's back, his legs a little wobbly from the unexpected flight. Rio bowed his head gracefully, as if taking a curtsy. Barnaby chuckled. He patted Rio on his head, thanking the bird for the incredible ride, feeling a deep sense of gratitude for the unexpected adventure. The seagull responded with a cheerful chirp and a flick of its wings before taking off into the sky.

The beach was a spectacle in itself. The sand, a dazzling white, stretched as far as Barnaby could see, punctuated by the occasional colorful beach umbrella. The waves crashed against the shore with a rhythmic roar, their sound a constant, soothing lullaby. The water, a brilliant turquoise, was crystal clear, inviting him to take a dip. He could see schools of brightly colored fish swimming just beneath the surface. People strolled along the beach, their laughter and conversation mingling with the sound of the waves. Some were sunbathing, their skin glistening under the sun; others were swimming in the ocean, their bodies creating ripples in the tranquil waters. The atmosphere was one of vibrant energy and relaxed joy.

Barnaby, still clad in his warm mountain gear, felt a little out of place amidst the throng of beachgoers in their colorful swimsuits. He felt the warmth of the sun on his skin, a pleasant contrast to the biting cold he had recently endured. He removed his thick woolen gloves, revealing his small hands, chapped from the harsh mountain winds. He carefully placed the gloves in his backpack and took off his heavy backpack. He could smell the salty air; he could feel the warm sand beneath his feet and the sun on his face. It was a completely different world from the one he'd left behind, and the transformation was stunning.

He wandered along the beach, taking in the sights and sounds around him. He watched children build elaborate sandcastles, their tiny hands shaping the sand into fantastical structures. He saw couples strolling hand-in-hand, their silhouettes outlined against the setting sun. He listened to the rhythmic sound of the waves, the constant, soothing cadence a calming balm to his senses. He even saw a group of musicians playing samba music, their infectious rhythm making him want to tap his feet along. He wondered if anyone had ever experienced such a drastic and extraordinary transition, from the snow and ice of the Himalayas to the warmth and vibrancy of Rio de Janeiro, all in a matter of minutes.

As the sun began to set, casting a warm golden glow over the beach, Barnaby found a quiet spot to sit and reflect on his journey.

The contrast between the icy heights of the Himalayas and the warm sands of Rio was striking, a testament to the unexpected turns life could take. He felt a profound sense of peace and contentment washing over him. He had faced challenges, he had overcome obstacles, and he had been rewarded with experiences that transcended his wildest imagination. He had conquered a mountain, and now, he was basking in the warmth of a tropical beach. He pondered the photograph the Yeti had given him, a reminder of his triumph. He smiled. This unexpected journey to Rio was a perfect ending to his grand adventure, a perfect capstone to his many exploits.

The setting sun painted the sky in vibrant hues of orange, pink, and purple, mirroring the colors of the city that surrounded him. The air was filled with the sound of waves crashing against the shore, a constant, calming rhythm. He closed his eyes, savoring the warmth of the sun on his skin, the soft sand beneath his feet, and the salty air filling his lungs. This was paradise, and he was utterly content. He could smell the delicious scents of street food drifting on the warm breeze – he was definitely going to try some of those interesting treats later! The sunlit energy of the beach, the lively music, and the friendly faces filled him with delight. This was a new chapter, filled with opportunities for new adventures and discoveries.

The next morning, Barnaby explored Copacabana Beach. He marveled at the bustling activity, the numerous vendors selling their wares, the bright beach umbrellas, and the skillful artistry of the beach volleyball players. He even tried his hand at learning a few Samba steps, although his attempts were far from graceful. Still, the joy of participation and the infectious enthusiasm of the local dancers made him forget his clumsiness.

He spent the afternoon lounging on Ipanema Beach, watching the surfers ride the waves. The sheer skill and elegance of their movements inspired him. He imagined himself gliding across the water, feeling the exhilaration of riding a wave, but concluded that perhaps a seagull ride was enough for the time being.

His days in Rio were filled with discoveries – the colorful houses of Santa Teresa, the iconic Christ the Redeemer statue overlooking the city, the vibrant street art decorating the city's walls, and the exotic flora of the botanical garden. Each experience was a bold brushstroke added to the canvas of his remarkable journey, a journey that had taken him from the icy heights of the Himalayas to the warm sands of Rio. The contrast was sharp, unexpected, and deeply satisfying. It was a journey that had shown him the incredible diversity of the world and the extraordinary resilience of his own spirit.

As he prepared to move on, Barnaby looked back at his journey. The Himalayas, a testament to his physical and mental strength; Rio, a celebration of life's unexpected turns, a vibrant culmination of his adventurous spirit. He carried with him not only solid mementos—the photograph of him and Omar, the rune stone from the shepherd, the photograph from the Yeti, a few brightly colored shells, and several delicious Brazilian sweets—but also countless memories, lessons learned, and a deeply enriched perspective on the world and himself. His heart was full, his spirit soaring. The world stretched out before him, a vast and wondrous tapestry of experiences waiting to be explored. And Barnaby, the mountain conqueror, the beachcomber, the adventurer extraordinaire, was ready to embrace them all.

The air thrummed with a frenetic energy, a palpable
excitement that vibrated through the very ground beneath
Barnaby's feet. He had arrived in Rio just as Carnival was reaching
its fever pitch, a fact that Rio, the remarkably insightful seagull,
had helpfully pointed out with a series of excited squawks and
wing flaps. The beach, usually a haven of sun-drenched relaxation,
had transformed into a kaleidoscope of motion and sound. Instead
of sunbathers and surfers, it was teeming with people, a river of
humanity flowing in a joyful, chaotic dance.

The colors were breathtaking. Costumes, shimmering and
elaborate, exploded with rich hues – greens and golds reminiscent
of the rainforest, blues and whites echoing the ocean, and fiery
reds and oranges that seemed to capture the very essence of the
Brazilian sun. Feathers, sequins, and glittering beads adorned
every imaginable surface, transforming ordinary people into
dazzling, mythical creatures. Gigantic papier-mâché figures,
depicting everything from fantastical beasts to iconic Brazilian
personalities, weaved their way through the throng, their presence
adding another layer of surreal wonder to the spectacle.

The music was inescapable, an intoxicating wave of rhythm
and percussion that seemed to pulse through Barnaby's very being.
Samba music, a joyful explosion of sound, filled the air, its
infectious beat making it impossible to stand still. Drums pounded
a relentless rhythm, their hypnotic beat a primal call to movement;
trumpets blared cheerful melodies, their notes sharp and bright
against the deeper tones of the percussion; and the voices of
countless singers rose in a harmonious chorus, their voices a fusion
of joy and celebration. Barnaby found himself swept up in the
joyous energy, despite his initial apprehension at being surrounded
by such a huge crowd, a feeling of exhilaration bubbling up inside
him.

He watched, mesmerized, as dancers moved with astonishing grace and precision, their bodies a symphony of fluid motion. They glided and swayed, their steps perfectly synchronized, their movements a testament to the dedication and practice that had shaped their art. Their costumes were equally magnificent, each a small universe of vibrant color and intricate detail. They moved with such energy and infectious enthusiasm that it was impossible not to be captivated by their performance. Barnaby found himself tapping his feet, then his hands, then his entire body, swaying involuntarily to the rhythm of the samba.

He felt a strange sense of belonging, a connection to this dynamic community of dancers, musicians, and revelers. The feeling of unity was powerful; despite not understanding the language or the intricacies of the dance, he understood the essence of the celebration – pure, unadulterated joy. It was a feeling of freedom, of letting go of inhibitions, and surrendering to the rhythm of the moment. It was a shared experience, a moment of connection between countless strangers bound together by the collective euphoria of Carnival.

Feeling a surge of boldness, Barnaby decided to join in. He wasn't a dancer, not even remotely, but the infectious energy of the celebration was too powerful to resist. He awkwardly attempted to mimic the dancers' movements, his steps clumsy and uncoordinated, but his heart filled with a surprising sense of exhilaration. The people around him seemed to embrace his enthusiasm, smiling and laughing as he stumbled and swayed, his movements a testament to his lack of grace but also to his boundless joy.

A group of young women, their faces painted with striking designs and their costumes shimmering under the Carnival lights, spotted him and beckoned him closer. They encircled him, their laughter echoing through the air, and began teaching him some basic samba steps. Their patience and enthusiasm were remarkable, and despite his initial clumsiness, Barnaby slowly began to get the hang of it. He found a surprising rhythm within himself, a newfound grace that surprised even him. The music resonated deep within him, a primal pulse that guided his movements.

Hours passed in a blur of music, dance, and laughter. Barnaby, completely immersed in the festivities, felt a sense of freedom he had never experienced before. He lost track of time, the worries and anxieties of his life melting away in the face of the exuberant joy of Carnival. He danced until his feet were sore, his body aching with the effort, but his spirit overflowing with happiness. The experience was transformative, a journey into a realm of pure, unbridled joy.

As the sun dipped toward the sky's edge, painting the sky in hues of orange and purple, the intensity of the Carnival celebrations began to wane. The crowds gradually dispersed, leaving behind a trail of confetti and laughter. Barnaby, exhausted but exhilarated, found himself sitting on the warm sand, the sounds of the receding music a fading echo in his ears. He felt a deep sense of satisfaction, a sense of accomplishment that had nothing to do with climbing mountains or conquering icy peaks. This, he realized, was a different kind of conquest – a conquest of self, a surrender to the overwhelming joy of the moment.

He looked up at the stars beginning to emerge in the twilight sky, their light shimmering above the receding waves. He pondered the stark contrast between the serene quiet of the post-Carnival beach and the frenetic energy he had just experienced. The experience was a profound reminder of the duality of life, the balance between quiet reflection and exuberant celebration. It was a feeling that resonated deeply within him, a realization that both stillness and vibrancy had their place in the tapestry of life.

The following days were a quieter affair, a chance to recover from the exhilarating energy of Carnival. Barnaby explored the quieter corners of Rio, wandering through the charming streets of Santa Teresa, the colors of the houses a gentle contrast to the frenetic energy of the celebration. He visited the Christ the Redeemer statue, its majestic figure overlooking the sprawling city, offering a sense of peace and perspective after the vibrant chaos of Carnival. He found himself drawn to the quieter moments, the subtle beauty of everyday life, appreciating the contrast between the explosive joy of the festivities and the quiet contemplation of the city's everyday rhythm.

He even took a cooking class, learning to prepare some of the delicious Brazilian dishes he had sampled during the Carnival celebrations. The vivid colors and aromatic spices of the food mirrored the colors and rhythms of the celebration, each bite a nostalgic reminder of the joy and excitement he'd experienced. He collected small mementos – brightly colored feathers that had fallen from the dancers' costumes, pieces of confetti, and even a small, intricately carved mask. These were not just souvenirs, but reminders of a life-altering experience.

He found a small, quiet beach, far removed from the bustling energy of Copacabana and Ipanema, where he could sit and reflect on his journey. The rhythmic sound of the waves, a constant and soothing companion, washed away the lingering echoes of the Carnival music, replaced by the quiet murmur of the sea. He looked out at the horizon, the vast expanse of the ocean reflecting the vastness of his experiences. He thought of the Yeti and the

Himalayas, a world seemingly so far removed from this bustling city, yet strangely connected by the thread of his unexpected adventure.

His journey, from the icy heights of the Himalayas to the sun-drenched beaches of Rio, had come full circle. He had faced his fears, embraced the unknown, and discovered a depth of joy and resilience within himself. He was no longer simply Barnaby, the mountain climber. He was Barnaby, the adventurer, the dancer, the celebrant – a testament to the unpredictable and wonderful nature of life's journeys. He carried the memories of the Carnival, a symphony of color, music, and joy, tucked safely in his heart, a reminder that life's greatest adventures often lie in the unexpected turns of the road. And as he prepared for his next adventure, he knew that the spirit of Rio's Carnival, its zest and infectious joy, would always stay with him, a constant reminder of the unexpected beauty and wonder the world had to offer.

The rhythmic crash of waves against the shore was a soothing balm after the chaotic energy of Carnival. Barnaby, finally free from the throbbing pulse of samba drums and the swirling kaleidoscope of costumes, found himself drawn to the tranquil beauty of Rio's beaches. The sand, still warm from the sun's embrace, offered a welcome respite for his weary feet. Gone were the towering peaks and icy winds of the Himalayas; in their place was the gentle caress of the ocean breeze and the soft whisper of the surf.

He began by building a tiny sandcastle, a miniature replica of a majestic fortress he'd only dreamed of scaling. The grains of sand, fine and golden, slipped easily through his fingers, a stark contrast to the rough, jagged rocks of his previous adventures. He meticulously fashioned turrets and battlements, adding a moat – a small, perfectly formed channel – to protect his creation from the encroaching tide. As he worked, he hummed a soft, almost inaudible tune, the remnants of the samba rhythms still lingering in his subconscious.

Suddenly, a small voice piped up, "That's a magnificent castle, sir!"

Barnaby looked up to see a tiny figure, no bigger than his thumb, standing at the edge of his sandcastle moat. It was a miniature traveler, complete with a miniature backpack and a tiny, wide-brimmed hat. He was clad in miniature hiking boots and carried a walking stick almost as tall as himself. Beside him stood another miniature figure, this one sporting a bright red miniature sombrero and a miniature guitar slung across its back.

"Greetings!" Barnaby exclaimed, his voice barely a whisper. He felt a strange sense of camaraderie with these tiny adventurers, a shared bond forged in the common love of exploration and the spirit of adventure.

"We are Pip and Squeak," the first miniature traveler announced proudly. "We've been traveling the world, seeing all the wonders it has to offer."

"I'm Barnaby," he replied, crouching down to get a better look at them. "And I've been on quite an adventure myself. I've just come from the Himalayas."

Pip and Squeak exchanged excited glances. "The Himalayas!" Squeak exclaimed. "We've always dreamed of visiting, but our little legs aren't quite up to the challenge."

Barnaby chuckled. "It's quite a climb," he admitted, "but the views are worth it."

They spent the rest of the afternoon playing together on the beach. Barnaby, his giant size now a source of amusement rather than intimidation, helped them build miniature sandcastles, their tiny hands working alongside his much larger ones. Squeak strummed his tiny guitar, playing cheerful melodies that seemed to blend perfectly with the rhythm of the waves. Pip, meanwhile, regaled Barnaby with tales of their adventures, stories of miniature jungles, miniature mountains, and miniature oceans.

They played a game of miniature beach volleyball, using tiny seashells as volleyballs and miniature seaweed as nets. Barnaby, despite his clumsy attempts, managed to keep the game going, his laughter echoing across the beach. They built miniature rafts from seashells and seaweed, launching them into the gentle waves, watching as they bobbed and weaved their way out to sea.

As the sun began to set, Pip and Squeak prepared to leave. They thanked Barnaby for the wonderful afternoon, their tiny voices filled with gratitude.

"We'll never forget our time on Rio's radiant beaches," Pip said, his voice full of sincerity. "It was a truly magnificent adventure."

"You've made my day," Barnaby replied, his heart filled with warmth. "I'll never forget our time together either."

He watched them disappear into the sand, their tiny figures swallowed by the grains, leaving only a few scattered seashells as a testament to their brief but memorable visit. The setting sun cast long shadows across the beach, the gentle waves washing away the last traces of their miniature footprints.

The following days were filled with similar adventures. Barnaby continued to explore the beaches, discovering hidden coves and secluded stretches of sand. He built elaborate sandcastles, often incorporating shells, seaweed, and small pieces of driftwood into his designs. He spent hours watching the surfers, their movements fluid and graceful as they danced on the waves. He learned to identify different types of seashells, marveling at their intricate patterns and delicate colors. He even tried his hand at bodyboarding, though his initial attempts were somewhat less than graceful.

One day, he met a group of children playing a game of beach frisbee. Their laughter was infectious, their energy boundless. He joined them, his awkward movements and clumsy throws bringing peals of laughter from the children. Despite his lack of skill, he found himself enjoying the game immensely. The feeling of camaraderie and shared joy was invigorating, a powerful reminder of the simple pleasures of life.

He befriended a local fisherman, a weathered man with eyes as blue as the ocean. The fisherman shared stories of his life at sea, tales of epic storms and miraculous catches. He taught Barnaby how to identify different types of fish and how to tie intricate fishing knots. He even took Barnaby out on his boat one morning, sharing with him the serenity of the sunrise as they sailed along the coast.

Barnaby also spent time simply relaxing on the beach, letting the sun warm his skin and the waves wash over his feet. He read books, sketched in his notebook, and simply enjoyed the quiet tranquility of the surroundings. The rhythm of the waves, the cries of seagulls, and the gentle breeze created a soothing symphony that calmed his mind and refreshed his spirit.

He discovered a small, secluded cove where the waves were especially gentle. He spent hours there, swimming in the crystal-clear water, marveling at the underwater world teeming with colorful fish and coral. He felt a deep sense of peace and serenity, a feeling of being completely at one with nature. The ocean, vast and powerful yet also soothing and calming, became a source of inspiration and rejuvenation.

His time on Rio's beaches was a period of reflection and rejuvenation. It was a chance to heal and rest after his challenging mountain adventures. The warmth of the sun, the gentle caress of the waves, and the companionship of new friends helped him to process his experiences and to find a renewed sense of purpose and direction. He carried with him the memories of these quiet moments. With their vibrant colors, gentle waves, and the spirit of adventure that permeated the air, the beaches of Rio had become a cherished part of his incredible journey.

The sun dipped lower, casting long shadows across the golden sand. Barnaby, feeling the satisfying tiredness of a day well spent, noticed a small kiosk nestled amongst the beach umbrellas. The aroma drifting from it was intoxicating – a sweet, rich scent that promised deliciousness. He approached cautiously, his curiosity piqued.

The kiosk was a riot of blues and greens, contrasting with the warm hues of the setting sun. A kindly old woman with a smile as warm as the Brazilian sun sat behind the counter, her hands nimble as she arranged tiny, chocolate-covered balls on a tray. These were brigadeiros, miniature spheres of pure chocolate indulgence, each one a perfect bite-sized treasure.

"Bom dia," Barnaby greeted her, his Portuguese still a bit shaky, but his enthusiasm evident. The woman chuckled, a sound as warm and comforting as the crackling fire he'd once sought shelter beside in the Himalayas.

"Bom dia, meu amigo," she replied, her voice like honeyed molasses. "Would you care for a taste of Brazil?"

He nodded eagerly. She offered him a small spoon and a tray of the glistening brigadeiros, each one dusted with sprinkles that shimmered like tiny jewels. He cautiously picked one up, its smooth surface yielding slightly to the pressure of his finger. He popped it into his mouth, the chocolate melting instantly on his tongue. It was intensely rich, a decadent explosion of bittersweet chocolate, with a subtle hint of condensed milk that lingered deliciously on his palate. He closed his eyes, savoring the moment. This was a far cry from the energy bars he'd subsisted on during his Himalayan trek.

He ate another, then another, each one a tiny burst of joy. The old woman smiled, watching him with evident pleasure. She pointed to another display, this one filled with vibrant purple bowls. These were açaí bowls, she explained, a refreshing blend of frozen açaí berries, topped with granola, banana slices, and a drizzle of honey.

He selected an açaí bowl, its deep purple color a striking contrast to the golden sand. The açaí itself was tart and refreshing, a perfect counterpoint to the richness of the brigadeiros. The granola added a satisfying crunch, and the banana slices provided a touch of sweetness. The honey drizzled on top completed the symphony of flavors, a perfectly balanced harmony of sweet, tart, and crunchy textures.

The açaí bowl was a welcome respite from the heat of the day. It was cool and refreshing, a delicious energy booster that filled him with renewed vitality. He felt the tiredness melting away, replaced by a sense of invigorated excitement. He finished the bowl, feeling both satisfied and exhilarated.

The woman offered him a small glass of fresh guava juice, its tangy sweetness a final flourish to the culinary experience. As he sipped the juice, he felt a deep sense of contentment. The simple pleasure of savoring these delicious treats had a profound impact on him. It was a reminder that even the smallest joys could bring immense happiness.

He spent the next few days exploring the culinary delights of Rio's beaches. He sampled pastel, delicate savory pastries filled with various ingredients, from cheese and beef to shrimp and vegetables. Each bite was a miniature adventure, a taste of local culture and tradition. He tried coconut water, straight from the coconut, its sweet, refreshing liquid quenching his thirst on the hot days. He discovered the sweet, creamy texture of queijo coalho, a firm cheese grilled to perfection, its salty flavor a pleasing contrast to the sweetness of the tropical fruits.

He found himself drawn to the bustling food stalls that lined the beaches, each one a richly hued showcase of Brazilian cuisine. The air buzzed with the sounds of sizzling meat, the chatter of vendors, and the joyous laughter of tourists and locals alike. He discovered the subtle nuances of different types of pão de queijo, the ubiquitous Brazilian cheese bread, each with its own unique texture and flavor. He learned to identify the distinct aromas of various spices, the earthy scent of cumin, the sharp tang of chili, and the sweet fragrance of cinnamon.

He even ventured into a small local bakery, where he sampled a variety of freshly baked breads and pastries. He tasted pão de mel, a honey cake, its rich, spiced flavor a comforting hug on a cool evening. He tried bolinhos de chuva, small, golden-brown rain cakes, so named for their appearance during rain showers, each one light and airy, melt-in-your-mouth deliciousness.

Each culinary experience was more than just a meal; it was a journey into the heart of Brazilian culture. It was a chance to connect with the people, to share in their traditions, and to experience the vibrancy of their spirit. The food was a source of nourishment, both physically and emotionally. It fueled his adventures, providing the energy he needed to explore the beaches, to build sandcastles, to play games with new friends. It was a testament to the simple pleasures of life, the joy of sharing a meal with friends, the satisfaction of savoring a delicious treat, and the comforting warmth of human connection.

The sweetness of the treats, the jewel-toned colors, the tantalizing aromas – they all combined to create a symphony of sensory experiences that resonated deeply within him. It was a stark contrast to the austere simplicity of his meals in the Himalayas, a reminder of the richness and diversity of life, the abundance that nature provides, and the joy to be found in the simplest of things. The culinary landscape of Rio's beaches was a delightful adventure in itself, a perfect complement to the natural beauty and the spirit of adventure that permeated every corner of this incredible city. He realized that the journey wasn't just about physical exploration; it was about embracing new experiences, discovering new tastes, and connecting with the world and its people on a deeper level. The radiant beaches of Rio, with their culinary treasures, had further enriched his already extraordinary adventure. The memories of these tastes, just like the memories of the Himalayas, would forever be etched in his mind, reminders of the unforgettable journey he was on. Each bite, each sip, was a moment to savor, a piece of the tapestry that was his life. He knew that these delicious memories would be a source of comfort and inspiration, fueling him for the adventures that lay ahead.

The sun beat down on Ipanema Beach, the sand shimmering like a million tiny diamonds. Barnaby, his hair slightly windblown and his face flushed with sun and exhilaration, was building a magnificent sandcastle, its turrets reaching for the sky. Around him, the beach buzzed with activity – children shrieked with laughter as they chased the waves, families picnicked under colorful umbrellas, and the rhythmic pulse of samba music drifted on the gentle sea breeze.

Suddenly, a flash of bright color caught his eye. A parade of Carnival figures – dazzling costumes shimmering in the sunlight, feathers fluttering, and music spilling into the air – snaked its way through the throng of beachgoers. They were a fluid harmony of movement and sound, a whirlwind of joyous energy that swept Barnaby up in its wake.

He found himself laughing along with a group of children, who were captivated by the dancers' spectacular costumes. One dancer, a woman with a dazzling smile and a headdress adorned with sparkling jewels, stopped to chat with him. She spoke rapidly in Portuguese, her words a torrent of cheerful enthusiasm that Barnaby, despite his limited grasp of the language, understood perfectly. She offered him a small, brightly colored trinket – a miniature replica of a samba dancer, its tiny details meticulously crafted. He accepted it gratefully, a smile spreading across his face.

A short while later, another figure joined the group – a man with a kind face and twinkling eyes, carrying a large, professional-looking camera. He was an artist, he explained, sketching and photographing the vibrant life of Rio's beaches. He introduced himself as Ricardo, his voice warm and welcoming. He was captivated by the scene unfolding before him – Barnaby, surrounded by the dazzling Carnival characters, his face alight with infectious joy.

Ricardo explained that he often captured moments like this, freezing them in time to preserve their ephemeral beauty. He said that his art aimed to convey the energy and vibrancy of Rio, the spirit of its people, and the beauty of its natural landscape. He felt a strong connection to the city and its culture, and his art was his way of expressing that bond.

He asked Barnaby if he would mind posing for a photograph. Barnaby, still somewhat overwhelmed by the vibrant scene, readily agreed. Ricardo carefully positioned himself amidst the colorful Carnival characters, making sure to capture the radiant energy of the moment. He explained how he would adjust lighting and composition to enhance the picture's storytelling ability, drawing the viewer in to experience the scene as if they were truly there. He spoke about the importance of capturing emotion and ensuring the photograph spoke to the viewers' feelings, not just their eyes.

The click of the camera echoed through the air, a fleeting sound in the animated symphony of the beach. Ricardo reviewed the image on his digital camera, his face beaming with satisfaction. He showed Barnaby the picture, a poignant testament to their fleeting encounter. It was more than just a photograph; it was a moment frozen in time, a glimpse into the heart of Rio's dynamic culture. Barnaby's smile radiated brightly, his eyes sparkling with amusement, while around him, the Carnival characters seemed to dance and twirl even in the static frame.

Ricardo carefully printed a copy for Barnaby, explaining that he planned to use the photograph for his next art exhibition, a show dedicated to showcasing the joy and energy of Rio's beaches. He explained that the exhibition would not only be a visual spectacle but also an opportunity to highlight and celebrate the cultural diversity and spirit of the people of Rio. He hoped his art would inspire others to visit and appreciate the beauty of the city.

The printed photograph felt warm to the touch, almost radiating with the same energy and vibrancy as the moment it captured. It was a reminder of his adventure, a souvenir that went beyond the usual postcards and trinkets. This wasn't just a picture of Barnaby; it was a narrative, a story woven from the colors, the sounds, and the sheer joy of the moment. It showcased the unexpected connections made, the spontaneous friendships formed, and the sheer energy that flowed through the heart of Rio.

He carefully tucked the photograph into his backpack, next to his collection of pressed flowers and sketches from his travels. It joined a growing collection of memories, each one a tangible piece of his journey. The photograph wasn't simply a record of a moment; it was a symbol of his transformation, a testament to the growth he had experienced, both personally and creatively. It spoke to his ability to connect with people from different backgrounds and cultures, to embrace the unfamiliar, and to find beauty in the unexpected.

Later that evening, Barnaby sat on his balcony, looking out at the ocean. He held the photograph in his hand, tracing the outlines of the Carnival characters and his own smiling face. The image served as a reminder of his extraordinary journey, its colors a testament to the richness and vibrancy of his experiences.

He reflected on the warmth and generosity of the people he had met, the kindness of strangers, and the serendipitous encounters that had enriched his life. He thought about Ricardo, the artist who had captured this fleeting moment, transforming it into a timeless piece of art. He considered Ricardo's perspective on capturing emotion in art, and how his own journey was all about capturing moments, creating memories and building experiences. His travels, in a way, were his own artistic expression, reflecting his personality and experiences. He marveled at the fact that a simple beach encounter could result in such a poignant and meaningful memory.

Barnaby realized that his journey wasn't merely about reaching a destination; it was about the journey itself, the connections made, and the memories created along the way. The photograph served as a powerful symbol of this truth. It was a reminder that even the smallest encounters could have profound and lasting impacts, shaping perspectives, forming bonds, and leaving an indelible mark on the heart.

The photograph, a seemingly simple snapshot, was actually a portal to a rich tapestry of memories, emotions, and personal growth. It was a testament to the extraordinary adventure he was living, the unexpected friendships he had forged, and the unforgettable moments he had experienced. He knew he would carry this photograph, and the memories it represented, with him always, a reminder of the magic and wonder that awaited around every corner of his incredible journey. As he drifted off to sleep, the colors and joyful energy of the photograph danced in his mind, a comforting reminder of the incredible journey he was undertaking. The vibrant beaches of Rio, with their kaleidoscope of people and experiences, had imprinted themselves on his soul, adding another layer to his richly textured life. The memory of the photograph and the day it represented would remain a treasured and cherished memory, forever etched into the album of his life's adventures. Each time he saw the photo, he'd be transported back to that moment, to the feeling of joy, to the warmth of the sun, to the energy of the carnival, and to the genuine connection he made

with Ricardo and the other people he met on that memorable day.
And he knew, with absolute certainty, that this was just the
beginning of many more unforgettable adventures to come.

Chapter 6:

Australian Outback

The salty tang of the Rio air was replaced by the dry, dusty scent of the Australian Outback. Barnaby, clutching his precious photograph of the Rio Carnival, felt a thrill of anticipation mixed with a healthy dose of apprehension. He'd traded the vibrant chaos of Ipanema Beach for the seemingly endless expanse of red earth and scrubby vegetation. His journey from Brazil to Australia had been a whirlwind of unexpected connections and spontaneous decisions, a testament to the impulsive yet strangely well-planned nature of his grand adventure.

He'd arrived in Sydney Harbor, the iconic Opera House a breathtaking backdrop to his arrival. The city, bustling with energy, had been a stark contrast to the tranquil beaches of Rio, but held its own unique charm. He spent a few days exploring the city's floursihing culture, sampling exotic foods, and soaking in the atmosphere before setting his sights on the Outback – a vast, untamed wilderness that beckoned with both promise and peril.

His plan, conceived during a conversation with a seasoned backpacker in a Sydney hostel, was as unconventional as it was daring. He was to hitch a ride on a kangaroo.

Not just any kangaroo, mind you, but a particularly large and agile specimen named Kevin, who, according to his owner, a weathered rancher named Rusty, possessed a surprisingly calm temperament and an uncanny sense of direction. Rusty, a man whose face bore the map of a thousand sunrises and sunsets, chuckled when Barnaby explained his audacious plan.

"Kevin's seen more of this outback than most humans," Rusty had said, stroking Kevin's thick, reddish-brown fur. "He's got a nose for water and a knack for finding the best shortcuts. But," Rusty added with a knowing wink, "it ain't a comfortable ride. You'll be bouncing more than a didgeridoo at a bush dance."

Barnaby, ever the adventurer, was undeterred. He'd learned to embrace the unexpected, to find joy in the challenge. And besides, he reasoned, what better way to truly experience the Outback than from the back of a kangaroo?

The journey began at dawn. The sun, a fiery ball rising over the horizon, cast long shadows across the parched earth. Kevin, a magnificent beast with powerful legs and a surprisingly gentle nature, stood patiently as Barnaby, with Rusty's help, carefully secured himself onto his back with sturdy straps and a well-worn saddle.

The initial bounce was jarring, a shock to Barnaby's system. He clung on tightly, his knuckles white, as Kevin launched himself forward with a powerful thrust of his legs. The landscape blurred into a tapestry of red earth, sparse vegetation, and the occasional distant eucalyptus tree.

The hours melted away as they hopped across the seemingly endless expanse. Barnaby, initially terrified, gradually found a rhythm, his body swaying with Kevin's graceful hops. The sun beat down relentlessly, the heat shimmering off the red sand. The air, dry and dusty, filled his lungs, but the exhilaration of the experience overpowered any discomfort.

He saw things he'd only ever dreamed of: wedge-tailed eagles soaring high above, their shadows gliding across the landscape; colorful lizards darting across the sand; and the occasional distant glimpse of a dingo, its lean form a testament to the harsh beauty of its environment. Kevin, his powerful muscles rippling beneath his fur, seemed to effortlessly navigate the terrain, his long strides eating up the miles.

But the journey wasn't without its challenges. There were moments of sheer terror as Kevin leaped across gullies, his massive frame momentarily suspended in mid-air. There were stretches of scorching heat that tested Barnaby's endurance, and moments of intense thirst that made him long for the cool waters of Rio's beaches. He learned to conserve his water, to find shade under the meager cover of the sparse vegetation, and to appreciate the resilience of Kevin, his unlikely steed.

One evening, they came across a watering hole, a small oasis in the vast desert. Kevin, sensing Barnaby's thirst, lowered himself gracefully to drink, his long tongue lapping up the precious water. Barnaby, too, drank deeply, feeling the life-giving liquid rehydrate his parched throat.

As they continued their journey, Barnaby found himself developing a deep respect for Kevin, his powerful yet gentle nature, and his unwavering dedication to the task. Kevin wasn't just a mode of transportation; he was a companion, a steadfast friend in this vast, unforgiving landscape. He felt a connection to the Outback, a sense of belonging in this wild and untamed place.

The stars emerged, a million pinpricks of light in the inky blackness, casting their ethereal glow on the sprawling desert. The night air, cool and crisp after the day's intense heat, was filled with the eerie sounds of the outback – the distant howl of a dingo, the rustling of unseen creatures in the scrub, and the rhythmic thump of Kevin's powerful feet on the earth.

The journey, though challenging, was filled with a unique kind of beauty. The vastness of the landscape, the silence broken only by the sounds of nature, and the unique connection he formed with Kevin created a deep sense of wonder and awe. It was a journey that tested his limits, stretched his resilience, and ultimately, enriched his soul. He was no longer just Barnaby, the boy from Rio; he was Barnaby, the adventurer, the voyager, the one who'd traversed the vast Australian Outback on the back of a kangaroo. He knew this experience would stay with him forever, etched into his memories as vividly as the Rio Carnival photograph nestled safely in his backpack. And as he drifted off to sleep under the starlit sky, cradled by the rhythmic thump of Kevin's powerful leaps, he knew that his journey was far from over. There were still many more adventures awaiting him, many more stories to be written in the album of his incredible life. The next chapter, he felt, would be equally as thrilling and unexpected as this one. The photograph from Rio, a reminder of another extraordinary adventure, felt warm in his pocket.

The rhythmic thud of Kevin's powerful leaps gradually subsided as the first rays of dawn painted the sky in soft pastels. They had reached a grove of eucalyptus trees, their silvery-grey leaves shimmering in the early morning light. The air, thick with the scent of eucalyptus, was a welcome change from the dry, dusty air of the open plains. Kevin, sensing the change in terrain, slowed to a gentle amble, his large, brown eyes scanning the surroundings with an almost human curiosity.

As he dismounted, carefully and gratefully, he felt a stiffness in his muscles he hadn't anticipated. His legs, unaccustomed to the constant bouncing, felt like jelly. But the exhilaration of the journey far outweighed any physical discomfort. He stretched, inhaling the refreshing scent of the eucalyptus leaves, feeling a sense of accomplishment wash over him. This was truly an experience unlike any other.

It was then that he saw him. High up in the branches of a towering eucalyptus tree, nestled amongst the silvery leaves, was a koala. He was a magnificent creature, his thick, grey fur blending seamlessly with the bark of the tree. His large, round eyes, dark and expressive, seemed to hold an ancient wisdom. He looked down at him, his gaze steady and unblinking, as if he'd been expecting him.

For a moment, they simply looked at each other, a silent understanding passing between them. Then, to his astonishment, the koala slowly descended the tree, moving with a surprising grace and agility. He ambled towards him, stopping a few feet away, his posture relaxed and seemingly unafraid.

"G'day," he said, his voice a low rumble that seemed to emanate from deep within his furry chest. "You're a long way from Rio, aren't you?" Barnaby was speechless. He had never imagined that he would have a conversation with a koala, let alone one that spoke perfect English. He could only nod, his jaw agape.

"Don't be startled," the koala chuckled, a sound like dry leaves rustling in the breeze. "We koalas are quite sociable, in our own way. Name's Bruce. And you are?"

"I'm Barnaby," he replied, still slightly dazed. "I'm… I'm travelling from Brazil."

Bruce nodded, his large ears twitching slightly. "A long journey indeed. Kevin told me you were coming. He's a good bloke, that Kevin. Though a little rough on the suspension, if you catch my drift."

They sat down together under the shade of the eucalyptus tree, its fragrant leaves offering a welcome respite from the harsh Australian sun. Bruce, it turned out, was a fountain of knowledge about the Outback. He spoke of the unique flora and fauna of this ancient land, of the delicate balance of nature, and of the vital importance of conservation.

He spoke of the eucalyptus trees, explaining their vital role in the ecosystem, providing food and shelter for countless creatures. He told Barnaby about the various species of birds that called this grove home, their vibrant colors and melodious songs a testament to the rich biodiversity of the Outback. He pointed out a tiny, brightly colored lizard darting across the ground, explaining its unique adaptations to the harsh environment.

Bruce told Barnaby about the dingos, their role as apex predators in maintaining the delicate balance of the ecosystem. He spoke of their cunning and their resilience, their ability to survive in this challenging landscape. He spoke with a deep respect for these creatures, emphasizing their importance in the circle of life.

He also shared stories of the Aboriginal people, their deep connection to the land, their ancient traditions and their profound understanding of the Outback's delicate ecosystem. He spoke of their knowledge of the land, their ability to read the subtle signs of nature, and their abiding respect for the animals and plants that shared this ancient land.

"We koalas," Bruce explained, "we've been here for millennia, witnessing the changes, the challenges, the resilience of this land. We've seen periods of abundance and times of scarcity.

We've learned to adapt, to conserve our energy, to live in harmony with this environment."

He went on to speak about the threats facing the Outback – the encroachment of human settlements, the impact of climate change, and the devastating effects of habitat loss. He spoke with a sadness in his voice, a concern that resonated deeply within Barnaby.

"Many of our kind are facing extinction," he said, his voice heavy with emotion. "Our habitat is shrinking, our food sources are dwindling, and our future is uncertain. It's a crisis that affects not just us koalas, but all the creatures of this land."

His words struck a chord within Barnaby. He had travelled thousands of miles, experiencing the wonders of the world, but he had never truly grasped the importance of conservation until this moment. He had seen the beauty of Rio, the bustling energy of Sydney, but here, in the quiet solitude of the eucalyptus grove, he realized the fragile beauty of the Australian Outback and the urgent need to protect it.

Bruce continued, his eyes twinkling with a mischievous light. "But it's not all doom and gloom. There are many things we can do to help. By understanding the delicate balance of nature and taking steps to protect it, we can play a vital role in conservation. Simple things, like reducing our carbon footprint, supporting organizations that work towards protecting wildlife and their habitats, and spreading awareness about the importance of sustainability, can make a huge difference."

He showed Barnaby different types of eucalyptus leaves, explaining how each offered a slightly different nutritional value for the koalas and other animals who depended on them. He described the intricate root systems of the trees, how they helped to prevent soil erosion and conserve water in this arid landscape. He pointed out the different types of insects, birds and other animals that thrived within this ecosystem, explaining how their interconnected lives formed a complex web of interdependence.

As the sun climbed higher in the sky, casting its warm rays through the eucalyptus leaves, Bruce shared his wisdom about the importance of living in harmony with nature. He talked about patience, resilience and the need to observe carefully the rhythms of the natural world. He showed Barnaby how to identify different animal tracks in the sand, how to read the signs of weather patterns, and how to respect the animals that shared this environment with him.

They spoke for hours, losing track of time as they delved into the wonders and challenges of the Outback. Barnaby learned so much from Bruce, not just about the flora and fauna of this ancient land, but about the importance of conservation and the vital need to protect this fragile ecosystem. He instilled in Barnaby a deep appreciation for the delicate balance of nature and the interconnectedness of all living things. He made Barnaby understand that they are all part of a larger web of life and that their actions have far-reaching consequences.

As the day drew to a close, painting the sky in hues of fiery orange and deep purple, Bruce slowly climbed back up his eucalyptus tree. He paused at the top, looking down at Barnaby with his wise, dark eyes.

"Remember, Barnaby," he said, his voice soft but firm, "the Outback is a precious gift, a treasure to be cherished and protected. Your journey here is a testament to your spirit of adventure, but it's also a call to action. Spread the word, my friend. Let others know the importance of preserving this incredible place for generations to come."

With a final wave of his paw, he settled into the branches of the tree, blending seamlessly with the silvery leaves. As Barnaby watched him disappear into the foliage, he felt a profound sense of gratitude for this unexpected encounter. His journey through the Australian Outback had been transformed from a simple adventure into a valuable lesson in conservation. The photograph of the Rio Carnival, a symbol of another incredible adventure, felt slightly less important than it had before. The true adventure now felt like it was just beginning. The memories of his incredible journey and the knowledge Bruce had shared with him would stay with him forever. He knew, with a certainty that surprised him, that his next adventure would be driven by a newfound sense of purpose. The world, he realized, was a place filled with wonder, but it also needed their help, their care, and their understanding.

The sun, a malevolent eye in the vast, cerulean sky, beat down mercilessly. The air shimmered with heat, the ground radiating an almost palpable warmth that threatened to bake Barnaby's boots to his feet. Bruce's words about the Outback's resilience echoed in his mind, but the reality of surviving the heat was far more immediate and demanding than any philosophical discussion. His water supply, already dwindling, felt like a precious jewel, its weight in his pack a constant reminder of his vulnerability.

His shirt, soaked through with sweat, clung uncomfortably to his skin. Each step felt like wading through thick molasses, the effort sapping his energy. He longed for the shade, the cool respite offered by the eucalyptus grove, but the landscape stretched before him, an endless expanse of ochre and burnt sienna, devoid of any significant cover.

Panic, a cold tendril, slithered around his heart. The sheer scale of the Outback, its unforgiving beauty, felt overwhelming.

He had underestimated the power of the Australian sun, its ability to drain the life from a body in a matter of hours. His meticulously planned itinerary, which seemed so comprehensive just days ago, now appeared hopelessly inadequate. He needed a plan, and he needed it fast.

His gaze fell upon a solitary acacia tree in the distance, its umbrella-like crown offering a sliver of hope. It was a distant beacon in a sea of heat, but any respite from the direct sunlight would be a godsend. With a renewed surge of determination, he pushed himself forward, each step a small victory against the relentless assault of the sun.

The journey to the acacia was torturous, every muscle screaming in protest. His throat felt parched, his tongue thick and swollen. He could feel the sun's rays penetrating his skin, the heat seeping into his very bones. The world seemed to blur, the landscape dissolving into a hazy, shimmering mirage.

Finally, he reached the acacia tree, its shade a cool balm on his scorched skin. He collapsed beneath its protective branches, his body heaving with exhaustion. The relief was immediate, a tangible shift from the searing heat to a more tolerable warmth. He drank deeply from his dwindling water supply, savoring each drop, feeling the life slowly returning to his parched body.

Observing the acacia, he noticed tiny beads of moisture clinging to the undersides of its leaves. An idea sparked in his mind, a primitive survival instinct kicking in. Carefully, he gathered some of the leaves, holding them close to his mouth and gently squeezing. Tiny droplets of moisture collected, each a precious elixir in this arid wasteland. It wasn't much, but it was enough to moisten his lips and ease the burning in his throat.

This newfound method of water collection became his salvation, a lifeline in the face of dehydration. He spent the remainder of the day under the acacia's shade, replenishing his moisture stores with each precious droplet. He watched the shimmering heat haze, learning to read the subtle nuances of the landscape, recognizing the signs of potential danger and the promise of survival.

As the sun began its slow descent, he felt a renewed sense of hope. The intense heat had tempered his spirit, honed his survival instincts, and instilled in him an enhanced respect for the power of nature. He had learned to listen to the whispers of the Outback, to decipher its secrets and to adapt to its challenges.

The following days were a blur of sun-drenched landscapes, punctuated by fleeting moments of respite in the shade of other trees. He honed his survival skills, developing a keen awareness of his surroundings and an innate ability to locate sources of water, however meager. He learned to recognize the subtle signs of approaching storms, the shift in the wind, the darkening of the sky, which offered temporary relief from the relentless sun.

During one such storm, he witnessed a spectacular display of nature's power. Torrential rain poured from the sky, transforming the parched landscape into a temporary oasis. He collected rainwater in whatever receptacles he could find – even his hat served as a temporary vessel. The water was cool and refreshing, washing away the dust and grime of days spent battling the heat. He felt reborn, invigorated, his spirit soaring with the rejuvenating rain.

The nights were a welcome reprieve, offering cooler temperatures and a chance to rest and recharge. The stars blazed in the inky sky, their brilliance a stark contrast to the sun-drenched days. The silence of the Outback at night was unusual, broken only by the occasional howl of a dingo in the distance.

His journey continued, each day bringing new challenges and new lessons. He learned to identify edible plants, to navigate by the sun and stars, and to recognize the signs of animal life, the faint tracks in the sand, the rustling in the dry grass, the fleeting glimpse of a lizard darting across the sun-baked ground. His body, once weak and vulnerable, had grown stronger and more resilient. His mind, once consumed by fear, was now filled with a newfound clarity and determination.

One evening, as he sat beneath the shade of a large boab tree, watching the sunset paint the sky with breathtaking colors, he reflected on his journey. He had come to the Outback seeking adventure, but he had discovered something far more meaningful—a deep appreciation for the resilience of the human spirit and the enduring power of nature. The intense heat, initially a source of fear and dread, had become a crucible in which his character was forged. He had faced his limitations and emerged stronger, wiser, and humbled by the experience.

The knowledge gained during those days of intense heat proved invaluable. He learned to respect the sun, to seek shelter when needed, to conserve his resources wisely, and to trust his instincts. His survival wasn't simply a matter of luck or circumstance; it was a result of adapting, learning, and mastering the challenges presented by the environment. This newfound understanding shaped his journey, transforming it from a purely physical endeavor into a spiritual one, a testament to the indomitable human spirit's ability to persevere and overcome.

The journey through the Australian Outback was far from easy, but it was a profoundly transformative experience. The memory of the intense heat, the relentless sun, and the constant struggle for survival would remain with him always, a reminder of his own strength, his resilience, and the power of the human spirit to overcome even the most formidable challenges. The lessons he learned in the face of the Outback's harsh conditions were far more valuable than anything he could have imagined. They were etched into the very fabric of his being, shaping his perspective, refining his character, and leaving him forever changed. It was a journey of survival, yes, but it was also a journey of self-discovery, a pilgrimage into the heart of the Australian Outback and, even more importantly, into the depths of his own soul.

The fire crackled merrily, casting dancing shadows on the weathered faces gathered around it. The scent of eucalyptus smoke mingled with the earthy aroma of the red dust, creating a heady perfume unique to the Australian Outback. Barnaby, huddled amongst the group, felt a warmth spreading through him that had nothing to do with the flames. It was the warmth of shared stories, of ancient wisdom whispered on the wind.

Bruce, his grizzled face etched with the stories of a thousand sunrises and sunsets, had introduced him to the elders of the local Aboriginal community. They welcomed him with open arms, offering him food, water, and the most precious gift of all – the sharing of their Dreamtime stories.

These weren't just ordinary tales; they were the very fabric of their existence, passed down through generations, each story a thread in the rich tapestry of their culture. They spoke of the creation of the world, of the spirits that inhabit the land, the sky, and the water, and of the deep spiritual connection between the people and the environment.

The first story Bruce translated was about the Rainbow Serpent, a powerful being that shaped the land with its mighty body. It slithered through the earth, creating valleys, rivers, and waterholes, its movements carving the very landscape they now inhabited. Barnaby could almost feel the power in Bruce's voice as he described the serpent's journey, the way it created life wherever it passed. He imagined the earth trembling under its weight, the land contorting and reforming under the serpent's mighty passage.

The next story was about the ancestors, the spirits of the first people who walked the land. These ancestors, the elders explained, were not simply figures from the past but ever-present forces, their energy interwoven into the very fabric of the earth. They protected the land, guiding the animals and ensuring the balance of nature. Barnaby was struck by the immense respect shown towards these ancestral spirits. He learned that the people didn't merely live on the land, they lived with it, an integral part of the vibrant ecosystem. Their actions were guided by their deep understanding of the interconnectedness of all things.

Another story described the creation of the stars, how they were formed from the ashes of great fires, each star a tiny spark of ancestral energy, still burning brightly in the vast, celestial expanse. Barnaby listened in rapt attention, his imagination soaring beyond the confines of the Outback, into the breathtaking immensity of the universe. The Aboriginal people weren't simply observing the stars; they were understanding their significance, their connection to the stories of creation and the continuing journey of life.

The stories weren't simply narratives; they were lessons in survival, in respect for the land, and in understanding the delicate balance of the natural world. The elders spoke of the importance of respecting the animals, of only taking what was needed, and of living in harmony with the environment. Barnaby learned about the traditional methods of gathering food and water, of reading the signs of the land, of understanding the weather patterns, and of respecting the cycles of life and death.

One story told of the emu, its long legs carrying it across the plains, its journey mirroring the journey of the people across the land. Barnaby learned that the emu wasn't simply an animal to be hunted; it was a powerful symbol, a part of their history and cultural heritage. The elders spoke of the importance of sharing, of caring for one another, and of maintaining the harmony within the community. These weren't just ethical principles; they were deeply ingrained in their way of life, stemming from a core understanding of their place within the larger ecosystem.

As the night deepened and the stars blazed brilliantly in the sky, the stories flowed, each one a testament to the resilience and adaptability of the Aboriginal people. They spoke of the challenges faced by their ancestors, of the droughts, the floods, and the harsh conditions of the Outback. But the stories also spoke of their triumphs, their ingenuity, and their enduring spirit. They told of how they had survived, adapted, and thrived in one of the harshest environments on earth, maintaining their connection to the land and their unique cultural heritage.

Barnaby learned that the Dreamtime wasn't simply a period in the past; it was a continuing presence, an ever-present force that shaped their lives, guided their actions, and connected them to the ancestors, the land, and the spirits. He learned about the importance of paying attention to the natural world, of recognizing the signs and signals that it provides, and of living in harmony with the delicate balance of nature.

The stories were also full of humor, laughter echoing around the fire as the elders recounted amusing anecdotes of their ancestors. Barnaby learned that the stories weren't just about the past; they were also about the present, a way of passing on knowledge, wisdom, and cultural values from one generation to the next. These were living, breathing stories, constantly evolving and adapting to the changing times, yet remaining deeply rooted in their ancient traditions.

The next morning, Barnaby awoke with a renewed sense of purpose. The Dreamtime stories had not only fascinated him but had also deeply affected him. He had seen the land through a new lens, recognizing the ancient energy and spiritual significance that connected the people to their environment. He now understood that survival in the Outback wasn't just about physical endurance; it was about understanding and respecting the intricate web of life that connected everything. He began to see the wisdom in their practices, the deep understanding of nature's rhythms, and the spiritual significance of every aspect of their lives.

He continued his journey, but he did so with a greater awareness, a deeper appreciation for the land, and a newfound respect for the Aboriginal people and their connection to the Outback. He carried with him the echoes of the Dreamtime stories, the whispers of the ancestors, a reminder of the resilience of the human spirit and the importance of living in harmony with the natural world. Each sunset painted across the vast expanse of the Outback now held a deeper meaning for him, a reflection of the ancient wisdom he had been privileged to witness. The harshness of the sun seemed softened, the vastness of the landscape imbued with a sense of ancient power and enduring spirituality.

The journey hadn't been easy, but it had changed him. The landscape wasn't just a backdrop; it was a living entity, a canvas upon which the Dreamtime stories were continuously unfolding. The acacia trees stood as silent witnesses to the passing of generations, their roots extending deep into the earth, connecting the present to the ancient past. Every rustle of the dry grass whispered tales of the ancestors, every star a spark of ancestral energy.

He started to notice details he had missed before – the subtle shifts in the wind, the patterns of animal tracks in the dust, the way the light played upon the landscape. These weren't just random occurrences; they were messages from the land, echoes of the Dreamtime stories, guiding him on his journey. The seemingly desolate landscape was, in fact, vibrant with life, humming with a powerful spiritual energy that connected him to something ancient and majestic. His understanding of survival expanded beyond the physical. He learned to read the signs of the land, to listen to its whispers, to become part of its rhythms.

Even the heat of the sun seemed to hold a different meaning now. It was not simply a source of discomfort; it was a powerful force of nature, a reminder of the relentless energy that shaped the land and sustained life. The sun's relentless energy, once an enemy, now seemed to resonate with the enduring spirit of the Aboriginal people, their ability to thrive despite the harsh conditions.

Barnaby's journey through the Outback was no longer just a physical challenge; it was a spiritual pilgrimage. He had embarked on a journey to understand the land, but he had unexpectedly discovered an enriched understanding of himself, his place within the world, and the enduring power of ancient wisdom. The stories of the Dreamtime had become woven into the fabric of his own being, shaping his perspective, guiding his steps, and enriching his soul. He felt a deep connection to the land, a sense of belonging that he had never experienced before. The Outback was no longer a hostile environment; it was home.

The sun beat down relentlessly, a fiery furnace in the clear, cloudless sky. Uluru, a colossal monolith of ochre and russet, loomed before Barnaby, a silent sentinel guarding the secrets of the ages. Its smooth curves, sculpted by millennia of wind and rain, seemed to ripple in the shimmering heat haze, an illusion of movement in the still air. The sheer scale of the rock overwhelmed him; it dwarfed everything else, a breathtaking testament to the power of nature. He felt utterly insignificant, a tiny speck against the immense canvas of the Outback.

Bruce, ever watchful, approached, his weathered face creased into a smile. "Ready for your picture, Barnaby?" he asked, his voice carrying the familiar rasp of the desert wind. He held up a well-worn camera, its body scuffed and scratched, a testament to countless journeys across this unforgiving land. It wasn't a sophisticated device, nothing like the sleek digital cameras Barnaby was used to, but it had captured countless moments of beauty and hardship in the Outback.

Barnaby nodded, a surge of excitement and anticipation coursing through him. This photograph wouldn't just be a snapshot; it would be a symbol, a representation of his journey. It would encapsulate the vastness of the land, the challenges overcome, and the priceless lessons learned. He adjusted his shirt, brushing off the clinging red dust that had become a part of him, an almost invisible layer of the Outback itself.

He stood before Uluru, his back to the sun, its golden light casting long shadows behind him. The rock seemed to emanate an ancient energy, a palpable sense of history and power. He could almost feel the weight of time, the millennia of stories etched into its surface, whispered on the wind. The silence was piercing, broken only by the occasional rustle of dry grass and the distant call of a bird.

Bruce framed the shot carefully, his experienced eyes assessing the light and the composition. He adjusted the focus, his movements precise and deliberate, honed by years of practice. Then, with a click, the camera captured the moment: Barnaby, a lone figure silhouetted against the imposing majesty of Uluru, his shoulders slightly hunched against the sun, the vast, desolate beauty of the Outback stretching out behind him.

The image was magnificent. It captured the immensity of the landscape and the maginitude of Barnaby's journey. Uluru dominated the background, its imposing presence dwarfing everything else. The red hues of the rock contrasted starkly with the deep blue of the sky, a vivid tableau of outback colors. Barnaby himself was a small figure, a testament to the overwhelming scale of the land, but his posture spoke of resilience and determination. He stood tall, despite the overwhelming size of the landscape, his stance a quiet symbol of his triumph over the challenges of the Outback.

As Bruce reviewed the photograph, a sense of pride filled his eyes. He knew that this image would carry more than just a memory; it would carry the essence of Barnaby's experience, a silent testament to the transformative power of the Outback. It would be a reminder not only of the physical journey but also of the spiritual pilgrimage he had undertaken. The photograph encapsulated the silent conversation between the land and its visitor, a communion of spirit and earth.

Later, as they sat around a small fire, the flames reflecting in their eyes, Bruce showed Barnaby the developed photograph. It was even more striking than he had imagined. The image seemed to hold a depth, a quality that transcended the mere capturing of a moment. It resonated with the stories of the Dreamtime, the whispers of the ancestors, and the connection Barnaby had forged with the land.

Barnaby traced the outline of Uluru in the photograph, his fingertip lightly brushing the surface of the paper. The image was more than just a picture; it was a symbol of his transformation, a visual record of his growth and understanding. He had come to the Outback seeking adventure, but he had found so much more. He had found a deeper understanding of himself, his place in the world, and the enduring power of nature.

He looked at Bruce, his heart filled with gratitude. "Thank you," he whispered, his voice thick with emotion. "This is more than just a photograph; it's a memory of a journey that changed my life." Bruce simply smiled, his eyes twinkling in the firelight. He understood the depth of Barnaby's words; he had seen the transformation firsthand, witnessed the impact of the Outback on this young man's soul.

The image transcended the mere photographic representation. It embodied the spirit of the Outback, the resilience of its inhabitants, and the extraordinary power of the land to transform those who dared to journey across its vast expanse. It was a powerful symbol of the ancient Dreamtime, the stories of creation and resilience that were woven into the fabric of the Aboriginal culture. Uluru, in all its majesty, stood as a silent sentinel to this journey, its presence adding a boundless sense of history and weight to the photograph.

The photograph also captured the essence of Barnaby's inner transformation. His initial naiveté and apprehension were replaced by a newfound respect for the land, its inhabitants, and the wisdom inherent in their ancient traditions. He had learned to listen to the whispers of the land, to observe the subtle nuances of nature, and to find a deep sense of connection with the ancient spirits that inhabited this sacred place.

The photograph, therefore, represented more than just a single moment in time. It encapsulated the entire journey, the physical challenges, the spiritual growth, and the remarkbale transformation that Barnaby had experienced. It was a powerful reminder of the enduring spirit of the human heart, the ability to connect with nature on a deep and meaningful level, and the transformative power of embracing the unknown.

As Barnaby continued his journey, he carried the photograph with him, a precious talisman representing his experiences and his connection to the Outback. It was a constant reminder of the lessons he had learned, the wisdom he had gained, and the shifts that had taken place within him. The photograph became a bridge between his past life and his new reality, a link to the spiritual journey he had undertaken, and a symbol of the deep connection he now felt to the land.

The journey westward continued. The landscape shifted and changed, but the image of Barnaby silhouetted against Uluru remained a constant companion. Each sunrise, each sunset, echoed the colors of the photograph, reminding him of the strength and resilience he had discovered within himself. He looked at the photograph regularly, remembering the stories of the Dreamtime, the elders' wisdom, and the deep respect for the land he had learned. The image served as an anchor to his experiences, a reminder of the powerful connection he had established with the Outback and its ancient spirit.

Even as the landscape changed, the lessons learned remained. The photograph wasn't just a reminder of a place; it was a reminder of a transformation, a testament to the profound impact the Australian Outback had had on his life. He carried it as a representation of his journey, a symbol of his newfound understanding of the interconnectedness of all things, and a reminder of the extraordinary journey he had undertaken. The photograph remained a constant source of inspiration, guiding his steps and enriching his soul, reminding him always of the power of the Outback and the transformative potential of a journey into the heart of the Australian wilderness. The image became a visual diary, a beacon guiding him towards a deeper understanding of himself and his place in the vast, magnificent world.

Chapter 7:

Amazonian Explorations

The vastness of the Australian Outback faded behind Barnaby as he boarded a flight to a completely different world—the Amazon rainforest. He felt a thrill of anticipation, a stark contrast to the quiet contemplation that had accompanied his time amidst the red earth and ancient rocks. The Outback had been a lesson in solitude and resilience; the Amazon promised a vibrant explosion of life and color.

The journey itself was an adventure. He didn't travel by jeep or even a small plane this time, but on the back of a magnificent blue-and-gold macaw named Skydancer. Skydancer, with her iridescent plumage gleaming in the sunlight, was surprisingly gentle and patient, her large, intelligent eyes seeming to understand Barnaby's excitement. She was provided by a friendly tribe of indigenous people Barnaby encountered on a brief stop in a small Amazonian village, a group whose wisdom and connection to the land echoed the Aboriginal elders he'd met in the Outback. They'd assured him that Skydancer would be a reliable and safe guide.

Their journey began at dawn, the sun painting the rainforest a breathtaking spectrum of greens and golds. From Skydancer's vantage point, high above the forest floor, the view was absolutely extraordinary. The canopy stretched as far as the eye could see, a quilt of leaves of every shade of green imaginable. Rivers, like shimmering ribbons of silver, snaked through the verdant landscape, reflecting the sunlight in dazzling flashes. The air was thick with the scent of damp earth, decaying leaves, and a thousand exotic blooms, a perfume both intoxicating and invigorating.

As they soared through the dense canopy, Barnaby marveled at the sheer diversity of life. Monkeys chattered and swung from branch to branch, their movements fluid and graceful. Brightly colored birds flitted amongst the leaves, their songs a symphony of exotic melodies. Giant butterflies, their wings like stained glass, floated lazily on the air currents. Parrots of every hue imaginable screeched greetings from their lofty perches. The vibrant life pulsed with an energy that felt almost palpable.

Skydancer expertly navigated the dense foliage, her powerful wings effortlessly carrying them through narrow gaps and over towering trees. Barnaby held on tight, his heart thrumming with excitement and a touch of apprehension. He'd never experienced anything quite like this before, the exhilaration of flight intertwined with the breathtaking beauty of the Amazon. The sensation of wind whipping through his hair, the striking colors swirling below, the almost deafening chorus of the jungle – it was an overwhelming sensory experience.

Occasionally, they would dip lower, giving Barnaby glimpses into the shadowy depths of the rainforest floor. He could see giant ferns, their fronds unfurling like emerald umbrellas. He glimpsed the sinuous movement of snakes, their scales gleaming like polished jewels. He even spotted a jaguar, its sleek, spotted coat barely visible amongst the dense undergrowth, a fleeting glimpse of raw power and untamed beauty.

The journey wasn't without its challenges. At one point, a sudden storm raged through the rainforest, a ferocious downpour that sent Skydancer struggling against the wind. Rain lashed down, soaking Barnaby to the bone, but Skydancer, incredibly strong, battled through the tempest, her powerful wings cutting through the driving rain. Barnaby clung tightly, his knuckles white, but Skydancer's determination reassured him.

Eventually, the storm subsided, leaving behind a landscape cleansed and refreshed. The air, washed clean by the rain, was filled with the scent of petrichor, a clean, earthy fragrance that was both calming and invigorating. A rainbow arched across the sky, a spectacular bridge between the earth and the heavens.

As they continued their journey, Barnaby's awe deepened. He learned to recognize the different calls of the birds, the rustle of unseen creatures in the undergrowth. He began to understand the intricate ecosystem of the rainforest, the delicate balance of life that sustained it.

One evening, they landed on a secluded riverbank, the setting sun casting long shadows across the water. Skydancer settled onto a branch, her plumage glowing in the fading light. Barnaby sat beside her, watching the sunset paint the sky in bold hues of orange, purple, and crimson, a fiery masterpiece that was as breathtaking as the sunrises he'd witnessed in the Outback. Here, however, the colors were even more intense, even more vibrant, almost unreal.

He reflected on the journey, the stark contrast between the vast, desolate beauty of the Outback and the exuberant, teeming life of the Amazon. Both landscapes, in their own way, were a reflection to the power and wonder of nature, each holding lessons of resilience, and the enduring beauty of the natural world. In both places, he had learned to listen to the whispers of the land, to respect the ancient wisdom held within its very being.

The Amazon, however, offered a different kind of lesson. It was a lesson in abundance, in the diversity and complexity of life, in the intricate balance of a vibrant ecosystem. It was a journey of intense sensory experience, a symphony of sights, sounds, and scents that overwhelmed and invigorated in equal measure. It was a world brimming with life, an assortment of creatures, both familiar and exotic, all interconnected in a complex, delicate web.

As the stars emerged, illuminating the Amazon night, Barnaby felt a deep sense of gratitude. He had come seeking adventure, but he had found so much more. He had found a deeper connection to the natural world, an appreciation for the beauty and wonder of life in all its forms. He had learned that the journey itself was the reward, the experience of exploring the earth's magnificent diversity, the profound lessons learned from the silent wisdom of both the Outback and the Amazon. His journey had connected him to places far beyond his wildest expectations, showing him that while the landscapes differ, the spirit of nature is unchanging. His heart swelled with gratitude, his senses still buzzing from the overwhelming beauty of this lush, vibrant land. He knew this journey, like the one through the Australian Outback, would forever be etched in his memory, a testament to the incredible power and wonder of the natural world, a lesson in resilience, understanding, and the boundless beauty of our planet. The photograph of himself against Uluru remained in his pack, a constant reminder of his first transformative journey. Now, Amazon has added another rich and vibrant chapter to its journey of self-discovery. The world was vast and wondrous, and he had only just begun to explore it.

The next morning, a chorus of chattering and squeaking woke Barnaby. He opened his eyes to a breathtaking sight: dozens of monkeys, an array of browns, greys, and the occasional flash of orange, were swinging through the trees surrounding the riverbank. They moved with astonishing grace and speed, their limbs a blur of motion as they leaped from branch to branch. Some swung using their tails as counterweights, performing acrobatic feats that would make any circus performer envious.

He watched, mesmerized, as they interacted with each other. There were playful chases, affectionate grooming sessions, and occasional squabbles over the juiciest fruits. He noticed a clear hierarchy within the troop, with older, larger monkeys seeming to command respect and attention. Younger monkeys, full of boundless energy, played incessantly, their antics a constant source of amusement.

One particularly bold monkey, a young male with mischievous eyes and a tuft of unruly hair, caught Barnaby's eye. The monkey, seemingly curious about the unfamiliar human, leaped onto a lower branch, its gaze fixed on Barnaby. The monkey's gaze was intelligent, questioning, and not at all afraid. Barnaby, emboldened by the monkey's apparent lack of fear, offered a slow, deliberate smile.

To his surprise, the monkey responded with a series of chattering sounds, almost like a greeting. It extended a hand–or rather, a paw – towards Barnaby, its fingers surprisingly delicate. Hesitantly, Barnaby reached out and gently touched the monkey's paw. The monkey responded with a soft chirp and a quick lick to Barnaby's fingers.

This seemingly simple gesture broke down any barrier between them. Soon, other monkeys were venturing closer, their initial curiosity overcoming any apprehension. They were remarkably gentle, their touches light and playful. One particularly small monkey, with fur the color of burnt caramel, climbed onto Barnaby's lap, nestled against him, and promptly fell asleep.

Barnaby spent the rest of the morning playing with the monkeys. He discovered that they were incredibly intelligent and social creatures. They seemed to understand his intentions, responding to his gestures and movements with playful antics of their own. He learned that they communicated through a complex system of vocalizations, body language, and gestures. He watched them share food, groom each other, and defend their territory with impressive displays of agility and coordinated movements.

The monkeys' social structure fascinated Barnaby. He observed how they worked together to find food, defend their young, and navigate the complex environment of the rainforest. The older monkeys, the apparent leaders of the troop, seemed to guide the younger ones, teaching them essential survival skills and social rules. He witnessed moments of intense cooperation, as well as occasional squabbles over resources, highlighting the dynamic nature of their social system.

He learned about their diet, observing them expertly extract insects from the bark of trees, pluck ripe fruits from overhanging branches, and skillfully peel away the tough outer layers of nuts. He watched in wonder as they used tools – sticks and stones – to pry open particularly stubborn nuts, showcasing a level of ingenuity that surprised him.

One particularly memorable incident involved a particularly large and grumpy-looking monkey who seemed to be the undisputed alpha male of the troop. This monkey, whom Barnaby nicknamed "Grumbles," initially seemed hostile, displaying threatening behavior whenever Barnaby came too close. However, after a series of carefully-crafted gestures and offers of fruit,

Barnaby managed to gain Grumbles' trust. The monkey eventually allowed Barnaby to groom him, a clear sign of acceptance and trust within the troop's social hierarchy.

Barnaby spent hours observing the monkeys, learning about their lives, their interactions, and their unique way of navigating the Amazonian rainforest. He learned to interpret their various calls—a sharp bark indicated danger, a soft cooing sound signified affection, and a rapid series of chattering signified excitement or playful interaction. The forest floor below became a stage for their captivating performances, a thrilling spectacle of acrobatics and social interactions.

As the day progressed, the playful energy of the troop slowly subsided. The monkeys began to prepare for the evening, searching for suitable sleeping spots in the highest branches of the trees. The setting sun cast long shadows through the forest, turning the leaves into a shimmering mosaic of gold and green. The air grew cooler, and the sounds of the rainforest shifted – the daytime cacophony giving way to a more subdued, nocturnal hum.

As darkness fell, Barnaby bid farewell to his newfound friends. He felt a deep sense of connection with these intelligent, playful creatures, an understanding born from shared moments of interaction and observation. The monkeys, for their part, seemed equally content, their curious gazes following Barnaby as he walked back to Skydancer. They chattered softly, a farewell chorus echoing through the darkening forest.

Barnaby spent that evening reflecting on his day. He realized that his journey into the Amazon had expanded beyond the sheer adventure. He had not only observed but had actively interacted with the ecosystem. He had come to understand the intricate social lives of the monkeys, their complex communication systems, and the dynamic relationships within their troop. He had seen their playful interactions, their cooperative efforts, and their individual personalities, forging a deeper appreciation for the diversity and beauty of the Amazonian rainforest. He knew he would remember these playful, clever creatures for years to come. The experience had deepened his understanding of the interconnectedness of all life, a theme that had resonated throughout his adventures, both in the Australian Outback and now, in the heart of the Amazon.

As he slept under the canopy of stars, the sounds of the rainforest-the rustling leaves, the chirping insects, the occasional distant monkey call–lulled him into a peaceful slumber. He dreamt of swinging through the trees with his new friends, their laughter echoing in the quiet depths of the Amazonian night, a reminder of the joyful encounters of the day. His heart swelled with the joy of discovery, the fulfillment of adventure and the wonder of the natural world. His journey continued, fueled by a deeper understanding of the delicate balance and the magnificent beauty of the planet he was so privileged to explore. He felt connected not only to the Amazon rainforest but also to the resilient spirit of nature, which echoed in both the vastness of the Australian Outback and the lively heart of the Amazon.

The morning sun, a molten gold coin rising above the emerald canopy, cast a shimmering light upon the Amazon River. Barnaby, perched precariously yet confidently on a giant, perfectly formed lily pad, felt a thrill course through him. This wasn't just any lily pad; it was his vessel, his chariot, his unlikely raft for navigating the mighty Amazon. The river teemed with life, a kaleidoscope of vibrant colors and sounds.

His makeshift paddle, a sturdy branch he'd expertly sharpened the previous evening, felt comfortable in his hands. He pushed it against the current, the lily pad responding with a gentle rocking motion. The water, dark and mysterious, swirled around the edges of his leafy boat, reflecting the sky above like a fractured mirror. The air hummed with the sounds of the rainforest – the chirping of unseen insects, the calls of unseen birds, the rustling of unseen creatures in the dense undergrowth lining the riverbanks.

The current, at times a gentle nudge, at others a forceful push, challenged Barnaby's skill. He learned quickly to anticipate its changes, adjusting his paddling rhythm to maintain his precarious balance. He navigated around fallen tree trunks, their decaying wood slick with moisture, their surfaces teeming with vibrant green moss and curious insects. He expertly avoided swirling eddies that threatened to pull him off course and skillfully steered clear of submerged branches, their jagged ends lurking just beneath the surface.

The river was a living entity, its currents a constant reminder of its immense power. He saw playful otters diving and surfacing, their sleek bodies glistening in the sunlight. He glimpsed the flash of a brightly colored fish darting between the aquatic plants. Giant water lilies, their pads larger than his, floated serenely, their delicate blooms unfurling in the warmth of the morning.

Barnaby's journey was far from smooth. He encountered patches of particularly strong currents that tested his strength and endurance. He had to use every ounce of his strength to push against the relentless force of the water, his muscles burning with exertion. At one point, a sudden downpour soaked him to the bone, turning his lily pad into a miniature, bobbing island amidst a storm. He clung to it tightly, his heart pounding, as the rain lashed down, blurring his vision and obscuring his view of the river. Yet, he persevered. The sense of adventure, the thrill of the challenge, fueled his determination.

As the rain subsided, the sun peeked through the clouds, painting the river with a fresh light. The rainforest, drenched and rejuvenated, exuded a vibrant energy. The air, cleansed by the rain, felt fresh and clean. Barnaby continued his journey, his spirits renewed. He paddled past towering trees whose roots snaked down into the river, their branches draped with lush vines. Monkeys chattered from their leafy perches, their calls echoing across the water. He saw colorful macaws flash through the sky, their wings a vibrant splash of blue and gold.

He noticed fascinating details along the riverbanks. He saw stunning orchids clinging to tree trunks, their delicate blooms a palette of colors. Butterflies, their wings like stained glass, flitted from flower to flower. He discovered tiny, brightly colored frogs hidden amongst the leaves, their skin slick with moisture. The rainforest seemed to unfold its secrets to him, revealing its hidden wonders and its intricate web of life.

One particularly memorable encounter involved a family of capybaras, grazing peacefully on the riverbank. These enormous rodents, larger than any dog he'd ever seen, seemed completely unfazed by his presence. They watched him with calm, curious eyes as he paddled past, their large bodies blending seamlessly with the lush vegetation. Their serene demeanor seemed to reflect the peacefulness of the rainforest itself.

As the day wore on, the river began to widen, the current becoming less forceful. Barnaby realized he was approaching a wider part of the river, where the water flowed more smoothly. He felt a sense of accomplishment, a pride in having navigated such a challenging stretch of water. He had learned to read the river, to anticipate its moods, and to adjust his movements accordingly. He had become one with the river, a part of its flow, its rhythm, its journey.

The afternoon sun, a gentler, warmer light, bathed the river in a golden hue. The air was filled with the sweet scent of blossoms and damp earth. Barnaby, weary but exhilarated, continued his journey, his gaze fixed on the horizon, his heart filled with the joy of discovery. He knew that the Amazon River held countless more secrets, countless more challenges, countless more wonders. He was ready. He was ready to explore. He was ready to discover. He was ready for whatever lay ahead, fueled by the confidence of his successful navigation and the awe-inspiring beauty of the Amazon.

As evening approached, the rainforest grew quieter. The vibrant energy of the day gradually faded, giving way to the hushed stillness of twilight. The monkeys grew silent, retiring to their sleeping places high in the trees. The birds ceased their singing, their cheerful melodies replaced by the chirping of crickets and the croaking of frogs. The river itself seemed to slow its pace, its surface reflecting the fiery colors of the setting sun.

Barnaby found a sheltered cove, nestled among the roots of a giant tree, where he could safely spend the night. He secured his lily pad to a sturdy branch, feeling a profound sense of gratitude for the day's successful voyage. He made a small fire, its flickering flames chasing away the growing shadows. As he gazed at the stars, their brilliance reflecting in the calm waters, he felt a strong connection with the Amazon River, a connection born from shared experiences, shared challenges, and shared victories.

The night brought with it a symphony of sounds unique to the rainforest. He listened to the calls of nocturnal creatures, sounds that were both intriguing and slightly unnerving. He learned to differentiate the rustle of leaves from the movement of animals, the chirping of crickets from the croaking of frogs. The rainforest was alive even in the dark, revealing its hidden life under the cloak of night. He felt privileged to be a part of this symphony, a silent witness to the teeming life of the Amazon at night.

As sleep finally claimed him, Barnaby dreamt of a fantastical river flowing with liquid starlight and lily pads as vast as islands. He dreamed of otters guiding his lily-pad boat and monkeys swinging from the branches, cheering him on. It was a dream born of a day spent in perfect harmony with the Amazon's rhythm. He woke to the soft sounds of the dawn, ready to continue his exploration, refreshed and invigorated, his heart brimming with the beauty and wonder of the Amazonian rainforest. His journey continued, not merely as a journey of exploration, but as a journey of connection, a journey into the very heart of the Amazon's soul.

The next morning dawned with a misty breath, the sun struggling to pierce the thick canopy. Dew clung to the leaves like tiny jewels, sparkling in the soft light. Barnaby, refreshed after a night of surprisingly peaceful sleep, pushed off from his sheltered cove, his lily pad once again his trusty vessel. He paddled further into the heart of the Amazon, the river widening into a broad, majestic expanse. The air was thick with the scent of damp earth and exotic blooms, a fragrance unlike anything he'd ever experienced.

It wasn't long before Barnaby's eyes were drawn to the riverbanks, ablaze with color. He saw plants he'd never even imagined existed. Unlike anything he'd seen in botanical gardens, vivid orchids clung to the giant trees, their petals a riot of purples, oranges, and yellows. Some orchids were small and delicate, their blooms resembling tiny butterflies; others were large and flamboyant, their petals a dramatic display of color and texture. He spotted a blush-pink orchid, its petals subtly veined with deeper crimson, a masterpiece of natural artistry. Another caught his eye, a golden yellow orchid with petals that seemed to glow with an inner light, as though imbued with the very essence of the Amazon sun.

He carefully guided his lily pad closer to the bank, mesmerized by these botanical wonders. He saw a cluster of red heliconia, their bracts shaped like lobster claws, standing proudly amongst the lush greenery. Their bright scarlet hue contrasted dramatically with the deep green of the foliage, creating a breathtaking spectacle. Hummingbirds, tiny jewels themselves, darted in and out of the heliconia's bracts, their wings a blur of motion.

Barnaby, ever the curious explorer, cautiously reached out and gently touched a velvety leaf of a large, broad-leaved plant. It felt cool and smooth to the touch, unlike any plant he had ever encountered. This turned out to be a giant water lily, even larger than the ones he'd seen earlier, its pads broad enough to easily support a small person. Its flowers, a dazzling white with a yellow center, were stunning in their simplicity and grandeur.

He noticed another plant nearby, its leaves a striking shade of deep purple, almost black. Tiny, iridescent blue flowers nestled amongst the foliage, adding another dimension of beauty to this mysterious plant. It had a delicate fragrance, sweet and slightly spicy, reminiscent of cinnamon and cloves. A small monkey, perched on a nearby branch, chattered inquisitively as Barnaby examined the plant.

As he continued his exploration, Barnaby discovered a plant with leaves that shimmered with an almost metallic sheen. The leaves were broad and heart-shaped, a deep emerald green with iridescent veins that shifted color in the sunlight. This was an example of Amazon's remarkable ability to produce plants with such startling visual displays. He learned later that this plant was known for its medicinal properties, its leaves used by indigenous communities to treat a variety of ailments.

He came across a vine with large, fleshy leaves, known locally for its ability to relieve inflammation. He carefully collected a few leaves, preserving them in a waterproof pouch he carried for just such purposes. He'd observed that many plants possessed valuable medicinal properties, a knowledge held within the heart of the Amazon for centuries. He knew it was crucial to learn about these plants, not only for his own benefit, but also to protect the rich biodiversity of this incredible ecosystem.

His explorations led him to a clearing where a variety of medicinal plants grew together, creating a natural pharmacy. He found a small tree with bright orange berries, which he identified, after careful research in his trusty guidebook, as a plant with anti-inflammatory properties. Nearby, a shrub with delicate white flowers possessed leaves used for treating stomach ailments. He noted their locations carefully, marveling at the incredible array of healing properties contained within these seemingly ordinary plants.

He learned that the color of a plant often indicated its properties. The bright red and orange hues often signaled a plant with powerful anti-inflammatory or antioxidant properties. Deep purples and blues were often associated with plants possessing antibacterial or antifungal qualities. Barnaby carefully documented each plant he discovered, sketching them in his notebook and making detailed notes of their appearances, locations, and any medicinal properties he could identify.

His explorations weren't without their challenges. He had to navigate through dense thickets of vegetation, carefully avoiding thorny vines and stinging insects. He learned to identify edible plants from poisonous ones, a skill that proved invaluable as the day wore on. He encountered areas where the air hung heavy with humidity, the thick air making it difficult to breathe. But the beauty and wonder of his discoveries kept his spirits high, driving him onward.

He discovered a species of carnivorous plant, its leaves shaped like delicate pitchers, filled with a clear liquid. These plants, hidden amongst the other vegetation, were remarkably efficient hunters. He observed a small insect inadvertently fall into one of the pitchers. The liquid quickly began to dissolve it, a testament to the plant's extraordinary adaptations.

He also encountered magnificent trees, their trunks adorned with a profusion of air plants and orchids, their branches draped with trailing vines. These majestic beings were themselves miniature ecosystems, home to countless species of insects, birds, and mammals. He spent a considerable amount of time observing these trees, recognizing the crucial role they played in the rainforest's delicate balance. He learned about the symbiotic relationships between different plants and animals, the intricate web of life that made the Amazon so unique.

As evening approached, the rainforest began to transition into its nocturnal state, the sounds of the daytime symphony fading into the soft chirping of insects and the croaking of frogs. The sky blazed with a fiery sunset, casting long shadows across the riverbanks, before settling into the soft embrace of twilight.

Barnaby, tired but exhilarated, found a suitable spot to rest for the night, his heart filled with the knowledge and wonder of the Amazon's diverse flora. He slept soundly that night, dreaming of vibrant orchids and towering trees, their leaves whispering secrets only the rainforest could reveal. The Amazon's secrets were slowly unfurling before him, one fascinating plant at a time. His journey was far from over; he knew that the rainforest still held countless more wonders waiting to be discovered. His experience had transformed from a simple exploration into a journey of learning and appreciation for the astonishing complexity and beauty of the Amazonian rainforest.

The sun, a molten orange orb sinking behind a curtain of emerald leaves, cast long shadows across the riverbank. Barnaby, his lily pad gently rocking in the current, felt a contented sigh escape his lips. The day had been a multitude of sights, sounds, and smells, a sensory overload that left him buzzing with excitement. He'd meticulously documented countless plants, each a unique masterpiece of nature's artistry. He'd sketched the intricate patterns on the leaves of the giant water lilies, the glowing hues of the heliconia, and the almost ethereal glow of the yellow orchids. His notebook, usually a pristine expanse of white paper, was now a riot of color and carefully labelled botanical sketches.

Suddenly, a flash of brilliant green and scarlet caught his eye. A large parrot, its plumage a mix of emerald, ruby, and sapphire, landed on a branch above him. It was a magnificent creature, its eyes bright and intelligent, its movements fluid and graceful. Barnaby, mesmerized, watched as the parrot cocked its head, seeming to assess him with curious interest. It hopped closer, its iridescent feathers shimmering in the fading light.

Then, something astonishing happened. The parrot tilted its head again, and Barnaby noticed a small, rectangular object clutched in one of its claws. It was a camera! A tiny, intricately carved wooden camera, no bigger than Barnaby's thumb. The parrot, with a surprising dexterity, aimed the camera at Barnaby, and with a small click, a tiny flash illuminated the scene.

Barnaby gasped. He'd seen cameras before, of course, back in his old life, but he'd never imagined witnessing such a thing in the heart of the Amazon. This was unbelievable! The parrot, apparently unfazed by its own technological marvel, chirped cheerfully, its bright eyes twinkling with mischief. It then proceeded to take several more photographs, expertly capturing Barnaby amidst the lush greenery. One photo showed him paddling his lily pad, surrounded by the majestic water lilies. Another captured him examining a cluster of luminous blue orchids. The third showed him surrounded by the lush greenery, the soft light of the setting sun illuminating the scene.

The parrot, seemingly satisfied with its photographic efforts, hopped back to its branch and with a final chirp, flew off into the deepening twilight, disappearing into the dense foliage. Barnaby stared at the spot where the parrot had been, his mind reeling. He could hardly believe what he had just witnessed. A parrot photographer? In the Amazon rainforest? It felt like a scene from one of his favorite adventure stories.

He carefully examined the area where the parrot had been perched. He found nothing except a single, perfectly formed feather. It was a vibrant scarlet, the color of a summer sunset, its delicate barbs perfectly intact. He picked it up gently, feeling the smooth texture, and placed it carefully in his notebook, next to his botanical sketches. It was a perfect memento of his extraordinary encounter.

As darkness descended, Barnaby prepared his bed of soft leaves under the shelter of a giant Cecropia tree. The night sounds of the Amazon began to fill the air – the chirping of crickets, the croaking of frogs, the rustling of unseen creatures in the undergrowth. He thought about the parrot and its amazing camera. How had it learned to use it? Who had taught it? He pondered this mystery as he drifted off to sleep, his mind filled with images of orchids and a mischievous parrot photographer.

The following days unfolded in a similar pattern of exhilarating exploration and surprising encounters. Barnaby discovered a hidden waterfall cascading down moss-covered rocks, the water crystal clear and refreshingly cool. He swam in the cool water, feeling the invigorating spray on his face. The mist from the waterfall created a mystical atmosphere, creating beautiful rainbows in the sunlight. The area surrounding the waterfall was a haven of biodiversity. He discovered rare orchids clinging to the damp rocks, their petals a dazzling array of colors, and delicate ferns unfurling their emerald fronds. He also spotted a family of monkeys swinging through the trees, their playful chatter echoing through the air.

He spent hours documenting the diverse flora and fauna of this hidden paradise. He noted the presence of several medicinal plants that weren't listed in his guidebook, their properties unknown. He carefully collected samples, preserving them in his waterproof pouch, knowing that his discoveries could contribute to a greater understanding of the Amazon's healing secrets. He learned to distinguish between different species of butterflies, their wings adorned with intricate patterns. Some butterflies were small and delicate, their wings adorned with pastel hues. Others were large and majestic, their wings ablaze with striking colors.

One evening, as he was preparing his camp, he heard a strange humming sound emanating from the depths of the forest. He followed the sound, his heart pounding with anticipation, until he stumbled upon a clearing bathed in a ethereal glow. In the center of the clearing stood a giant tree, its branches reaching towards the sky like gnarled fingers. The tree was covered in bioluminescent fungi, their glow illuminating the clearing in an otherworldly light. The humming sound seemed to originate from within the tree itself.

He cautiously approached the tree, his senses alert. The air around the tree felt strangely charged with energy. He noticed tiny insects flitting around the fungi, their bodies also emitting a faint light. It was like something out of a fairy tale. The sight was magical, the giant tree emitting a magical aura. The fungi were an ethereal display of the rainforest's diversity.

He spent hours observing the bioluminescent tree, captivated by its otherworldly beauty. He sketched the tree in his notebook, trying to capture the soft glow of the fungi, but his drawing could never truly capture the magic of the moment. He understood that there were many mysteries in the Amazon and many undiscovered wonders.

One day, while exploring a particularly dense part of the jungle, Barnaby came across a clearing where a group of indigenous people were carrying out a traditional ceremony. He watched from a distance, mesmerized by their rhythmic chants and the intricate movements of their dance. They were using medicinal plants in their ritual, emphasizing the deep connection between the indigenous people and the rainforest's flora. He felt a sense of awe and respect for their ancient knowledge and their heartfelt connection with the natural world. He realized that the true heart of the Amazon lay not only in its incredible biodiversity but also in the wisdom and traditions of the people who have called it home for centuries.

Barnaby learned to respect the Amazon, to appreciate its intricate web of life and to understand the delicate balance between its inhabitants. He learned that every plant, every animal, and every insect played a crucial role in maintaining the rainforest's health and diversity. He also learned the importance of respecting the indigenous knowledge and traditions that have been passed down through generations.

His time in the Amazon was coming to an end. As he prepared to leave, he felt an overwhelming sense of gratitude and awe. His journey had been more than just an adventure. It had been a constantly evolving experience that had broadened his understanding of nature's magnificence and the interconnectedness of all living things. The bold colors, the sounds of the rainforest, the many plants he'd discovered, and the friendly parrot with its camera would remain etched in his memory forever. The Amazon had left an indelible mark on his soul, a reminder of the beauty and wonder that still existed in the world, a reminder that needed to be preserved for generations to come. He left the Amazon a changed person, his heart full of gratitude for the incredible experiences he'd encountered, vowing to return someday to continue his exploration and to share the wonders of this magnificent place with others.

Chapter 8:

African Safari

The scent of damp earth and decaying leaves, so familiar from the Amazon, faded, replaced by the dry, dusty aroma of the African savanna. Barnaby, his spirit still soaring from his Amazonian adventures, found himself standing at the edge of a seemingly endless expanse of golden grass, punctuated by the occasional acacia tree. The air hummed with a different kind of energy, a vibrant pulse of life that was both exhilarating and slightly overwhelming. He felt a thrill, a mixture of anticipation and nervous excitement, course through him. This was Africa, a continent he'd only ever dreamt of visiting, a place brimming with legendary creatures and breathtaking landscapes.

He'd arrived in Africa through a series of remarkably fortuitous events, a chain of coincidences that felt almost orchestrated by fate. After bidding farewell to the Amazon, he'd found himself unexpectedly befriending a group of traveling musicians, their instruments strapped to the backs of brightly colored camels. They were heading towards the Serengeti, and, after sharing stories around crackling campfires and exchanging laughter under a sky bursting with stars, they had graciously offered Barnaby a ride, promising him a grand adventure across the African continent.

The journey itself had been an adventure. They had traversed bustling cities, crossed shimmering deserts under the scorching midday sun, and navigated winding mountain passes where the air grew thin and the stars shone with unparalleled brilliance. He'd learned to play a simple melody on a handcrafted flute, his fingers clumsy at first, but gradually gaining dexterity and rhythm. He'd helped prepare delicious meals over open fires, the taste of exotic spices awakening his palate to new and exciting sensations. He'd listened to enchanting tales of ancient kings and legendary heroes, his imagination fired by the rhythmic beat of their drums and the haunting melodies of their songs.

Finally, they reached the savanna, the air thick with the promise of wildlife encounters. Barnaby, his heart pounding with anticipation, dismounted his camel, feeling the soft, yielding earth beneath his feet. His eyes scanned the horizon, taking in the vastness of the landscape, the rolling hills stretching towards a distant haze, the acacia trees standing like sentinels against the fiery backdrop of the setting sun. The sounds of the savanna were a symphony of rustling grass, the distant call of birds, and the low rumble of unseen creatures.

Then, a sight that took his breath away. A giraffe, its coat a patchwork of rich browns and creamy beige, gracefully emerged from behind a cluster of acacia trees. Its long, elegant neck arched as it gazed at Barnaby with curious, gentle eyes. It was a creature of extraordinary beauty, its height dwarfing everything around it. The giraffe was as elegant and calm as any creature he'd ever witnessed; its poise filled Barnaby with a sense of tranquility. The sun glinted on its dark eyes and the delicate patterning on its coat.

Before Barnaby could even react, the giraffe lowered its head, its massive brown eyes meeting his. It then gently nudged him with its long neck, as if extending an invitation. Barnaby, his heart filled with a mixture of awe and excitement, hesitantly reached out and touched its velvety soft skin. The giraffe let out a soft sigh, a sound that resonated deep within Barnaby's chest.

The giraffe knelt gracefully and, much to Barnaby's astonishment, offered him its back. This graceful giant, this majestic creature of the African savanna, was inviting him for a ride! He scrambled onto its broad back, gripping its soft fur for support. The giraffe rose effortlessly, its movements fluid and powerful. The height was thrilling, the panoramic view breathtaking.

From his elevated perch, Barnaby witnessed the beauty and wonder of the African wildlife unfold before him. Herds of zebras, their stripes a mesmerizing pattern against the golden grass, grazed peacefully. A pride of lions, majestic and powerful, lazed under the shade of an acacia tree, their tawny coats blending seamlessly with their surroundings. A family of elephants, their colossal forms moving with surprising grace, ambled through the tall grass, their young playfully chasing each other. He watched a cheetah, a blur of golden fur, stalk its prey with breathtaking speed and precision. The air throbbed with the sounds of nature – the trumpeting of elephants, the snorting of rhinos, the chirping of crickets, the melodic calls of various birds.

He saw a pair of giraffes playfully sparring with each other, their necks entwined in a gentle dance. The sight was both majestic and endearing. He witnessed a family of meerkats emerging from their burrows, their tiny bodies erect as they scanned their surroundings with keen eyes. The sun set, creating a beautiful display of color, orange, red, and purple filled the sky as the giraffe gracefully carried him across the savanna.

Barnaby spent days exploring the savanna with his new friend. The giraffe, which he eventually named Kipenzi (meaning "beloved" in Swahili), became his steadfast companion, navigating him through the vast landscape, introducing him to its hidden treasures and secret pathways. Kipenzi seemed to understand Barnaby's fascination with nature, patiently allowing him to document the plants, insects and animals they encountered. Barnaby's notebook grew thicker, filled with animated sketches, meticulous observations, and newfound understanding of this unique ecosystem. He observed the intricate patterns on the wings of butterflies, the delicate structure of desert flowers, and the social dynamics of different animal groups, noting that each played a crucial role in maintaining the intricate balance of the savanna.

One evening, painting the sky in orange, pink, and purple, Kipenzi led Barnaby to a watering hole. A variety of animals gathered at the watering hole to quench their thirst; zebras, wildebeests, giraffes, and elephants all congregated around the watering hole. The scene was a breathtaking demonstration of the savanna's biodiversity. Barnaby watched, mesmerized, as different animals, usually rivals, coexisted peacefully, their thirst outweighing their natural instincts.

Kipenzi allowed Barnaby to stay close by, observing the animals interacting in their natural habitat. The experience gave him a newfound respect for the delicate balance of the ecosystem. The sight left an indelible mark on his heart, reminding him of the incredible richness of life on Earth and the crucial importance of preserving it for future generations.

Barnaby's African adventure was more than just a safari; it was a transformative experience. It reinforced his love for nature, expanded his knowledge of the natural world, and ignited a deeper understanding of the delicate harmony of all living things. The memory of Kipenzi, the majestic giraffe who had become his friend and guide, would forever endure in his heart, a symbol of the beauty, wonder, and untamed spirit of the African savanna. He knew that he would carry the memories of his journey, the knowledge he gained and the friends he made with him always.

The next morning, Kipenzi woke Barnaby with a gentle nudge. The sun was already painting the sky with streaks of gold and rose, casting long shadows across the savanna. Kipenzi's breath, warm and slightly musky, tickled Barnaby's cheek. He felt a surge of excitement, eager to see what wonders the day would bring.

Their first encounter was with a herd of zebras, their black and white stripes shimmering in the morning light like a living kaleidoscope. They were surprisingly playful, their movements fluid and graceful as they grazed, their tails flicking rhythmically to keep away pesky flies. Barnaby watched, fascinated, as they interacted, their social dynamics complex and intricate. He learned from Kipenzi, through subtle gestures and nuanced body language, that the herd followed a strict social hierarchy, with older, more experienced zebras leading the way. Younger foals played amongst themselves, their playful nips and kicks a testament to their youthful energy.

Later that day, they stumbled upon a pride of lions, resting under the shade of a large acacia tree. The majestic creatures were breathtaking – their tawny coats blending seamlessly with the surroundings, their powerful bodies radiating an aura of quiet strength. Kipenzi, surprisingly, seemed unfazed by their presence, approaching them with a calm dignity that was both impressive and humbling. Barnaby observed the lions carefully, noting their muscular build, their piercing gaze, and their seemingly effortless grace. He learned that these apex predators were essential to the savanna's ecosystem, their hunting keeping the herbivore populations in check, thus maintaining the delicate balance of nature. He sketched them diligently, capturing the subtle nuances of their expressions, their powerful forms, and the way the sunlight glinted on their fur.

Their exploration led them to a family of elephants, their colossal forms moving with surprising grace through the tall grass. The matriarch, a wise and ancient-looking elephant, led her family with quiet authority, her every movement a symphony of strength and wisdom. The younger elephants, playful and energetic, chased each other, their joyous trumpeting echoing across the savanna. Barnaby observed the elephants' intricate communication, the subtle nuances of their rumbling calls, their touching interactions, and the way they used their trunks to communicate and assist each other. He was particularly struck by the family unit, the way they looked out for each other, their bond unbreakable. It reinforced his growing appreciation for the complex social structures that existed within the savanna's animal community. He learned that the elephants played a critical role in shaping the landscape, their movements spreading seeds and creating waterholes.

One afternoon, while resting in the shade of a baobab tree, they witnessed a breathtaking spectacle – a cheetah hunt. The cheetah, a blur of golden fur, moved with incredible speed and precision, stalking its prey with deadly efficiency. Barnaby watched, his breath caught in his throat, as the cheetah pounced, its movements a marvel of nature's engineering. The hunt was successful, and the cheetah, its sleek body glistening with sweat, enjoyed its hard-earned meal. Kipenzi explained that cheetahs were solitary hunters, relying on their speed and agility to catch their prey. He learned that their role in the savanna's ecosystem was to keep the antelope and gazelle populations healthy and balanced.

As days turned into weeks, Barnaby's fascination with the savanna's inhabitants deepened. He encountered many other fascinating creatures: the mischievous baboons with their cheeky antics, the graceful gazelles with their elegant leaps, the stealthy hyenas with their distinctive laughter, and the peaceful rhinoceroses, their thick hides proof to their resilience. Each creature had its own unique story to tell, its own role to play in the interconnected system of the savanna.

He observed the complex relationships between the animals, the predator-prey dynamics, the symbiotic partnerships, and the way they all contributed to the overall health of the ecosystem. He saw how the wildebeests' migrations influenced the growth of grasses, and how the dung beetles played a vital role in nutrient cycling. He learned that the ecosystem was a delicate balance, a complex interplay of interactions, each component vital for the survival of the whole.

Kipenzi patiently answered Barnaby's countless questions, providing insights into the animals' behavior, their communication, their social structures, and their ecological roles. He taught Barnaby about the importance of respecting the animals and their habitat, emphasizing the need for conservation and the preservation of this unique and irreplaceable ecosystem. Barnaby learned to interpret the subtle cues of the animals, understanding their postures, their calls, and their movements. He learned to approach them with respect and sensitivity, to observe without disturbing their natural behaviors.

Barnaby filled notebooks with detailed sketches and observations, meticulously documenting the wildlife he encountered. He learned to identify different bird species by their calls and plumage, he learned to distinguish the tracks of various animals, and he learned to appreciate the delicate beauty of the savanna's flora. He discovered a new passion for botany, carefully sketching the exotic plants, the vibrant flowers, and the resilient trees that thrived in this harsh yet beautiful environment. He found himself captivated by the interdependence of all living things, the fine-tuned system of life that sustained the savanna.

One evening, as they sat by a watering hole, watching a family of hippos cooling off in the mud, Barnaby realized the depth of his transformation. He had started his journey as a curious observer, but he had evolved into a passionate advocate for the preservation of the African savanna. He had not only experienced the raw beauty of the wild but also the delicate balance that kept it all thriving. The journey had instilled in him a immense respect for nature and a deep understanding of the fusion of all life.

He knew that his time in Africa was coming to an end, but he carried the lessons of his adventure with him, etched into his heart and mind. He vowed to share his experiences with the world, to inspire others to cherish and protect the wonders of the natural world, and to champion the cause of wildlife conservation. The memories of his encounters with the zebras, the lions, the elephants, the cheetahs, and all the other amazing creatures of the African savanna would remain with him, a reminder of the extraordinary beauty and the urgent need for preservation of our planet's incredible biodiversity. The memory of Kipenzi, his gentle, wise, and graceful giraffe friend, would forever be a beacon, reminding him of the magic that could be found in the most unexpected places and the lasting connection between humanity and the natural world.

The air vibrated with a low, resonant hum, a sound that seemed to emanate from the very earth itself. It was a sound that thrummed through Barnaby's chest, a primal rhythm that spoke of ancient migrations and the relentless pulse of life. Kipenzi, sensing Barnaby's growing anticipation, nudged him gently, his large, dark eyes reflecting the immensity of the spectacle unfolding before them.

We were perched atop a small rise, overlooking a sprawling expanse of grassland stretching as far as the eye could see. The sun beat down, turning the air shimmering and hazy, but the scene before us was far from indistinct. The land was alive, teeming with movement, a river of fur and hooves flowing across the plains.

It was the wildebeest migration, a phenomenon Barnaby had only read about in books, a breathtaking spectacle of nature's power and endurance. Thousands upon thousands of wildebeest, a seemingly endless stream of tawny bodies, stretched out before us, their thunderous hooves drumming a steady beat against the parched earth. The sheer scale of it was overwhelming – a moving tapestry of life that stretched to the horizon, a testament to the enduring power of nature.

The wildebeest moved in a seemingly chaotic yet organized fashion, a living river winding its way across the savanna. Young calves stumbled and wobbled, their mothers protecting them with fierce determination. Older bulls, their horns impressive and formidable, jostled for position, their grunts and bellows echoing across the plains. The air was thick with dust, the scent of sweat and earth filling Barnaby's nostrils, the cacophony of their movements a powerful symphony of survival.

Kipenzi explained that this migration was a life-or-death journey, a perilous trek undertaken every year in search of fresh grazing lands and water. It was a test of endurance, a race against time and predators. The wildebeest moved in massive herds, their numbers providing a measure of safety, their collective strength a defense against the dangers that lurked in their path.

As we watched, a pride of lions emerged from the tall grass, their movements silent and stealthy. The sight sent a shiver down Barnaby's spine, a stark reminder of the brutal reality of the savanna. The lions were silent hunters, their tawny bodies blending seamlessly with the dry grass, their powerful muscles coiled and ready to strike.

The wildebeest, sensing the danger, quickened their pace, their panicked bellows rising above the other sounds of the migration. The lions, masters of patience and strategy, chose their targets carefully, their powerful bodies erupting into action with surprising speed. Barnaby watched, his heart pounding, as the chase unfolded – a deadly ballet of predator and prey, a raw display of nature's unyielding forces.

Kipenzi explained that the lions were vital to the balance of the ecosystem. Their hunting thinned out the wildebeest herds, preventing overgrazing and ensuring the sustainability of the grasslands. He also pointed out the vultures circling overhead, patient scavengers awaiting their turn in the cycle of life and death.

The migration wasn't just about the wildebeest; it was about the harmony between all life on the savanna. Zebras mingled with the wildebeest, their striking stripes providing camouflage amidst the chaos. Ostriches, their long legs carrying them effortlessly, kept watch, their keen eyesight detecting danger from afar. Other herbivores, such as gazelles and impalas, joined the throng, benefiting from the collective safety of such a vast number.

The predators weren't limited to lions. Spotted hyenas, with their distinctive cackling laughter, patrolled the edges of the herd, opportunistic scavengers ready to take advantage of any weakness or misfortune. Cheetahs, with their remarkable speed, darted in and out, their lightning-fast attacks a testament to their hunting prowess. Even birds of prey, like eagles and hawks, took to the skies, seizing upon the opportunities afforded by the mass movement.

As the sun began to sink, the migration continued its relentless journey. Barnaby found himself awestruck by the sheer scale of the event, the power and beauty of it humbling him. He had witnessed a spectacle of nature that was both brutal and breathtaking, a striking testament to life's resilience and unbreakable spirit.

He sketched furiously, his pencil capturing the chaos and majesty of the scene – the swirling dust clouds, the vast herds, the deadly attacks, the relentless movement. He couldn't capture it all, of course, but he tried his best, his drawings filling his notebooks with images that would forever remain etched in his memory.

That night, under a sky teeming with stars, Barnaby reflected on the day's events. He'd seen life and death played out on a grand scale, a stark reminder of the delicate balance of nature. The wildebeest migration wasn't merely a spectacle; it was an illustration of the circle of life, the constant struggle for survival, and the intricate relationships between the various creatures of the savanna. He felt a profound respect for the animals, their tenacity, and their unwavering determination to survive.

He realized that the migration was a microcosm of life itself – a continuous journey filled with challenges, dangers, and moments of breathtaking beauty. It was a reminder that even in the face of adversity, life finds a way to persist, to adapt, and to endure.

The next day, we followed the migration further, witnessing more incredible sights. We saw a young wildebeest calf separated from its mother, its plaintive cries echoing across the plains. We saw a desperate struggle for survival, the calf's vulnerability exposed against the relentless power of the migration. But we also saw the strength and compassion of other wildebeest, some adults gathering near the calf, providing a semblance of protection, a testament to the complex social dynamics of these magnificent creatures.

We encountered a group of elephants, their massive forms moving through the midst of the migration, their presence both intimidating and reassuring. Kipenzi explained that elephants, too, followed seasonal migrations, although theirs were less dramatic and more leisurely. Their paths often crossed with the wildebeest, resulting in a fascinating juxtaposition of power and grace.

We witnessed a dramatic confrontation between a lion pride and a group of male wildebeest, who formed a protective circle around their weaker counterparts. The sight was a compelling reminder of the constant struggle for survival in this unforgiving landscape.

Throughout the migration, we saw other animals—cheetahs, hyenas, jackals—taking advantage of the chaos and abundance. Vultures followed close behind, patiently waiting for their opportunity. The entire ecosystem was on display, a complex web of interdependent species, each playing its critical role in the grand spectacle of life and death. It was a humbling experience, witnessing the raw power of nature and the delicate balance of its many interconnected parts.

Barnaby continued to sketch and record his observations. The sounds, smells, and textures of the migration were etched into his memory, and he vowed to use his art to capture and share this magnificent experience with others.

As the migration moved on, so did we, following its path across the vast African plains. Each day brought new challenges and exciting discoveries, deepening Barnaby's understanding of the workings of this remarkable ecosystem. The great wildebeest migration was far more than just a journey; it was a testament to life's tenacity, a powerful demonstration of nature's remarkable resilience, an experience that would forever shape Barnaby's perspective on life and the natural world. He knew, as the sun set on another day of this extraordinary journey, that the memories he was creating and the lessons he was learning would stay with him for a lifetime. He was witnessing not just an animal migration, but a spectacle of life itself, unfolding before him in all its glorious, brutal beauty.

The sun, a molten orange orb cast long shadows across the savanna as Kipenzi and I sat by a crackling fire. The day's spectacle, the breathtaking wildebeest migration, had left an indelible mark on my soul. But Kipenzi, with his quiet wisdom and deep understanding of the African bush, had something more to share, something that went beyond the sheer beauty and brutal reality of the migration.

He spoke of the shadows that fell upon this magnificent display of life; the insidious threat of poachers who stalked the herds, their motives driven by greed and fueled by the illegal wildlife trade. He described the silent, deadly traps they laid, the cruel methods they employed to claim their victims, leaving behind a trail of suffering and death. The powerful spectacle we had witnessed, was under constant threat, threatened not only by natural predators but by the actions of mankind.

Kipenzi spoke of the slow, creeping encroachment of human settlements and agriculture, pushing ever further into the animals' natural habitat. He showed me images on his tablet, pictures of once-vast grasslands shrinking to mere patches of green amidst a sea of human development. The wildebeest, he explained, required vast tracts of land for their migration; their survival depended on these unbroken pathways, these corridors of life that allowed them to traverse the landscape in their yearly pilgrimage. The shrinking of their habitat was squeezing the life out of this ancient ritual, creating bottlenecks, making them more vulnerable to predators and poachers.

He pointed to a map detailing the wildebeest migration routes, highlighting the areas where these crucial pathways were being threatened by human activity. Roads bisected their paths, fences restricted their movement, and the construction of dams and irrigation systems altered the flow of water, disrupting the delicate balance of the ecosystem. The consequences, he stressed, were severe, threatening not only the wildebeest but also the other species that depended on the health of the savanna.

He explained the ripple effect of habitat loss. The decrease in wildebeest numbers meant less food for the lions, impacting the lion population. The disruption of the migration routes changed the feeding patterns of other predators, leading to imbalances within the ecosystem. Even the plants and the very soil itself were affected. The migration was a keystone event, a fundamental process that maintained the health and balance of the entire savanna ecosystem. Its disruption threatened to unravel the whole fabric of life.

Kipenzi then turned his attention to the crucial role of conservation. He described the tireless work of conservation organizations, the rangers who risked their lives patrolling the vast wilderness, protecting the animals from poachers. He spoke of anti-poaching strategies, sophisticated technology used to track poachers' movements, and community engagement programs aimed at educating local people about the importance of protecting wildlife and fostering sustainable practices. He showed me images of community-based conservation initiatives, highlighting the successes of involving local communities in the protection of their natural heritage.

He explained that conservation wasn't just about protecting animals; it was about protecting the entire ecosystem, the intricate web of life that sustained the savanna. It recognized how deeply all living things rely on one another and the vital importance of biodiversity in sustaining the planet's health. He emphasized that conservation wasn't simply a matter of preserving a beautiful spectacle; it was essential for the future of the planet and for the well-being of generations to come.

The conversation sparked a fire in my own heart, a newfound determination to use my skills to contribute to the cause. I realized that my artwork could be more than just a record of my travels. It could be a powerful tool for raising awareness, for educating others about the beauty and fragility of the African savanna, and for inspiring people to support conservation efforts.

I spent the next few days sketching furiously, capturing the essence of what Kipenzi had taught me. I drew images of poachers' traps, stark reminders of the threats facing the wildlife. I depicted the shrinking grasslands, showing the encroachment of human development. I illustrated the tireless efforts of the conservation rangers, their unwavering commitment to protecting the animals.

And alongside these images, I painted vibrant scenes of the migration itself, celebrating the magnificent beauty of the wildebeest, the lions, and all the creatures that call the savanna home. I wanted to convey the urgency of the situation, to show the stark contrast between the breathtaking beauty of nature and the destructive forces that threatened to destroy it.

I began to understand the broader context of conservation, its importance not just for Africa, but for the entire planet. The savanna's problems mirrored issues faced by ecosystems worldwide, reflecting the growing threat of climate change, habitat loss, and biodiversity decline. The experience was a powerful wake-up call, a stark reminder of our responsibility as stewards of the earth. The migration, I realized, was more than a natural phenomenon; it was a living testament to the interconnectedness of life, a reminder of the fragility of ecosystems, and an urgent call for action.

My time in Africa had transformed me. I had witnessed the raw power of nature, the brutal beauty of the savanna, and the devastating impact of human activities. But I had also experienced the hope and inspiration that come from the dedication of those working tirelessly to protect this precious landscape. I learned that conservation was not just a noble cause, but a vital necessity, a fight for the survival of the planet and all its inhabitants. The wildebeest migration had become a symbol of this battle, a magnificent spectacle representing both the strength and vulnerability of life itself.

The final evening of our safari, sitting around the campfire under a star-studded sky, I reflected on everything I'd seen and learned. The vastness of the African plains, the breathtaking scale of the migration, the beauty of the animals, and the looming threat of human interference had left a lasting impression. I knew my role wouldn't just be to document this incredible journey, but to share my experience and inspire others to act. I would use my art to give voice to the silent cries of the endangered, to raise awareness about the urgent need for conservation, and to celebrate the incredible resilience of life on this extraordinary planet. My sketchbook was more than just a record of a journey; it was a manifesto for conservation, a powerful testament to the enduring spirit of the African savanna and a passionate call to action for the future. The images would not only capture the beauty of what I'd witnessed, but the urgency of preserving it for generations to come. The work had just begun.

The embers of the campfire glowed, painting dancing shadows on the canvas of the night. The air, thick with the scent of woodsmoke and the distant musk of wild animals, hummed with a quiet energy. Kipenzi, his face illuminated by the flickering flames, chuckled softly. He held up a small, worn leather-bound book, its pages filled with faded photographs.

"Barnaby," he said, his voice a low rumble, "I have something to show you." He turned a page, revealing a photograph – a sepia-toned image that seemed to hold the very essence of the African savanna. It was Barnaby himself, a small, intrepid figure dwarfed by the immensity of the landscape. He stood amidst a herd of zebras, their stripes blurred by the movement, their eyes wide and wary. The setting sun cast long, dramatic shadows, turning the golden grasses into a shimmering sea of light and shadow. In the background, acacia trees stood like silent sentinels, their branches reaching towards the fiery sky. Barnaby, with his wide-eyed wonder and his small backpack, looked utterly captivated, a tiny speck of humanity swallowed by the breathtaking scale of the African wilderness.

"Old Tembo, the wisest elephant in this whole wide land, took that picture," Kipenzi explained, his eyes twinkling. "He has a knack for capturing the soul of a moment, wouldn't you say?"

The photograph was indeed remarkable. It wasn't just a snapshot; it was a story. It captured the raw beauty of the savanna, the vibrant energy of the wildlife, and the sense of awe and wonder that Barnaby clearly experienced. The composition was exquisite, the lighting dramatic, the moment perfectly timed. It felt as though the very spirit of the African adventure was imprinted on the faded paper. I could almost feel the heat of the sun on my skin, hear the rustling of the grasses, and sense the watchful presence of the wild creatures surrounding Barnaby.

Kipenzi turned another page, revealing more photographs, each one a small window into the wonders Barnaby had encountered. There was a picture of him perched on a termite mound, observing a family of meerkats at play; their tiny bodies a whirlwind of activity. Another showed him sketching furiously, capturing the delicate details of a vibrant bird in flight. One image depicted him standing beside a majestic baobab tree, its ancient trunk a testament to the passage of time. Each photograph told a story, each one adding to the richness and depth of Barnaby's extraordinary journey.

"Tembo said Barnaby reminded him of himself when he was young," Kipenzi continued, a hint of amusement in his voice. "Always curious, always exploring, always eager to learn. He saw in Barnaby a kindred spirit, a soul drawn to the wild heart of Africa."

I looked again at the photograph of Barnaby amidst the zebras. The image was more than just a record of a moment; it was a symbol of the connection between humanity and the natural world.

It was an ode to the power of curiosity, the thrill of exploration, and the humbling experience of encountering the wild beauty of Africa.

Kipenzi spoke of Tembo, a creature of immense wisdom and gentleness. He described the elephant's vast knowledge of the savanna, his ability to sense danger, and his deep understanding of therelationships between all living things. Tembo, Kipenzi explained, wasn't just an animal; he was a guardian, a protector, a silent observer of the human journey through the heart of Africa.

"Tembo is a living legend," Kipenzi said reverently. "He's seen generations of animals come and go, witnessed the changes in the land, and felt the pulse of the savanna's heart. He remembers a time when the land was even wilder, when the herds were larger, and the migration was even more spectacular."

He paused, lost in thought, before continuing. "He often speaks of the balance of nature, how delicate it is, and how easily it can be disrupted. He sees the scars left by human encroachment, the effects of poaching, and the subtle shifts in the ecosystem that threaten the delicate web of life."

Kipenzi described how Tembo, in his quiet wisdom, had chosen Barnaby as a subject worthy of his photographic skill. He saw in the boy a reflection of his own youthful curiosity, a spark of wonder that was essential for understanding and appreciating the beauty and fragility of the natural world. The photograph, then, wasn't just a beautiful image; it was a message a calm reminder to stay mindful, the importance of respect for nature, and the urgent need for conservation.

We spent the rest of the evening poring over Tembo's photographs. Each image was a portal, transporting us to a different corner of the savanna, introducing us to a different facet of the wilderness. We saw playful baboons swinging through the trees, a lone giraffe silhouetted against the sunset, and a family of lions basking in the warmth of the afternoon sun. Every image was a story waiting to be told, every detail a testament to the rich biodiversity of the African landscape.

Kipenzi explained that Tembo had a unique perspective, a deep understanding of life. He saw the subtle relationships between different species, the intricate dance of predator and prey, and the delicate balance that sustained the ecosystem. His photographs were not merely records of individual animals; they were portrayals of the life that made up the savanna.

As the night deepened and the stars blazed across the inky sky, Kipenzi shared stories of Tembo's encounters with other creatures, his wisdom in navigating the challenges of the wild, and his unwavering devotion to the land he called home. He spoke of Tembo's deep connection to the earth, his understanding of the rhythms of nature, and his enduring respect for all living things.

Tembo's wisdom, Kipenzi emphasized, wasn't just about survival; it underscored the significance of seeing the links between all living things and the contribution each species makes to sustaining nature's delicate harmony. He taught that respecting nature wasn't just a moral imperative, it was essential for the survival of the planet.

I looked at the photograph of Barnaby once more, seeing it not just as a portrait, but as a symbol of hope. A testament to the power of human curiosity, the beauty of the natural world, and the urgent need to protect the planet's precious biodiversity. The photograph was a powerful reminder of the extraordinary journey Barnaby had taken and the important lessons he had learned. The journey was far from over, and the images, both captured and yet to be created, would continue to tell the story, inspiring others to protect this precious landscape for generations to come. The African savanna was far more than just a beautiful place; it was a living testament to the resilience and beauty of life itself. And in Barnaby's adventures, and in the wise old elephant's captured moments, lies a powerful message of hope and a call to action for the future. The adventure and the journey of understanding continued.

Chapter 9:

Antarctic Ice Cap

The embers of the campfire had long since faded to ash, leaving behind only the faintest whisper of warmth. The African savanna, with its vibrant tapestry of life, now seemed a distant memory, replaced by a vast, white expanse stretching to the horizon. Barnaby, bundled in layers of thermal gear, felt the biting Antarctic wind whip across his cheeks, a stark contrast to the sun-drenched heat he had recently known. He shivered, not entirely from the cold, but from the sheer magnitude of the landscape before him. This was a world utterly different from the African savanna, a world of ice and snow, of penguins and seals, a world that whispered secrets of ancient glaciers and untold mysteries.

His journey to Antarctica had begun unexpectedly. After bidding farewell to Kipenzi and the memories of the African savanna, Barnaby found himself on a research vessel, sailing across the tempestuous Southern Ocean. The voyage was a thrilling rollercoaster of high seas and wild storms, but Barnaby, ever the adventurer, reveled in the challenge. He spent hours on deck, mesmerized by the rolling waves and the albatrosses that soared effortlessly above the churning water. He learned about the currents, the winds, and the intricate dance of the ocean's ecosystems from the ship's crew, his insatiable curiosity leading him to devour every piece of information they offered.

Days turned into weeks, and the icy continent of Antarctica slowly materialized on the horizon – a breathtaking expanse of pristine white, punctuated by towering icebergs that resembled majestic castles carved from crystal. The air grew colder, the waves calmer, and subtle anticipation filled Barnaby. He felt as if he were approaching a forgotten realm, a place where time seemed to stand still, where nature reigned supreme.

Upon reaching the Antarctic research base, a bustling hub of scientific activity, Barnaby was greeted by a team of friendly researchers who quickly embraced his infectious enthusiasm. They shared their knowledge, showed him their sophisticated equipment, and explained their ongoing studies of the Antarctic ecosystem. Barnaby, ever the keen observer, was enthralled by their work. He learned about the delicate balance of the Antarctic food chain, the impact of climate change on the region's fragile ecosystem, and the importance of conservation efforts in protecting this pristine wilderness.

One day, while exploring the snowy plains near the research base, Barnaby stumbled upon a colony of Emperor penguins. These magnificent birds, with their sleek black and white plumage and their upright posture, were a sight to behold. They waddled gracefully across the ice, their movements a captivating blend of elegance and clumsiness. Barnaby watched them, mesmerized, as they interacted with each other, their calls echoing across the vast expanse of white.

As he observed the penguins, a particularly playful one, with an unusually bright yellow patch on its chest, caught Barnaby's eye. The penguin, seemingly aware of Barnaby's presence, tilted its head, its dark eyes gleaming with curiosity. It took a few steps closer, then, with a sudden burst of energy, it slid across the snow with remarkable speed, its belly skimming the icy surface. Barnaby couldn't help but chuckle at the penguin's antics. It was as if the bird was inviting him to join in the fun.

Emboldened by the penguin's playful invitation, Barnaby, ever the adventurous soul, cautiously sat down on the ice. He slid forward, mimicking the penguin's graceful glide. The playful penguin, delighted by Barnaby's imitation, began to lead him on a thrilling ice-sliding journey across the snow-covered landscape. Barnaby whooped with laughter as they slid. It was a journey that acknowledged the delicate charm of unexpected kinship between animals and humans. They glided across the pristine expanse, leaving behind a trail of laughter and delight. The icy wind whipped around them, but their shared joy warmed them from within.

Their trek led them past breathtaking glaciers, their colossal forms shimmering under the pale Antarctic sun. They slid past colonies of seals, their sleek bodies basking in the cold sun, and passed fields of snow, their surfaces sparkling with millions of tiny ice crystals. The playful penguin, ever the guide, led Barnaby deeper into the heart of the icy wilderness, revealing hidden wonders at every turn.

The cold intensified as they ventured further into the interior of the continent. The temperature dropped significantly, the wind grew stronger, and the snow became deeper. But Barnaby, shielded by his warm gear and filled with the joy of the adventure, hardly noticed the chill. The sheer beauty of the landscape, the playfulness of his newfound penguin companion, and the thrill of exploring a new world filled him with a sense of exhilaration.

Their journey was punctuated by moments of quiet contemplation, as Barnaby took in the stunning vistas around him.

He marveled at the intricate patterns of ice crystals, the sheer scale of the glaciers, and the endless expanse of the snow-covered plains. He spent hours sketching the penguins, capturing the elegance of their movements and the playful sparkle in their eyes. Each sketch was a manifestation of the unique beauty of this icy wilderness, a tribute to the resilience of life in the most extreme environments.

The sun, a pale disc in the vast sky, cast long shadows across the snow, giving the landscape a surreal quality. The air hummed with the sounds of nature – the calls of penguins, the cries of seals, the creak and groan of the glaciers. It was a symphony of sounds that spoke of a world untouched by human hands, a world of pristine beauty and untamed power. Barnaby, wrapped in the stillness of this icy realm, felt a keen sense of connection to nature, a profound understanding of its raw, majestic power.

As the day ended and the pale sun dipped below the horizon, casting a soft, ethereal gleam over the snow, Barnaby and his penguin companion found a sheltered spot near a rocky outcrop. They huddled together, sharing the warmth of their shared adventure and the deep contentment of a time well spent. The stars, blazing brilliantly in the crisp, clear sky, seemed to wink down upon them, as if in approval of their extraordinary bond. Barnaby, exhausted but filled with an overwhelming sense of joy and wonder, drifted off to sleep, lulled by the soothing sounds of the Antarctic night.

The next morning, Barnaby awoke to a breathtaking sunrise, the sky ablaze with a kaleidoscope of colors. He looked around him, at the pristine snow, at the playful penguin nestled beside him, and felt a deep gratitude for the adventure he had been given. There was still much to explore, much to learn, and much to appreciate in this remarkable realm of ice and snow. He knew this journey had changed him in ways he was still beginning to comprehend. The African savanna had filled him with an appreciation for life's abundant vitality, while this icy continent emphasized the enduring power of nature's quiet tenacity.

His experience in the Antarctic had opened his eyes to a new understanding of the planet's delicate ecosystem. The vibrant life of the savanna and the silent fortitude of the Antarctic were two sides of the same coin, showing him the importance all life on earth. The memory of the old elephant's wisdom echoed in his heart. The balance of nature was a precious thing, a delicate tapestry woven from countless threads, each one as important as the next. He returned to the research base, ready to share his experience and his heightened understanding of the planet's fragile beauty with others. The next chapter of his adventures lay ahead, and he knew, with unwavering certainty, that it would be an extraordinary one. He understood that he now had a responsibility. He had been privileged to see the world's wonders, and he was now charged with protecting them for future generations.

The playful penguin, whose bright yellow chest patch seemed to glow even in the dim light, nudged Barnaby's hand with its beak. It was a surprisingly gentle touch, almost a caress. Barnaby chuckled, a warm sound that echoed faintly in the vast, silent landscape. He reached out a gloved finger, and the penguin, with surprising dexterity, gripped it with its small, surprisingly strong beak.

For hours, Barnaby simply watched them. He observed their social structures, the way they huddled together for warmth, sharing body heat in a collective effort against the brutal cold. He watched the adults meticulously care for their chicks, shielding them from the wind with their bodies, their protective instincts evident in every movement. He saw the playful chases, the squabbles over territory, and the intricate dance of courtship rituals. It was a world of its own, a microcosm of society, functioning with remarkable efficiency and elegance.

He noticed details he'd never considered before. The way the penguins' feathers repelled water created a natural, waterproof barrier against the icy winds and snow. The way they used their flippers to navigate the slippery ice, their movements were fluid and surprisingly graceful. The way their black and white plumage provided effective camouflage against the stark landscape, blending seamlessly with the snow and ice. The penguins' adaptations to the harsh Antarctic environment were nothing short of miraculous, a sign of the power of natural selection.

One particularly engaging penguin, whom Barnaby started to think of as "Sunny" due to that bright yellow patch, seemed especially fascinated with him. Sunny would waddle close, tilting its head as if trying to decipher the strange, large creature before it. Sometimes, Sunny would perform an almost comical "bow", bending its neck low to the ice before straightening up with a playful chirp. It was as if Sunny was attempting to communicate, to bridge the gap between two vastly different worlds.

Barnaby decided to try sketching Sunny. He carefully pulled out his waterproof sketchbook and charcoal pencils, his gloved fingers fumbling a little with the cold. The penguins continued their activities around him, seemingly unperturbed by his presence. Sunny, however, watched him intently, his dark eyes following the movements of his hand across the paper.

He sketched Sunny's sleek body, its elegant posture, and the way its flippers moved with a surprising grace. He tried to capture the sparkle in Sunny's eye, that inherent playfulness which hinted at a rich inner life. He sketched several other penguins, capturing their unique personalities in his drawings. There was the grumpy-looking one who seemed to be always complaining, the intensely protective parent guarding its chick, the energetic one leading a group in a playful chase, and the one that seemed rather contemplative, sitting on a small ice floe observing its surroundings. Each sketch was unique, a peek into the layered, lively world of the penguin colony.

As he sketched, he noticed the other penguins exhibited a range of emotions, from the playful antics of the youngsters to the cautious alertness of the adults. He saw the tender care between parents and chicks, the fierce competitiveness during feeding time, and the quiet companionship of huddled groups weathering the icy storms. Their society was complex, full of unwritten rules and unspoken rituals. The penguins' resilience, their ability to thrive in one of the harshest environments on Earth, filled Barnaby with awe and respect. He realized that their seemingly simple lives were deeply fascinating and sophisticated.

He spent the entire day immersed in the penguin colony. The sun, a pale disk in the vast sky, slowly made its way across the horizon, casting long shadows across the ice. The wind howled, but the penguins seemed impervious to its icy breath, their feathers providing perfect insulation. He watched them glide effortlessly on the ice, their movements elegant and fluid, a captivating spectacle against the backdrop of the stark, white landscape. He learned to identify their different calls – the chirps of the chicks, the squawks of the adults, the almost musical sounds they made during courtship rituals.

As dusk approached, the temperature plummeted. Barnaby, despite his many layers of thermal clothing, felt the cold creeping into his bones. But the penguins didn't seem to notice. They huddled together, sharing body heat, creating a warm, protective circle against the elements. Barnaby felt a deep sense of kinship with these creatures, a connection that transcended the boundaries of species. They were both enduring the same harsh conditions, yet they found ways to survive and even thrive. He was learning from them, not just about their environment, but about resilience, adaptation, and the power of community.

He packed up his sketches, carefully tucking them into a waterproof bag. As he stood up, Sunny nudged his hand again, this time leading him towards a sheltered crevice in a nearby ice formation. Barnaby followed, understanding that Sunny was showing him where to take shelter for the night. This penguin, unusually unafraid of human interaction, had become his guide, his companion in this extraordinary adventure.

Barnaby spent the night in the small crevice, sheltered from the wind and snow. He listened to the symphony of the Antarctic night – the cries of penguins, the howling wind, the distant roar of the ocean. It was a soundtrack to his extraordinary adventure, a affirmation to the power and beauty of the natural world.

The next morning, Barnaby awoke to the sight of Sunny perched at the entrance of the crevice. The penguin's bright yellow chest patch seemed to radiate warmth, even in the cold morning light. He smiled, feeling a cozy sense of peace and contentment. He knew he would always treasure this moment, a reminder of the incredible beauty of life in the most extreme environments. He'd learned about the power of community, the importance of adaptation, and the unexpected bonds that could form between different species. The Antarctic, once a symbol of cold and isolation, now felt like a place of warmth and connection, thanks to the playful penguins and the experience they had shared. He knew his time in Antarctica was not over. He still had much more to discover and explore. He would dedicate his life to protecting and sharing the marvels of nature he had witnessed, inspired by the penguins' unwavering spirit and the planet's astonishing power.

Sunny, the intrepid penguin guide, led Barnaby towards a looming ice formation, its surface shimmering with an ethereal, icy glow. A narrow opening, barely visible against the blinding white of the Antarctic landscape, hinted at a hidden world within. Curiosity piqued, Barnaby followed his feathered companion, his heart pounding with anticipation.

The entrance was surprisingly low, requiring Barnaby to crouch and almost crawl to enter. The air inside was noticeably warmer than the biting wind outside, a welcome change that immediately eased the chill that had been clinging to his bones. The transition was dramatic; from the stark, blinding white of the Antarctic expanse to a world bathed in a soft, diffused light filtering through the ice above.

The ice cave opened into an immense cavern, its walls sculpted by millennia of wind, water, and frost. Towering formations of ice, sculpted into fantastical shapes by the relentless forces of nature, rose from the floor and reached towards the ceiling, creating a breathtaking cathedral of ice. Some formations resembled towering spires, others resembled delicate curtains, hanging frozen in time. The sheer scale of the cavern was overwhelming, a continual reminder to the power of nature.

Barnaby gasped, his breath misting in the frigid air. The light within the cave danced and shimmered, creating an otherworldly effect. It was as though he had stepped into a magical realm, a secret kingdom hidden beneath the frozen surface of Antarctica. He felt an intense, solemn admiration, a feeling of insignificance in the face of such grandeur.

The cave floor was uneven, covered in a layer of smooth, polished ice. Barnaby carefully picked his way through the cavern, his boots crunching softly on the frozen surface. He noticed intricate details he had never imagined. Delicate patterns, like frozen lace, adorned the walls and ceilings, each a unique masterpiece crafted by the hand of nature. Some formations looked like frozen waterfalls, their icy tendrils frozen mid-cascade. Others resembled giant ice crystals, their facets glittering with an inner light.

He reached out a gloved hand to touch one of the formations, feeling its smooth, cold surface. The ice felt strangely alive, resonating with a subtle energy. It was a tangible connection to the slow, relentless processes that had shaped this subterranean world. Barnaby could almost feel the passage of time, the eons it had taken for these formations to form. He imagined the water seeping into cracks in the ice, freezing and expanding, slowly chipping away at the rock, creating these incredible, intricate shapes.

As he ventured deeper into the cave, Barnaby discovered more breathtaking formations. He found chambers hidden behind curtains of ice, each one unique and captivating. Some chambers were small and intimate, while others were vast and expansive. He discovered a hidden lake, its surface frozen over, a mirror reflecting the luminous light filtering from above. The silence was palpable, broken only by the occasional drip of melting ice, a sound that echoed through the cavern with surprising resonance.

Sunny, waddled ahead, its small body seeming insignificant against the grandeur of the cave. The penguin seemed perfectly at home in this icy kingdom, moving with effortless grace across the slippery surface. Barnaby watched in amazement, marveling at the penguin's agility and its seemingly innate understanding of this hidden world. Sunny paused occasionally, chirping softly, as if sharing its own sense of wonder with Barnaby.

He noticed subtle changes in the colors of the ice, ranging from crystal-clear transparency to a deep, almost sapphire blue. He found delicate patterns of trapped air bubbles, creating an effect similar to a frozen starry night. The formations were not simply ice; they were sculptures, crafted by the hand of nature over thousands of years. The ice seemed to glow from within, illuminated by a subtle, inner light.

Barnaby sketched furiously in his waterproof sketchbook, trying to capture the beauty and complexity of the ice cave. He filled pages with sketches of towering spires, delicate curtains of ice, frozen waterfalls, and the patterns woven into the ice. His charcoal pencils struggled to keep up with his enthusiasm, capturing the essence of this magical underground world. He felt a powerful connection to the cave, a sense of awe and wonder that transcended the mere observation of its beauty. It was a world untouched by human hands, a symbol of the raw power and artistry of nature.

He spent hours exploring the ice cave, his sense of wonder growing with each new discovery. He climbed over smooth, sculpted ice mounds, carefully navigated narrow passages, and marveled at the sheer scale of the cavern. Every corner revealed a new surprise, a fresh masterpiece sculpted by the forces of nature.

The experience was awe-inspiring, humbling him in the face of the Earth's raw power and the beauty of its hidden worlds.

As the daylight began to wane, casting long shadows even within the cave, Barnaby knew it was time to return. He felt a deep sense of gratitude for this unexpected adventure, a journey into the heart of the Antarctic ice cap. The experience had expanded his understanding of the planet's incredible diversity and the resilience of life in even the harshest environments. He had witnessed a hidden world, the enduring power of nature, a realm of magic and wonder sculpted by time and ice.

He retraced his steps, carefully making his way back to the entrance, the memory of the cave's beauty etched firmly in his mind. Sunny waited patiently at the entrance, its bright yellow patch seeming to glow even in the fading light. As they emerged into the frigid Antarctic air, Barnaby felt a pang of sadness at leaving this wondrous place behind.

Yet, he carried with him a wealth of memories, the images of the ice cave seared into his mind, along with a renewed respect for the planet and its hidden wonders. The journey had been arduous, but the rewards were immeasurable. The Antarctic, once a symbol of cold isolation, now held a new significance for Barnaby. It was a land of extraordinary beauty, a place of hidden wonders, and a home to creatures that had shown him the true meaning of adaptation and survival. His experience in the ice caves had been nothing short of magical, a journey into the heart of a hidden world. His adventure continued, fueled by the wonder he had experienced and a desire to share its beauty with the world. The penguins, particularly Sunny, had shown him a path, not just through the frozen landscape, but to a deeper understanding of himself and his place within the awe-inspiring natural world. The sketches, a mere record of his journey, could not hope to capture the true essence of what he had experienced within those crystalline caverns, but they served as a gentle reminder.

Emerging from the ice cave, the biting Antarctic wind whipped around Barnaby, a stark contrast to the sheltered warmth of the cavern. Sunny, ever vigilant, huddled close, its feathers ruffled by the gusts. Barnaby shivered, not just from the cold, but from a lingering sense of awe, the memory of the crystalline cathedral still echoing in his mind. He pulled his thick parka tighter, the warmth a small comfort against the icy expanse.

As twilight deepened, painting the sky with hues of lavender and rose, a subtle shift occurred. A faint, celestial glow began to appear on the horizon, a soft shimmer at first, barely discernible against the darkening sky. Sunny, sensing Barnaby's gaze, tilted its head, its bright eyes fixed on the horizon. It chirped softly, a sound that seemed to vibrate with anticipation.

The glow intensified, spreading across the sky like a celestial painter unleashing a torrent of color. Greens, blues, purples, and pinks danced and swirled across the heavens, a magical spectacle that stole Barnaby's breath. It wasn't just light; it was movement, a living, breathing canvas of vibrant hues that shifted and transformed before his very eyes. Curtains of emerald green flowed into shimmering oceans of turquoise, while streaks of crimson and violet painted fiery brushstrokes across the canvas.

The Aurora Australis, the Southern Lights, unfolded before Barnaby in all its breathtaking glory. He had seen pictures, read descriptions, but nothing could have prepared him for the sheer magnificence of the real thing. It was a breathtaking display of nature's power, a celestial ballet performed across the vast Antarctic sky. The colors were impossibly vibrant, the movements fluid and hypnotic. He felt a profound sense of wonder, a feeling of insignificance in the face of such grandeur. This was a spectacle that transcended words, a visual poem written across the night sky.

Barnaby stood mesmerized, his jaw slack with astonishment. He felt a strange sense of connection to this star-lit spectacle, a feeling of being part of something larger than himself, something ancient and powerful. The aurora seemed to pulse with a subtle energy, as if breathing, its colors shifting and changing with each breath. He could almost feel the energy emanating from the display, a palpable connection to the cosmos.

The light show continued for what felt like hours, though Barnaby later learned it had lasted for several. The aurora danced and swirled, creating ever-changing patterns of light and color. Sometimes, it looked like silk curtains touched by light, drifting smoothly through the air and flowing gracefully across the sky. At others, it formed arcs and bands, stretching from horizon to horizon. Occasionally, the display would intensify, erupting in bursts of brilliant light before fading back into a gentler glow.

Sunny, perched on a nearby snowdrift, watched the aurora with the same rapt attention as Barnaby. The penguin seemed to understand the significance of the event. It occasionally chirped softly, as if commenting on the ever-changing display. Barnaby felt a deep connection to the penguin, sharing this moment of awe and wonder in the heart of the Antarctic wilderness.

Barnaby pulled out his sketchbook, his fingers numb with cold, but his spirit burning with inspiration. He tried to capture the beauty of the aurora, the impossible colors, the fluid movements, but he knew his charcoal pencils could never truly do it justice. The aurora was a spectacle that transcended representation, a visual experience too grand, too vibrant, too dynamic to be captured on paper.

Yet, he sketched furiously, filling page after page with attempts to capture the essence of the display. He experimented with different shading techniques, different color combinations, trying to capture the shimmering movements, the vibrant hues. His sketches were imperfect, but they served as a record of his experience, a reminder of the breathtaking beauty he had witnessed.

As the aurora began to fade, its colors slowly diminishing, Barnaby felt a pang of sadness. The spectacular display was coming to an end, leaving behind a lingering sense of wonder and awe. The colors slowly retreated, leaving behind a clear, star-studded sky. The stars, usually obscured by the light pollution of civilization, shone with a brilliance Barnaby had never seen before.

He spent a long time simply gazing at the stars, feeling the vastness of the cosmos. The aurora had opened his eyes to a new level of appreciation for the natural world, an heightened understanding of the interconnectedness of everything. The stars seemed to whisper secrets, hinting at the vastness of space and the mysteries it held.

The experience had been more than just a visual spectacle. It had become a pivotal moment, a journey into the heart of nature's grandeur, a reminder of the planet's incredible beauty and the majesty of the universe. It was a moment he would carry with him always, something to be cherished and shared. The Aurora Australis had painted a masterpiece across the night sky, a masterpiece that would stay forever in Barnaby's memory, a symbol of the beauty and wonder of the Antarctic wilderness.

As the first rays of dawn touched the horizon, Barnaby and Sunny began their journey back to their base camp. Barnaby felt a sense of peace, a quiet contentment that came from witnessing such a spectacular event. The ice cave, the aurora – these were experiences that would stay with him forever, shaping his understanding of the world and his place within it. He knew that this journey had changed him. His adventure had opened up a new world of wonder and possibility. The sketches in his notebook, now filled with images of ice caves and auroras, were only a faint echo of the immense beauty he had witnessed, but they served as a reminder of a journey that had transcended the physical, touching the soul. He carried with him not just memories, but a deepened appreciation for the planet's breathtaking beauty and a connection to the natural world and the boundless wonders of the universe.

The crisp Antarctic air bit at Barnaby's cheeks as he and Sunny continued their trek back towards base camp. The vibrant colors of the Aurora Australis had faded, leaving behind a sky dusted with a million glittering stars, each a tiny pinprick of light in the vast, inky blackness. The memory of the celestial display, however, remained vivid. He felt a deep sense of gratitude, a quiet joy that settled in his heart like the first snowflakes of a gentle blizzard. It was an experience that transcended words, a communion with the raw, untamed beauty of the natural world.

As they walked, a peculiar sound caught Barnaby's attention – a series of clicks and whirs, followed by a soft splash. He glanced around, his eyes scanning the icy landscape. And then he saw it: a seal, a sleek, dark creature with intelligent, curious eyes, balanced precariously on a small ice floe. The seal was unlike any Barnaby had ever seen before; its fur was a deep, rich brown, almost black, and its eyes held a spark of mischief.

The seal regarded Barnaby with an almost human-like curiosity, its head cocked to one side as if assessing him. Then, to Barnaby's utter astonishment, the seal raised a small, flipper-like appendage and pointed it towards him. From the appendage, a small, almost invisible device extended – a miniature camera! Before Barnaby could even react, the seal snapped a picture. The flash, tiny but bright, momentarily illuminated the ice cap, capturing Barnaby and Sunny in a single, unforgettable frame.

The photograph, as Barnaby later saw it, was remarkable. It wasn't just a snapshot; it was a work of art. The icy white of the ice cap formed a dramatic backdrop, highlighting the radiant colors of Barnaby's parka and the sleek, dark form of Sunny. The setting sun cast long shadows, adding depth and texture to the scene. Barnaby's expression, a mixture of awe and wonder, was perfectly captured; Sunny's gaze was fixed on the camera, its expression one of curious alertness.

The seal, seemingly pleased with its work, let out a happy bark – a sound like a series of playful clicks and whistles – before sliding gracefully back into the icy water. It disappeared beneath the surface, leaving only a few ripples to mark its passing. Barnaby stood there, speechless, staring at the spot where the seal had been. He couldn't help but laugh, a mixture of amazement and incredulity bubbling up inside him. A seal, with a camera? It was the most extraordinary thing he'd ever witnessed.

The memory of the encounter was a bizarre and wonderful footnote to his incredible Antarctic adventure. It added another layer of magic to the already extraordinary experience. The photograph, a reminder of this whimsical encounter, became a treasured keepsake – proof that even in the most remote and seemingly barren landscapes, life found a way to surprise and delight. He wondered often about the seal and its mysterious camera, imagining it snapping pictures of other adventurers, each photo a unique and precious record of the Antarctic wilderness.

The journey back to base camp was filled with quiet contemplation. Barnaby pondered the experiences of the last few days – the awe-inspiring beauty of the ice cave, the breathtaking spectacle of the Aurora Australis, and now, this unexpected encounter with the photographer seal. Each event seemed to build upon the other, adding layers of wonder and astonishment to his Antarctic expedition. He realized that the Antarctic was a realm of magic and enchantment, a place where the ordinary could transform into the extraordinary in the blink of an eye.

As they neared the camp, Barnaby noticed the subtle shifts in the landscape. The white expanse of the ice cap gave way to rolling hills of snow, sculpted by the wind into fantastical shapes. The air, though still biting, felt less harsh, perhaps because Barnaby was now filled with a warm glow of contentment and wonder. He couldn't wait to share his stories, his sketches, and even the story of the photographer seal with everyone back home.

He envisioned the reactions – the disbelief, the laughter, the shared sense of wonder. He knew that his words could only capture a fraction of the experience, but the photographs and sketches would serve as a visual testament to the magic he had witnessed. The photographs would not merely document his Antarctic journey; they would become the narrative itself, a visual story of adventure, discovery, and unexpected encounters.

The base camp appeared on the horizon, a cluster of brightly colored tents against the white landscape. A wave of warmth, both physical and emotional, washed over Barnaby as he saw the familiar sight. He knew that he would be returning to a different world, a world that seemed suddenly less ordinary, less mundane. The memories of his journey would stay with him forever, shaping his perception of the world, his understanding of nature's power and beauty, and his belief in the extraordinary possibilities that exist, even in the most unexpected places.

He felt a deep sense of gratitude for the opportunity to have experienced such an extraordinary adventure. The journey hadn't just been about seeing the sights; it had been a journey of self-discovery, a deepening of his connection to the natural world, and an appreciation for the wonders of the planet. The Antarctic wilderness, with its seemingly barren landscape, had proven to be a realm of surprising beauty, unexpected encounters, and transformative experiences. The cold, the wind, and the vastness of the ice cap had only served to amplify the magical elements of his expedition.

Barnaby reflected on the ice cave, a crystalline cathedral sculpted by nature's hand, and the vibrant spectacle of the Aurora Australis, a cosmic ballet played out across the night sky. These experiences, together with the curious photographer seal, had left an indelible mark on his soul. He realized that sometimes the most significant and memorable experiences are the ones that challenge our expectations, the ones that defy easy explanation, the ones that simply leave us speechless with wonder.

He felt a surge of anticipation as he looked towards the tents. He couldn't wait to share his stories with his fellow explorers. He knew that his tales would fill them with the same sense of wonder and inspiration that had gripped him during his Antarctic expedition. The stories would become a part of the collective memory of the expedition, an honor to the extraordinary adventures that awaited those who dared to venture into the heart of the unknown.

The photographs, especially the one taken by the curious seal, would be the visual anchors of his stories, adding an extra layer of credibility and wonder. He imagined showing the picture to his friends and family – their astonished expressions as they marveled at the seal's surprising skill and the dramatic beauty of the background would be a reward in itself. The picture would be a conversation starter, an icebreaker, a reminder that the world is full of unexpected wonders and extraordinary possibilities, waiting to be discovered by those with open minds and adventurous spirits.

The journey had not only expanded his understanding of the Antarctic wilderness; it had expanded his understanding of himself, his capacity for wonder, and his appreciation for the world's hidden treasures. The memory of the seal's photograph would be a constant reminder of this extraordinary journey, a testament to the boundless possibilities of nature's artistry and life's unexpected encounters. It was a perfect culmination of his expedition, a final, unforgettable memory that solidified the Antarctic wilderness as a place of magic, adventure, and breathtaking beauty – a place he would never forget. The Antarctic had shown him a different world, a world teeming with wonder, and he carried this new perspective with him as he approached base camp, his heart brimming with the joy of discovery and the thrill of an adventure well-lived.

Chapter 10:

South American Adventure

The Antarctic wind howled a farewell song as Barnaby boarded a surprisingly comfortable research vessel, bound for warmer climes. The transition from the harsh yet breathtaking, icy landscape to the bustling port city was jarring, a sensory overload after the quiet solitude of the ice cap. The air thrummed with the cacophony of unfamiliar sounds – the honking of horns, the chatter of people in a dozen different languages, the rhythmic clang of metal on metal from a nearby shipyard. It was a world away from the pristine silence of the Antarctic.

Barnaby, still buzzing from his Antarctic adventures, felt a thrill of anticipation. His next destination: South America. The thought conjured images of lush rainforests, towering mountains, vibrant cultures, and creatures he'd only ever dreamed of seeing. He'd pored over maps and books, his imagination fueled by tales of exotic birds, playful monkeys, and the mysterious depths of the Amazon.

The voyage itself was an adventure. The ship, a sleek research vessel named the *Aurora Borealis* (a fitting name, he thought, given his recent experiences), sliced through the waves, leaving a churning white wake in its path. Barnaby spent hours on deck, the salty spray kissing his face, the wind whipping through his hair. He sketched the ever-changing seascape – the playful dolphins leaping and diving, the dramatic sunsets painting the sky in an array of shades. Each sunset seemed more spectacular than the last, a testament to the Earth's boundless artistry.

He befriended a seasoned ornithologist named Dr. Amelia Hernandez, a woman whose passion for birds was infectious. She shared countless stories of her expeditions, her voice filled with the wonder and respect she held for the natural world. Amelia regaled him with tales of hummingbirds, their iridescent feathers shimmering like jewels, their wings beating so fast they were almost invisible. She described their incredible agility, their ability to hover in mid-air, and their acrobatic feats as they darted through the jungle canopy. Barnaby, already captivated by the Antarctic wildlife, was instantly enthralled by the sheer diversity and beauty of the South American avifauna.

The ship finally reached the coast of Ecuador. The air was thick with humidity, fragrant with the scent of exotic flowers and damp earth. The colors of the landscape were a sharp difference to the monochrome palette of the Antarctic. Everywhere Barnaby looked, life flourished – lush green vegetation, cascading waterfalls, and an abundance of vibrant wildlife. He felt a surge of exhilaration, a sense of boundless possibility.

His South American adventure truly began when, while exploring a remote rainforest region, he encountered a hummingbird unlike any he'd ever seen before. It was a dazzling creature, its feathers shimmering with an iridescent sheen that shifted colors in the sunlight – emerald green, sapphire blue, ruby red, all swirling together in a breathtaking display. It hovered before him, its tiny heart beating rapidly, its eyes sparkling with an unnerving intelligence.

Then, to Barnaby's astonishment, the hummingbird extended a tiny, delicate leg, beckoning him closer. He cautiously approached, his heart pounding with a mixture of excitement and apprehension. The hummingbird chirped, a sound like the tinkling of tiny bells, and then, to Barnaby's utter amazement, it offered him a ride!

Barnaby, never one to shy away from an adventure, accepted the offer. He carefully perched on the hummingbird's back, his fingers gently grasping its delicate feathers. The hummingbird launched into the air, its tiny wings whirring like a miniature helicopter. Barnaby held on tight, his eyes wide with wonder as he soared through the lush rainforest canopy.

The view was spectacular. The forest floor stretched out below him, a tapestry of emerald green, dappled with sunlight filtering through the leaves. He saw monkeys swinging effortlessly through the trees, their calls echoing through the forest. He spotted brightly colored parrots, their squawks filling the air, and colorful macaws, their plumage a riot of hues

The hummingbird navigated the dense foliage with astonishing skill, dodging branches and weaving through the trees with effortless grace. It soared over the waterfalls, their thundering roar a powerful symphony in the heart of the rainforest. It flew past towering mountains, their peaks piercing the clouds, their majestic presence dominating the landscape.

The journey was a whirlwind of sights and sounds. Barnaby sketched furiously, his pencil struggling to keep up with the sheer profusion of beauty. He filled his notebook with drawings of exotic flowers, strange insects, and the fantastical creatures that inhabited this ever-changing ecosystem.

The hummingbird led him to hidden waterfalls, secret groves, and breathtaking vistas. He saw orchids of unimaginable beauty, their delicate petals displaying a spectrum of colors, from the purest white to the deepest purple. He saw butterflies with wings like stained glass, their delicate patterns shimmering in the sunlight.

The flight lasted for what felt like hours, though it was probably only a few. The hummingbird finally landed on a branch, gently nudging Barnaby to dismount. Barnaby thanked his tiny steed, marveling at its unwavering loyalty and astonishing navigational skills. He knew that he would never forget this once-in-a-lifetime experience.

He continued his South American explorations, trekking through lush rainforests, scaling towering mountains, and exploring ancient ruins. He encountered playful monkeys swinging through the trees, their antics a constant source of amusement. He befriended a family of sloths, their languid movements a soothing contrast to the frenetic energy of the rainforest. He swam in crystal-clear rivers, the cool water a refreshing respite from the tropical heat. He marveled at the diversity of life – the colors, the exotic sounds, the sheer abundance of creatures, both great and small.

He learned about the rich cultures of South America, listening to the stories of the indigenous peoples, their traditions, their myths, and their deep connection to the land. He tasted exotic fruits, sampled spicy foods, and learned a few phrases in Spanish and Portuguese. Each interaction, each new experience, added another layer of richness to his South American adventure.

He observed the lively, flourishing landscape of South American life; a region teeming with color, vitality, and charm. He witnessed the spectacle of the Andean Condor soaring high above the mountains, a majestic sight, and heard the songs of the myriad birds, a melodic symphony echoing through the landscape. Every sunset offered a breathtaking spectacle.

His journey through South America was not just a geographical expedition, but a journey of the spirit. It was a celebration of the natural world, an affirmation of life's boundless beauty. The memories he created would remain with him forever, a constant reminder of the extraordinary possibilities that exist when we embrace adventure and open our hearts to the magic of the world. The image of the hummingbird, his unlikely steed, remained a symbol of that adventure of the unexpected connections and incredible journeys that life can offer.

Barnaby, still buzzing from his hummingbird flight, found himself standing at the edge of a seemingly endless expanse of emerald green. The rainforest air hung heavy and humid, a blanket woven with the scent of damp earth, decaying leaves, and a thousand unseen blossoms. The sounds were a symphony of the wild – the chatter of unseen monkeys, the rustling of leaves underfoot, the chirping of insects, and the distant calls of unseen birds, a chorus of life both familiar and utterly alien.

He plunged into the rainforest's heart, his boots sinking slightly into the soft, damp earth. Towering trees, their trunks thick as ancient oaks, clawed at the sky, their canopies forming a dense, almost impenetrable ceiling. Sunlight struggled to fill the thick foliage, creating dappled patterns on the forest floor. The air was still, except for the constant rustling and creaking of the living world around him.

The first thing that struck Barnaby was the sheer abundance of life. Giant ferns unfurled their emerald fronds, their delicate textures a stark contrast to the rough bark of the ancient trees. Vines, thick as pythons, snaked their way through the undergrowth, their tendrils reaching for any available support. He saw orchids clinging to branches high above, their vibrant blossoms explosions of color against the deep green backdrop. Their petals were delicate, translucent, almost ethereal, showcasing a spectrum of colors that seemed to shift and change with every subtle movement of the light. Some were a brilliant, almost electric purple, others a soft, creamy yellow, and still others were a dazzling, iridescent mix of colors.

He spotted a family of sloths clinging to a branch high above, their slow, deliberate movements a calming contrast to the frenetic energy of the forest floor. Their fur was a patchwork of greens and browns, providing excellent camouflage against the foliage. They seemed almost oblivious to his presence, their placid expressions an indication their laid-back lifestyle.

A troop of monkeys swung effortlessly through the branches, their chattering calls echoing through the trees. They were a whirlwind of energy, leaping from branch to branch with astonishing agility. Their fur was a rich, dark brown, and their eyes shone with intelligence and mischief. Barnaby watched them for a long time, captivated by their playful antics.

He discovered a clearing where butterflies with wings like stained glass fluttered amidst a profusion of exotic flowers. The colors were diverse – vibrant blues, fiery oranges, and deep purples, all swirling together in a kaleidoscope of patterns. He spent a long time sketching them, captivated by their delicate beauty and intricate designs. Their wings seemed almost too delicate to support their bodies, yet they fluttered effortlessly, their movements graceful and precise.

He encountered a variety of insects, some familiar, others utterly alien. Giant iridescent beetles crawled across fallen logs, their shells shimmering with an opalescent sheen. He saw brightly colored frogs, their skin smooth and glistening, perched on broad leaves. He watched in fascination as a group of ants marched in a perfectly ordered line, carrying crumbs of food many times their size.

The sounds of the rainforest continued to enthrall him. He heard the shrill calls of unseen birds, the rustling of leaves, and the chirping of crickets, all blending together into a rich auditory symphony. The air itself hummed with energy, as if the very forest itself was alive and breathing. He felt a sense of peace and tranquility amidst the seemingly chaotic abundance of life.

As he ventured deeper, Barnaby discovered a hidden waterfall, cascading down moss-covered rocks into a crystal-clear pool. The water was cool and refreshing. He sat by the pool, listening to the roar of the waterfall, the sounds washing over him like a soothing balm. He sketched the scene, capturing the beauty of the waterfall, the lush vegetation surrounding it, and the sunlight filtering through the trees.

He continued his exploration, his senses overwhelmed by the abundance of sights, sounds, and smells. He felt an intense connection to the rainforest, a sense of awe and wonder at the beauty and complexity of this vibrant ecosystem. He understood, in a way he never had before, the importance of preserving this precious environment for future generations.

He found himself tracing the path of a river, the water crystal clear and flowing swiftly over smooth, grey stones. The banks were lined with green vegetation, and the air was filled with the songs of many birds, their melodic calls harmonizing perfectly. He observed the many small creatures in the water as tiny fishes darted between rocks, their silver scales flashing in the sunlight. The river felt like the lifeblood of this incredible rainforest.

As dusk settled, Barnaby found a clearing bathed in the soft light of the setting sun. He built a small fire, the warmth a welcome comfort as the temperature cooled. The sounds of the night emerged, owls calling softly, and crickets chirping their rhythmic song. As night fell, the rainforest seemed to hold its breath, a dense silence descending. He looked up at the starlit sky, the immensity of the universe echoing the vastness of the rainforest that surrounded him.

He spent the night sheltered in the heart of the jungle, protected by the very ecosystem that he had been exploring. He slept soundly, lulled by the sounds of the night. The experience was unforgettable, a connection to the earth and the natural world unlike any he'd ever known. He woke with the dawn, feeling renewed and invigorated. The rainforest's life unfolded before him, a magnificent testament to the beauty and resilience of nature. His South American adventure continued, his experiences richer and deeper than he could ever have imagined. The rainforest had revealed its secrets, not only to his eyes, but also to his heart and soul.

Barnaby left the rainforest behind, the verdant green a fading memory as he began his ascent into the Andes Mountains. The change was dramatic. The humid, heavy air thinned with every step, replaced by a crispness that invigorated his lungs. The lush green gave way to a landscape of rugged beauty, where towering peaks scraped the sky, their rocky surfaces a patchwork of browns, greys, and ochre. The vibrant symphony of the rainforest was replaced by a quieter, more austere melody – the whistle of the wind, the distant cry of a condor, and the crunch of his boots on the rocky trail.

He climbed steadily, the path winding its way through a landscape sculpted by time and the elements. He passed through forests of hardy, wind-swept trees, their branches gnarled and twisted by the relentless mountain winds. The trees were shorter, more stunted than those in the rainforest, clinging tenaciously to the rocky slopes. Here and there, patches of wildflowers defied the harsh conditions, their colors a splash of brilliance against the muted tones of the mountains. The air grew thinner, and the scent of damp earth was replaced by the sharp, clean smell of pine and mountain air.

The views began to unfold gradually, initially in glimpses between the trees, then as vistas that took his breath away. Valleys spread out below him, carpeted in a patchwork of greens and browns, rivers snaking through them like silver ribbons. In the distance, other peaks rose majestically, their snow-capped summits glistening under the sun. The scale of the expanse was overwhelming. He felt small, insignificant, yet strangely exhilarated by the vastness of it all.

He paused frequently, mesmerized by the unfolding vista. The colors shifted throughout the day, the mountains bathed in the golden light of dawn, then cast in the deep shadows of the afternoon. The clouds drifted lazily across the peaks, their forms constantly changing, creating ever-shifting patterns of light and shadow. Sometimes, they clung low to the mountains, shrouding the peaks in a misty veil, creating an air of mystery and intrigue. Other times, they were swept away by the wind, revealing the full majesty of the Andes in all their breathtaking glory.

He encountered llamas along the trail, their soft, woolly coats a comforting contrast to the harsh, rocky landscape. They were graceful and sure-footed, moving effortlessly along the steep, winding paths. Their large, expressive eyes seemed to hold a wisdom born of their intimate relationship with the mountains. He watched them graze peacefully, their gentle movements a calming rhythm in the vast, expansive landscape. He learned that the local people depended on these gentle creatures for their wool, meat, and as pack animals, their role in the Andes culture was deeply significant. He also noted the many smaller creatures, mountain foxes with their alert expressions and nimble paws; tiny birds flitting about with a surprising energy.

He found himself tracing ancient Inca trails, their stone pathways still remarkably intact after centuries. The precision of their construction was incredible, a testament to the ingenuity and skill of the Inca people. He imagined the Inca travelers who had once walked these very paths, carrying goods and messages across the mountains, their lives intertwined with the rhythm of the Andes. He found himself deeply touched by the connection to the past, a sense of history woven into the very fabric of the landscape.

The higher he climbed, the more dramatic the views became. He could see for miles, the world stretching out below him like a giant map. He spent hours sketching the landscape, attempting to capture the beauty and grandeur of the mountains in his drawings. He found that words failed him; his pen struggled to accurately capture the immense scale and the subtle beauty of the scenery.

As he climbed, he noticed subtle shifts in the vegetation. The hardy trees gradually gave way to alpine meadows, their colorful grasses and wildflowers creating vibrant mosaics of color. He discovered a small lake, nestled high in the mountains, its waters reflecting the surrounding peaks like a mirror. The silence here was broken only by the occasional cry of a bird or the whisper of the wind. The stillness was captivating, a sense of peace washing over him, allowing him to truly appreciate the solitude of the heights. He drank from the icy cold water, its taste refreshing and pure.

One evening, he found himself on a high pass, the wind whipping around him, the air thinning considerably. Below him, clouds drifted across the valleys, their white forms creating a breathtaking contrast against the deep greens and browns of the landscape. As twilight deepened, he watched the mountains became silhouettes against the sky, their shapes becoming increasingly dramatic as the light faded. The experience was overwhelming as he witnessed the majesty of nature.

Once darkness fell, the temperature plummeted. He huddled by a small rock outcropping, shielded from the wind, marveling at the starlit sky above. The stars were brighter here, more numerous than he had ever seen them before. The Milky Way stretched across the heavens like a river of light, a breathtaking vision in the inky black. The vastness of the universe mirrored the vastness of the mountain range around him, a humbling experience. The night brought a deep stillness, broken only by the wind and the distant call of a nocturnal animal. He felt connected to the earth and the heavens, a part of the ancient echoes of the mountains.

The next day, he continued his ascent, pushing his limits, his body challenged by the altitude and the steep inclines. But with every step, the sense of achievement was immense. The views continued to reward him, each new vista more breathtaking than the last. He crossed rivers, navigated tricky paths, and even had to traverse some snowfields, his sense of exhilaration growing with each new challenge.

He eventually reached his goal, a high vantage point that offered a panoramic view of the Andes stretching as far as the eye could see. The air was thin, and he needed to take frequent breaks, but the view was beyond anything he could have imagined. The mountains formed a majestic, jagged horizon, their snow-capped peaks glistening under the sun. Below him, valleys cascaded down, their slopes a blend of colors and textures. The world stretched out before him, a breathtaking panorama of unimaginable scale. He felt an overwhelming sense of accomplishment, a sense of having conquered not only the physical challenge but also a sense of self-discovery that was deeply fulfilling. The Andean Mountains had tested his physical endurance, his resilience, and his spirit. He had emerged not just with stunning memories but a deeper appreciation for the power and the beauty of nature, a realization of the bond between humanity and nature.

The crisp mountain air carried the scent of woodsmoke and something subtly sweet, a promise of warmth and welcome. Rounding a bend in the trail, Barnaby came across a small village nestled in a sheltered valley, a cluster of adobe houses clinging to the mountainside like swallows' nests. Smoke curled lazily from their chimneys, painting the clear morning air with a gentle haze. The sight was a welcome change from the rugged beauty of the high peaks, a comforting reminder of human presence in this vast, wild landscape.

As he approached, children, their faces bright and curious, emerged from the houses, their laughter echoing through the quiet valley. They were dressed in brightly colored clothing, their ponchos a fusion of reds, blues, and yellows, a contrast of the muted tones of the mountains. They spoke a language Barnaby didn't understand, but their gestures were universally welcoming, their smiles open and infectious. He offered a tentative wave, and they responded with delighted shrieks, rushing towards him with a joyful abandon that instantly put him at ease.

An older woman, her face etched with the wisdom of years spent under the Andean sun, emerged from one of the houses. Her eyes, deep and knowing, held a warmth that transcended language barriers. She approached Barnaby with a gentle grace, her movements fluid and deliberate, despite the apparent stiffness of her aged joints. She spoke to him in rapid Spanish, her words a melodious cascade, punctuated by the lilting sounds that only the native tongue can capture. Barnaby, despite his limited Spanish, understood the warmth of her greeting, the genuine welcome in her eyes.

She gestured towards a nearby house, where a steaming pot sat over a crackling fire. The aroma of something delicious, perhaps a hearty stew or a rich soup, wafted towards him, a fragrant invitation. Inside, the warmth of the room was a welcome contrast to the crisp mountain air. The walls were adorned with woven tapestries, their intricate designs telling silent stories of Andean history and tradition. The air buzzed with a gentle hum of conversation, the rhythmic sound of knitting needles clicking in time with the crackling fire.

Several other villagers joined them, each with a unique story to share, though Barnaby could only grasp fragments of their conversation. He learned of their lives, their reliance on the land, and the fragile balance they maintained with nature. They spoke of their crops, the challenges of farming at high altitude, and the rituals they performed to ensure a bountiful harvest. He learned of their deep respect for the mountains, their belief in the spirits that inhabited the peaks, and the ancient traditions that had been passed down through generations.

One man, a wiry figure with calloused hands and a twinkle in his eye, showed Barnaby his intricate carvings, miniature llamas and condors fashioned from the wood of the mountain trees. His craftsmanship was exquisite, each detail meticulously carved, a testament to the skill and dedication of his work. He explained, through a combination of gestures and a few carefully chosen Spanish words, the meaning behind each carving, the symbolic representation of Andean culture and mythology.

An elderly woman, her face a roadmap of wrinkles shared stories of her childhood, her voice a low, resonant hum. She spoke of her grandmother, a wise woman who had taught her the ancient ways, the traditions that connected them to their ancestors. She spoke of the stars, their movements a celestial clock that guided their lives, and their influence on the rhythms of the earth. Her words were imbued with a deep connection to the land and to the spirit of the Andes.

The villagers shared their food with Barnaby, a simple meal of hearty stew and freshly baked bread. The food was delicious, its flavors a reflection of the land, the earthiness of the potatoes and the sweetness of the corn. He felt a sense of kinship with these people, their generosity and warmth melting away any feelings of loneliness or isolation. He shared his own stories, drawing pictures in the dirt to convey his travels, his experiences in the rainforest, and his awe of the mountains. Though language was a barrier, the shared experience of human connection transcended words.

As the sun began to set, casting long shadows across the valley, Barnaby prepared to leave. The villagers presented him with a small, intricately woven tapestry, a parting gift, a token of their friendship. He felt a deep sense of gratitude, a profound appreciation for their kindness and generosity. He left the village with a heavy heart, but also with a renewed sense of purpose, his understanding of the Andean culture greatly enriched by their stories.

The next day, Barnaby continued his journey, but the memory of the village, the warmth of its people, and the beauty of their traditions remained with him. He carried with him not only the vivid image of the snow-capped peaks and the rugged beauty of the Andes, but also the stories of the people he had met, their resilient spirits and their deep connection to the land. He realized that the mountains were not just a geographical feature, but a living entity, a sacred place where the past, present, and future intertwined. The people were not merely inhabitants of this vast landscape, but its guardians, their lives interwoven with the rhythm of the mountains, their culture a vibrant expression of their relationship with nature.

His journey through the Andes had been a physical challenge, but it was also a journey of discovery, of deepening his understanding of the natural world and the human spirit. He had witnessed the majestic beauty of the mountains, but he had also been touched by the warmth and generosity of the people who called them home. The memory of his time spent in that small Andean village would remain ingrained in his heart always, a treasure more precious than any physical souvenir. It was a reminder that the greatest rewards of exploration were not always found in the vastness of nature, but also in the heartfelt connections made with the people who shared their lives with the land. The Andean people were not just part of the landscape; they were the very heart and soul of it, a living testament to the endurance of the human spirit and the enduring magic of human connection.

The sun dipped lower, casting long shadows that stretched and danced across the valley floor. The air, already crisp with the mountain chill, grew even colder, a subtle reminder that it was time to continue my journey. But before Barnaby left, there was one more experience to be had, a final memory to capture of this incredible Andean adventure.

Barnaby had befriended a llama, a creature of remarkable gentleness and surprising intelligence. This wasn't just any llama; this was Lorenzo, a fluffy, caramel-colored fellow with eyes as soft as velvet and a surprisingly photogenic nature. He'd been watching Barnaby with quiet curiosity all afternoon, his large, expressive eyes following my every move. It was as if he understood Barnaby's unspoken desire to capture this moment, this perfect picture-postcard scene, forever.

He was surprisingly docile, and a quick glance at his harness revealed a tiny, intricately carved wooden camera attached to it. Not a real camera, of course, but a miniature replica, perfectly crafted from polished mountain wood. Its lens was a tiny, perfectly smooth piece of obsidian, gleaming like a black jewel. Barnaby couldn't help but smile at the whimsical nature of it all. This wasn't just a llama; this was a llama with a flair for photography.

Lorenzo nudged Barnaby arm gently, his soft wool brushing against Barnaby's cheek. He seemed to be urging Barnaby into position. Barnaby chuckled, a sound that echoed faintly in the stillness of the valley. He was directing Barnaby, arranging his pose with surprising skill. He positioned Barnaby against the backdrop of the majestic Andes, the snow-capped peaks rising in the distance, painted in hues of rose and gold by the setting sun.

The villagers, gathered around a crackling fire, watched with amusement. They laughed, their voices a melodic chorus against the backdrop of the mountain wind. Barnaby felt a warmth spread through him, a feeling of belonging, of shared joy in this breathtaking landscape. It was a moment of pure, unadulterated happiness, a memory that would forever be etched in his soul.

Lorenzo, with the patience of a seasoned professional, adjusted my stance, coaxing Barnaby to turn slightly to the left, then slightly to the right, ensuring the perfect angle to capture the majestic view behind me. He even managed to adjust Barnaby's hat – a wide-brimmed straw hat Barnaby had purchased in a bustling market in Cusco – so it cast a flattering shadow across his face.

His attention to detail was astounding. It was as if he understood the principles of photography, the art of composition, and the importance of light and shadow. He was a natural. Barnaby could almost imagine him studying Ansel Adams's work, carefully analyzing the play of light and shadow in his photographs, perfecting his craft.

He then carefully adjusted his miniature wooden camera, focusing with surprising precision on me, the mountains, and the setting sun. Barnaby held his breath, anticipating the "click" of the shutter – a sound that, of course, never came. But in that moment, Barnaby knew that the picture was taken, not just in the physical sense, but in Barnaby's heart and mind.

After what felt like an eternity, Lorenzo beamed, as if he had successfully captured the perfect shot. A satisfied sigh seemed to puff from his nostrils as he lowered the little camera back down to his side. He gave a satisfied nod, his large, dark eyes twinkling, as if he knew he had captured the essence of the moment. It was a moment that transcended words, a perfect synthesis of human and animal connection against the breathtaking backdrop of the Andes.

The photo itself, a product of a llama's artistry, wasn't a tangible thing. It existed only in Barnaby's memory, in the feelings evoked by that perfect moment. It was a picture of more than just a man standing against a mountain range. It was a picture of wonder, of shared joy, of the magical reality that often unfolds when we least expect it.

As the last rays of sunlight faded behind the peaks, Barnaby turned to the villagers, expressing his gratitude with a mixture of gestures and heartfelt smiles. Their warm smiles and nods of approval confirmed what he already felt deep down – the Andean people have a way of making even the most fantastical moments feel perfectly natural, almost expected.

The villagers presented him with a small, hand-woven bag, its design depicting a majestic condor soaring over snow-capped peaks. Inside, nestled amongst soft, fragrant alpaca wool, was a tiny, hand-carved llama – a miniature version of Lorenzo, perhaps – perfectly capturing his gentle, wise expression. It was a precious souvenir, a symbol of the unique bond forged in that breathtaking moment by the Andes.

That night, under the vast expanse of the starlit Andean sky, he lay awake, the image of myself, silhouetted against the majestic peaks, forever in his memory. It was a picture more vivid and memorable than any photograph could ever be, honoring the unique and unforgettable experiences that await those who dare to embrace the unexpected adventures that life throws in someone's way.

Barnaby's South American adventure was drawing to a close, but the memories-the vibrant colors of the rainforests, the stark beauty of the high Andes, the warmth and generosity of the people he met, and the unexpected photographic talents of a llama–would remain. Each memory, a tender brushstroke on the canvas of his life.

The journey had reshaped him, stripping away the layers of preconceived notions and revealing a deeper appreciation for the world's beauty and the resilience of the human spirit. The mountains were no longer just geological formations; they were guardians of stories, keepers of ancient wisdom, and silent witnesses to the passage of time. The people were not just inhabitants of this vast landscape; they were its soul, their lives intricately woven with the rhythm of nature.

And then there was Lorenzo, the llama photographer, whose image, along with his miniature wooden camera, forever resided in my memories, a constant reminder of the magical and surprising moments that make life's adventures truly unforgettable. His legacy wasn't just a picture; it was the embodiment of the unexpected connections people make, the spontaneous friendships that form, and the shared experiences that deepen their understanding of themselves and the world around them.

Leaving the Andes was bittersweet. Barnaby carried with him not just physical souvenirs, but a treasure trove of memories, experiences, and a renewed perspective on life. The Andes had shown him the power of human connection, the beauty of simplicity, and the magic that unfolds when we embrace the unexpected. The journey he took through the Andes, defined by the stunning scenery and the generosity of those he met, would stay with him for the rest of his life.

The journey home was long, but the memories kept him company, each one a comforting reminder of the breathtaking beauty and unexpected friendships he had found in South America. And somewhere in that tapestry of memories, a llama with a wooden camera would always hold a special place, a symbol of the magical, unpredictable, and profoundly rewarding nature of travel and adventure.

Chapter 11:

Return Journey

The airport buzzed with a chaotic energy, a stark contrast to the serene quiet of the Andean highlands. The air, thick with the scent of jet fuel and anticipation, felt strangely alien after weeks of breathing the crisp mountain air. Barnaby clutched his worn backpack, its contents a reminder of his incredible journey – a hand-woven Andean blanket, a small, hand-carved llama, and the ever-present memory of Lorenzo, the llama photographer.

He boarded the plane, finding a window seat that offered a panoramic view of the sprawling city below. As the plane ascended, the city shrank, transforming into a miniature model, its bustling streets and towering buildings reduced to a fascinating tapestry of colors and shapes. He watched, mesmerized, as the urban landscape yielded to the sprawling expanse of the earth, its patchwork fields and winding rivers stretching out like a painter's canvas.

The journey was long, a seemingly endless succession of meals served on trays, movies watched on tiny screens, and whispered conversations between fellow passengers. But Barnaby's mind remained far away, still drifting through the breathtaking landscapes he'd once explored. He found himself revisiting the constantly evolving colors of the rainforest, the lush green canopy teeming with life, and the sparkling glimmers of exotic birds darting through the leaves. He recalled the thrill of navigating the

Amazon River, the feeling of the warm, humid air on his skin, and the sounds of nature's symphony enveloping him.

He remembered the welcoming smiles of the indigenous communities he had encountered, their generosity and kindness extending beyond the mere exchange of goods and services. He recalled their stories, their traditions, their deep connection to the land, and the respect they held for the natural world. These interactions had broadened his understanding of different cultures and perspectives, and their impact continued to resonate with him even as he flew thousands of miles away.

Then came the Andes, their majestic peaks piercing the clouds, their snow-capped summits gleaming under the sun. The crisp mountain air, the breathtaking views, the challenging climbs – each moment was etched in his memory, a vivid reminder of the physical and mental strength he had discovered within himself. He recalled the humbling experience of being dwarfed by the sheer scale and magnificence of the mountains, a powerful reminder of the vastness and power of nature.

He smiled, recalling the mischievous glint in Lorenzo's eye, the llama's surprising skill in posing him for that unforgettable "photograph." It was a moment of pure, unadulterated joy, a reminder that life's greatest moments often arise from the most unexpected sources. The memory of the soft wool brushing against his cheek, the villagers' laughter echoing in the stillness of the valley, and the warmth of their shared experience filled him with a sense of profound contentment. Lorenzo wasn't just a llama; he was a symbol of the unexpected connections we make, a testament to the beauty of spontaneity, and a constant reminder of the joy found in the simplest things.

The hours flew by, filled with reflections on how his journeys had changed him. They had not only expanded his horizons geographically but also deepened his understanding of himself, his capabilities, and his place in the world. He had learned to appreciate the simple things – the beauty of nature, the warmth of human connection, and the unexpected joys that life has to offer.

As the plane began its descent, the familiar glow of city lights emerged from the darkness below, a stark contrast to the starlit Andean skies he had grown accustomed to. A wave of emotion washed over him – a mix of excitement at returning home and sadness at leaving behind the magic of the Andes. He felt changed, irrevocably altered by the experiences he had encountered.

He was no longer the same person who had embarked on this journey. He carried within him the echoes of the rainforest, the silent majesty of the mountains, and the warmth of the Andean people. He had discovered a deeper appreciation for the natural world, a renewed sense of self-discovery, and a vast understanding of the richness and diversity of human cultures.

He knew the world awaited him with new challenges and opportunities, but he carried with him the wisdom and lessons learned in the Andes. His memories would serve as a compass, guiding him through life's journey. He would always remember the lessons he learned and the connections he formed.

The airplane descended, the landscape below slowly drifting from a patchwork quilt of clouds to a familiar green and brown. Barnaby pressed his face against the window, a thrill of anticipation coursing through him. He hadn't realized how much he'd missed the subtle nuances of his own land, the gentle undulations of the hills, the way the sunlight kissed the fields at different angles. The Andes, with their majestic peaks and breathtaking vistas, had captivated him completely, but the familiar comfort of home was a powerful draw. He felt a pang of sadness, a wistful ache for the vibrant culture he was leaving behind, but it was tempered by an overwhelming sense of joy at the prospect of returning to his own little corner of the world.

He pictured his garden, a riot of colors and scents he had carefully cultivated over the years. He imagined the cheerful yellow sunflowers, their faces turned towards the sun, their sturdy stems swaying gently in the breeze. He could almost smell the sweet fragrance of his lavender bushes, a calming scent that always soothed his soul. The plump tomatoes, bursting with their summery sweetness, and the peppers, each with its unique shade of fiery red and orange, danced in his mind's eye. Even the slightly unruly patch of wildflowers, a haphazard blend of colors and textures, held a special place in his heart. They were a symbol of nature's untamed beauty, a reminder that perfection wasn't always necessary, and that sometimes, embracing the chaos was more rewarding.

Landing at the airport, the familiar sounds and smells of home washed over him – a comforting wave of normalcy after weeks immersed in the extraordinary. He walked out of the terminal, his heart filled with gratitude, his mind buzzing with memories. His journey home was a continuation of his journey itself, not an end. The experiences he had lived, the people he had met, the lessons he had learned – these were not just transient memories, but enduring legacies that would continue to shape him for years to come.

He looked up at the sky, remembering the endless expanse of the Andean sky, the brilliant stars that shone with such intensity. He felt a moving sense of connection sweep over him, a feeling that the mountains, the rainforests, and the people he had met were still with him, gently residing in his heart and mind. The long journey home was not just a physical one; it was also an internal journey, a process of integration and reflection, allowing him to fully assimilate the changes his wandering had brought about.

The world outside the airport seemed brighter, the air cleaner, the sounds livelier. He noticed details he had not noticed before, appreciating the everyday aspects of life with a renewed perspective. The ordinary had become extraordinary, transformed by the lens of his experiences. He knew that his life would never be quite the same, and he embraced this change with open arms. The journey was over, but its impact would reverberate through his life forever.

The taxi hummed along the highway, a jarring contrast to the silence of the Andean peaks. Barnaby leaned back against the plush leather seat, his gaze drifting out the window at the blurring landscape. He wasn't just returning home physically; he was carrying a world within him, memories of faces, and experiences that had irrevocably altered his perspective. The journey home was a contemplative one, a slow unwinding of the tightly woven tapestry of his adventure.

His thoughts drifted back to the rainforest, to the raucous chatter of the macaws echoing through the dense canopy. He remembered old Elara, the woman with eyes as deep and knowing as the Amazon itself, who had taught him to identify the medicinal properties of rainforest plants. He pictured her wrinkled hands, calloused from years of working the land, deftly preparing a potent remedy from a handful of leaves. Her stories, whispered in hushed tones, had painted vivid pictures of the rainforest's history, its ancient secrets, and the deep-rooted connection between her people and their environment. Elara's wisdom, her quiet strength, and her profound understanding of nature had left an indelible mark on his soul.

Then there was Mateo, the young boy who had guided him through the labyrinthine paths of the jungle, his laughter as infectious as the jungle's humidity. Mateo, with his boundless energy and insatiable curiosity, had shown Barnaby a world seen through the eyes of a child, a world where wonder thrived and imagination ran wild. He remembered Mateo's infectious grin as they navigated the dense undergrowth, pointing out colorful insects and elusive animals, his knowledge of the jungle seemingly limitless.

The memory of the Andean villagers flooded his mind. He thought of old Señora Elena, her wrinkled face etched with the wisdom of generations, who had welcomed him into her humble home with open arms, offering him steaming bowls of hearty stew and stories that spun tales of ancient gods and mythical creatures. Her kindness, her warmth, and her unwavering hospitality had transformed a simple meal into a cherished memory. The intricate patterns she had woven into her blankets, each stitch showcasing her dedication and skill, seemed to symbolize the harmony of life. Her stories, steeped in the rich folklore of the Andes, had unveiled some culture rich in tradition and history.

He recalled the hearty laughter of the villagers as they played their traditional games, their faces alight with pure joy. The rhythmic beat of their music, the vivid colors of their clothing, the shared moments of merriment and camaraderie – each detail painted a portrait of a community bound together by their shared history and unwavering spirit. Their unassuming generosity, their willingness to share their culture and traditions, had been a powerful lesson in the strength and resilience of the human spirit.

They had shown him that true wealth lies not in material possessions, but in the richness of human connections.

And of course, there was Lorenzo, the llama photographer, his mischievous glint still present in Barnaby's memory. Lorenzo wasn't just a llama; he was a symbol of the unexpected connections we make. The image of Lorenzo posing patiently for his photographs, his expressive eyes reflecting a surprising intelligence, brought a smile to Barnaby's face. Lorenzo's presence had added a touch of whimsy and humor to his journey, a lighthearted counterpoint to the sometimes challenging moments.

He thought of the challenges he had faced—the steep climbs, the torrential rains, the moments of self-doubt—and how he had overcome them. He thought of the friendships he'd forged, the connections he'd made, and the resilience he'd discovered within himself. These were not just fleeting encounters; they were chapters in his life story, adding depth, color, and meaning to his journey. The people he met along the way weren't just passing acquaintances; they were fellow travelers on his life's adventure, each contributing a unique perspective, a shared laughter, a moment of mutual understanding.

The taxi pulled up to his house. As Barnaby stepped out, he took a deep breath, the familiar scent of home filling his lungs. But home felt different now, richer, more textured, more meaningful. It was no longer just a place; it was a point of reference, a center from which he could now radiate outwards, connected to a wider world he had glimpsed and experienced firsthand.

He walked through the front door, the familiar sounds and smells of his home washing over him – a comforting wave of normalcy after weeks immersed in the extraordinary. He knew that the physical journey was over, but the internal journey was far from complete. The memories, vivid and ever-present, would serve as a compass, guiding him through life's journey.

He looked at the hand-carved llama, sitting on his desk, a symbol of his journey. He knew his life would never be quite the same, and he embraced this change, understanding the profound impact his Andean adventure would have on his future, shaping his choices, his relationships, and his appreciation for the world.

He smiled, a genuine sense of gratitude washing over him. He had returned home a changed person, richer for the experiences, friendships, and memories he had gained. The Andean adventure was over, but its legacy would live on. And as he settled into his chair, he knew, with absolute certainty, that the echoes of the Andes, the laughter of the villagers, the wisdom of Elara, and the mischievous glint in Lorenzo's eye would continue to shape his journey for years to come. The journey had changed him, but in doing so, it had made him whole. The world felt different now. Brighter. And filled with a deeper understanding of himself and the world around him. He was home. But he was also everywhere he had been, in every heart he had touched, and in every memory he carried within him. The journey had just begun.

The quiet hum of the refrigerator was the only sound in the otherwise silent house. Barnaby, still buzzing with the residual energy of his journey, found himself unable to simply sit still. He paced the length of his living room, his gaze lingering on the familiar objects that had once defined his world, now seen with fresh eyes, imbued with a new significance. The worn armchair, usually a haven of comfort, now felt like a symbol of a life lived somewhat narrowly before his adventure. The framed photographs on the mantelpiece, once snapshots of routine, now seemed like faded memories from a previous existence.

He picked up the hand-carved llama, its wood soft beneath his fingers. Each tiny detail, the subtle curve of its neck, the intricacy of its carved features, whispered tales of the Andean artisans who had poured their heart and soul into its creation. It was an authentic link to the people he had met, the landscapes he had traversed, and the lessons he had learned. He traced the lines of its face, feeling a surge of gratitude and a deep sense of connection to the vibrant culture he had encountered.

The lessons he had learned extended far beyond the practical skills he had acquired. He had learned the resilience of the human spirit, witnessing firsthand the unwavering strength of the Andean villagers in the face of adversity. Their lives, though seemingly simple by his standards, were rich with a depth of meaning he had only begun to understand. They had taught him the importance of community, the value of shared experiences, and the satisfaction of contributing to something larger than oneself.

He thought about Elara and her instinctive connection to the rainforest, her intimate understanding of the delicate balance of the ecosystem. He realized that his own understanding of the environment, previously limited to the abstract concerns of conservation, had been deepened by her wisdom. He now saw nature not just as a resource to be exploited, but as a living, breathing entity deserving of respect and protection. He was inspired by the way her people coexisted harmoniously with nature, understanding and honoring its rhythms and cycles. He had witnessed a way of living that was sustainable and respectful, an example to emulate rather than merely admire.

Mateo's infectious laughter echoed in his memory, a reminder of the simple joys of childhood. He had learned from Mateo the importance of maintaining a sense of wonder, the ability to see the world through the eyes of a child, to find joy in the smallest of things, be it a brilliantly colored insect or a breathtaking sunset. Mateo's unbridled curiosity had been contagious, reminding him of the power of asking questions, exploring possibilities, and never ceasing to learn.

The vibrant music, the joyous dances, and the shared meals all contributed to a richer understanding of the human experience. He had learned the importance of cultural exchange, the richness that comes from celebrating differences, and the unifying power of music and art. The simple act of sharing a meal, the laughter shared during a game, had cemented in his mind the concept of communal living and its powerful sense of belonging.

And Lorenzo, the mischievous llama photographer, had reminded him to embrace the unexpected, to find humor in life's absurdities, and to cherish the spontaneous moments that add spice and delight to our journey. He had demonstrated that even the most ordinary moments can be extraordinary with the right perspective.

His journey had also been a journey of self-discovery. He had faced physical challenges, pushing himself beyond his perceived limits, and in doing so, he had discovered a resilience he didn't know he possessed. He had learned to appreciate the value of perseverance, the importance of setting goals, and the satisfaction of overcoming obstacles. He had also learned the importance of self-reflection, of taking time to appreciate the beauty of the world around him, and of acknowledging his own limitations and growth areas.

His adventure had not been without its difficulties. He recalled moments of frustration, of loneliness, and of self-doubt. But these challenges, he realized, had only served to deepen his understanding of himself and the world around him. They had shown him that life is not always easy, but that even in the midst of adversity, there is always something to be learned, something to be gained, and something to be appreciated.

Back in his familiar surroundings, Barnaby felt a lasting sense of peace. His life was no longer solely his own. It had become intertwined with the lives of those he'd met and the landscapes he had journeyed through. He had returned home a changed man, wiser, more compassionate, and deeply grateful for the experiences that had shaped his life. The llama, still sitting on his desk, became his silent companion, a symbol of a journey that would continue, evolving and enriching his life in ways he couldn't even yet imagine. His home felt different, warmer, infused with the echoes of laughter, the wisdom of ages, and the spirit of adventure.

He saw his garden from the little window of his bedroom. His heart glistened with a sense of belonging, as if it was calling him. Immediately, he walked towards it. He paused, for a brief moment, his hand resting on the rough-hewn wooden gate, a silent moment of appreciation. The gate, slightly askew as always, creaked a familiar welcome as he pushed it open. It was as if the garden itself was breathing a sigh of relief, welcoming him back into its embrace. The air hummed with the gentle buzz of bees, diligently collecting nectar from the radiant blossoms. Butterflies, their wings shimmering with multicolored hues, fluttered lazily amongst the flowers. The entire garden felt alive, pulsating with energy, welcoming him home.

For him, his garden wasn't just a collection of plants; it was a sanctuary, a space where he could escape the pressures of daily life and reconnect with the earth. It was where he found solace in tending to his plants, feeling the cool soil beneath his fingertips, and observing the subtle changes in nature's rhythms. It was a space that reflected his own personality – a blend of order and chaos, of planned intention and spontaneous growth. He recalled the countless hours he had spent weeding, watering, and nurturing his plants, watching them grow from tiny seeds into flourishing specimens. Each plant stood as a testament to his patience, dedication, and deep-rooted love for the natural world.

Beyond the garden, he thought of his home, a small, charming cottage nestled amongst the trees. It wasn't grand or ostentatious; it was simple and unassuming, yet filled with warmth and character. The walls were adorned with paintings he'd made during his travels, each capturing a unique memory or emotion. The shelves were lined with books, each one holding a story, a journey, an experience. His home wasn't merely a structure; it was a container for his memories, his dreams, and his aspirations. It was a place where he could relax, reflect, and recharge. It was where he could be truly himself.

The thought of sharing his experiences with his friends and family added another layer of anticipation. He longed to recount the incredible adventures he'd had, to share the breathtaking landscapes he'd seen, and to introduce them to the fascinating people he'd met. He envisioned lively evenings filled with laughter, animated conversations, and the exchange of stories. He imagined their expressions of wonder as he described the dynamic Andean culture, the majestic mountains, and the warmth of the people he had come to know. He had collected small gifts, trinkets to share, each carrying a piece of his journey.

He planned on showing them his collection of intricately woven tapestries, each depicting scenes of Andean life, illustrating the stories Señora Elena had shared with him. He would tell them about the patience and dedication required to create such masterpieces, and the deep cultural significance they held. He would share the stories of the artisans he had met, each a unique character with their own skills and traditions. He was eager to demonstrate the techniques of Andean knot-tying, a skill he had meticulously practiced, passing on the knowledge he had gained.

He also couldn't wait to show them the photographs Lorenzo had taken. The quirky, humorous approach had captured so much more than just the landscapes. The images of Lorenzo, himself, posed with llamas in various amusing situations, were sure to provide endless laughter. They were a perfect visual representation of his journey, blending the beautiful with the unexpected and the funny. He would share the story of how he had met Lorenzo, an unlikely friendship forged amidst the majestic landscapes, demonstrating that companionship could blossom in the most unexpected circumstances.

He would relive the moments of challenge, the moments of doubt, and the moments of triumph. He would explain how he had pushed himself beyond his perceived limits and discovered a resilience within himself he never knew existed. He would share his lessons about perseverance, about embracing the unknown, and about finding strength in adversity. He'd describe how the simplicity of life in the Andes had shown him a different perspective, emphasizing the importance of appreciating what we have and the joy of sharing experiences with others.

He also wanted to share the deeper, more profound lessons he had learned. He wanted to speak of the interconnectedness of nature, of the profound wisdom of the Andean people, and of the importance of cultural understanding. He wanted to communicate the importance of respecting other cultures and learning from their ways of life. He wanted his friends and family to appreciate the lessons he had gained in humility, in gratitude, and in the value of connecting with the natural world. He anticipated their questions, their curiosity, and their shared wonder. He yearned to express how profoundly the journey had transformed him, to share its beauty, its wonder, and the enduring impression it had made on his soul.

As he walked, he noticed the subtle shifts in his garden – the way the sunflowers had grown taller, their faces tilted towards the setting sun, a golden halo in the late afternoon light. The lavender, once neatly pruned, now cascaded over the stone pathway, a fragrant purple wave. His tomatoes, plump and red, hung heavy on their vines, begging to be picked. Even the unruly patch of wildflowers seemed to have embraced the summer's warmth with a newfound exuberance, a chaotic explosion of color and texture. They were a welcoming committee, a boisterous greeting after months of absence.

He walked slowly through the rows of vegetables, feeling the cool, damp soil between his toes. The texture was familiar, comforting. He touched the leaves of his basil, inhaling their sharp, aromatic scent, a sensation that sent a wave of warmth through him. He ran his fingers gently over the velvety petals of his roses, their fragrant heads nodding in the slight breeze. It was a sensory symphony, a feast for his senses that surpassed any he'd experienced in the Andes. The simple act of touching the plants, feeling the earth, was a grounding experience, anchoring him to the familiar comfort of his home.

His gaze fell upon his small herb garden, a haven of aromatic plants tucked into a sunny corner. The rosemary, pungent and strong, thrived in its clay pot, its silvery-green leaves shimmering in the fading light. The thyme, with its delicate, almost lacy leaves, released its sweet fragrance with the slightest touch. And the mint, its leaves a crisp green, exuded a refreshing aroma. The herbs were a reminder of the simple pleasures in life – the comforting smells, the soothing textures, the sense of calm and tranquility they brought.

Moving further into the garden, he discovered a small patch of pumpkins nestled amongst the vines. They were round and orange, with deep grooves. He couldn't resist picking one, holding its weight in his hands, feeling its smooth, firm skin. The pumpkin was a symbol of harvest and abundance, a perfect representation of the fruits of his labor. The garden wasn't simply a collection of plants; it was an expression of his connection with nature, a reflection of his soul's quiet harmony.

He reached the back of the garden, where a small wooden bench sat beneath the shade of a sprawling oak tree. The tree had been here long before his cottage, its branches reaching skyward, a silent sentinel over his little haven. He sat down, letting out a long sigh of contentment. The gentle rustling of leaves, the chirping of crickets, the distant calls of birds – it was the soundtrack to his homecoming. He closed his eyes, letting the tranquility wash over him.

It wasn't just the physical act of returning that filled him with such profound contentment; it was the feeling of coming back to himself. The journey transformed him. It peeled away the routines and expectations he had followed, revealing a sense of self he had almost lost. He felt lighter, more grounded, and more appreciative of the simple things that life offered. The garden, his sanctuary, was a physical manifestation of that inner peace he had discovered.

He opened his eyes, the setting sun casting long shadows across the lawn. The light was soft, diffused. He could almost feel the warmth of the sun on his face, a gentle caress that seemed to embrace him with a quiet, benevolent energy. He felt a deep sense of gratitude for this space, this haven, this piece of earth that belonged to him.

As dusk settled, he finally made his way to his cottage. The door creaked open, a familiar sound that held a comforting resonance. Inside, the air was still and cool, the quiet hum of the refrigerator a welcoming sound. The warm glow of the lamps cast a soft light, illuminating the familiar walls, adorned with paintings from his travels. His books, his cherished companions, lined the shelves, each one a silent chronicle of past adventures and dreams yet to come. His home was more than just a place; it reflected everything he had seen, felt, and hoped for. It held his memories, his growth, and the quiet dreams he had carried with him. It was a sanctuary of comfort and calm, where he could truly be himself. He was home, and it felt deeply, unmistakably right. The journey had been long and filled with both challenges and rewards, but this feeling of return was the perfect conclusion. One chapter had ended, and another was just beginning.

Chapter 12:

Back in the Garden

The latch clicked, and Barnaby pushed open the cottage door, stepping into the cool, welcoming darkness. But before he could even fully register the familiar scent of woodsmoke and beeswax, a chorus of delighted shrieks erupted from the shadows. Tiny figures, barely taller than his thumbs, swarmed out from behind flowerpots and beneath sprawling leaves. They were the garden gnomes, his fellow inhabitants of this hidden world, their faces alight with joyous excitement.

Their leader, a stout gnome named Pipkin with a mischievous twinkle in his eye and a beard woven with wildflowers, rushed forward, his tiny arms outstretched. "Barnaby! You're back!" he cried, his voice surprisingly strong for such a small creature. He was followed by a gaggle of gnomes, each one as unique and individual as the flowers they tended. There was Willow, with her crown of woven ivy, and Thistle, whose clothes seemed to be perpetually dusted with pollen. Even Grumbles, the perpetually grumpy gnome who rarely spoke, cracked a smile, revealing a surprisingly charming set of crooked teeth.

Pipkin, ever the organizer, had already prepared a celebration. A tiny table, crafted from a discarded acorn cap, was laden with miniature delicacies. There were tiny berries, plump and juicy, arranged on moss-covered plates. Crumbs of a cake, baked from wild herbs and honey, were carefully placed beside a miniature pitcher of dandelion wine, its golden liquid shimmering under the glow of fireflies flitting amongst the flowers. It was a feast fit for the tiniest of kings.

"We missed you terribly, Barnaby," Willow chirped, her voice as delicate as a butterfly's wing. "The garden wasn't the same without you."

"The sunflowers drooped," Thistle added, "and even the roses refused to bloom as brightly."

Barnaby chuckled, his heart swelling with warmth. He'd never thought of his garden as anything other than a haven for himself, but the gnomes' words revealed a deeper truth. His garden was a community, a vibrant ecosystem where even the smallest creatures played a vital role. He had been a part of that community, and his absence had been felt.

The gnomes had spent their absence tending the garden with remarkable dedication. They had weeded, watered, and even engaged in elaborate conversations with the plants, urging them to thrive in his absence. They shared stories of their daily tasks, describing battles with slugs, the joy of watching a new flower blossom, and the challenges of coaxing reluctant seeds to germinate.

Grumbles, surprisingly, had taken on a leadership role during Barnaby's absence, organizing the gnome community with an unexpectedly efficient hand. He even confessed, in his gruff way, that he'd missed Barnaby's quiet presence and the way he hummed while tending to the herbs. His admission was met with a round of happy gasps from the other gnomes, a testament to Barnaby's quiet impact on their little community.

The feast was a whirlwind of laughter and tiny conversations. The gnomes shared stories of their adventures while Barnaby was away – a daring rescue of a trapped ladybug, a competition to see who could build the tallest mushroom house, and even a rather heated debate over the best method of attracting bumblebees. Each story was filled with the kind of childlike wonder and boundless energy that Barnaby had often forgotten existed in the adult world.

Their conversations painted a picture of a world buzzing with activity, a hidden realm where even the smallest creatures had a significant impact. It was a world filled with extraordinary details, the kind that most people missed in their hurried lives. The gnomes, in their own way, had kept the garden alive with their dedication, reminding Barnaby of the importance of appreciating the small things, of finding joy in the everyday miracles of nature.

As the moon rose, casting a silver glow over the garden, the celebrations began to wind down. The fireflies, tiny sparks of light, danced in the air, creating a magical atmosphere. The gnomes, tired but happy, began to disappear into their homes, nestled amongst the roots of plants and beneath the petals of flowers. Their goodbyes were a chorus of sleepy whispers and affectionate pats on Barnaby's hand.

Pipkin, before retiring for the night, presented Barnaby with a small gift – a miniature clay pot filled with freshly picked herbs, a symbol of gratitude and a reminder of the bond they shared. Barnaby held the pot in his palm, feeling its weight, the delicate fragrance of the herbs filling his senses. It was more than just a gift; it was a symbol of belonging, a warm welcome, a reaffirmation of his connection to this hidden world, a small piece of magic in an ordinary garden.

He looked around the garden, now bathed in moonlight, and felt a sense of peace. His journey had been long, his experiences transformative, but it was in this familiar setting, surrounded by his gnome companions, that he truly felt at home. His garden, once simply a place of retreat, had become something more. It was a sanctuary, a community, a reflection of his soul. And he, in turn, was a part of it all. The journey had come to an end, yet something equally meaningful was beginning. It was a time of new experiences, deeper connections, and the gentle joy of being exactly where he belonged.

The air was still, filled only with the gentle rustling of leaves and the soft chirping of crickets. The sounds were familiar and comforting, like an old, beloved song. Barnaby felt a profound sense of gratitude for this place, for the people – the gnomes, his unique, remarkable friends – and for the simple beauty of his garden. It was a feeling he knew would stay with him, long after the last firefly had blinked out for the night, a feeling that would nourish his soul and keep him grounded. The homecoming was complete. The garden was not just a space; it was a haven, a community, and a home. The journey to rediscover himself had led him, unexpectedly, back to the place where he had always belonged. The silence was filled with a quiet contentment, a gentle hum of happiness that vibrated through the very earth beneath his feet. This quiet joy, this sense of belonging, was a feeling that promised to blossom and grow, much like the wildflowers in his garden. The night was full of magic and the potential for many more beautiful adventures to come.

The next evening, Barnaby, settling comfortably onto a moss-cushioned log, pulled out a small, leather-bound album. The gnomes, their faces alight with curiosity, crowded around, their tiny bodies jostling excitedly. He carefully opened the album, revealing a series of photographs – tiny, meticulously crafted images capturing moments from his incredible journey.

The first photo showed him standing atop a towering mountain, the wind whipping through his hair, a vast expanse of snow-capped peaks stretching as far as the eye could see. The gnomes gasped, their tiny hands covering their mouths in awe. "Magnificent!" Pipkin exclaimed, his voice filled with wonder. "Did you climb all the way up there?"

Barnaby chuckled. "Indeed, I did, my friends. It was a long and challenging climb, but the view from the top was simply breathtaking." He pointed to a small, almost imperceptible figure in the distance, barely visible against the snow. "See that tiny speck? That's me, standing on the summit!"

The next photograph showed Barnaby navigating a dense jungle, vibrant green leaves forming a canopy overhead. Strange, exotic flowers bloomed in profusion, their colors vivid and unlike anything the gnomes had ever seen. "Are those...talking flowers?" Willow whispered, her eyes wide with fascination.

Barnaby smiled. "They were indeed very... expressive. Let's just say they had strong opinions on the best way to attract hummingbirds." He recounted a humorous anecdote about a particularly vocal orchid and its disdain for certain types of insects. The gnomes erupted in laughter, their tiny bodies shaking with mirth.

Another photograph depicted Barnaby sailing on a vast, shimmering ocean, his little boat bobbing gently on the waves. The sky was ablaze with the fiery colors of a spectacular sunset. "Did you see mermaids?" Thistle asked, her voice filled with hopeful anticipation.

Barnaby's eyes twinkled. "I'm afraid I didn't encounter any mermaids, but I did meet a colony of incredibly friendly dolphins! They escorted me for miles, showing me hidden coves and singing songs under the moonlight." He described the dolphins' playful antics, their sleek bodies gliding through the water with effortless grace. The gnomes listened, completely captivated, their imaginations soaring alongside Barnaby's tiny boat.

He showed them pictures of shimmering deserts, where the sand dunes stretched endlessly under a sky of brilliant stars. He described the quiet majesty of the desert nights, the silence broken only by the gentle whisper of the wind. He talked about the fascinating creatures he encountered – strange, nocturnal animals that only emerged under the cover of darkness. The gnomes were captivated by his tales of the desert, a landscape so foreign and yet so enchanting.

He showed pictures of bustling cities, with towering buildings that scraped the sky, their lights twinkling like a million fallen stars. He described the sights, sounds, and smells of the city, the constant movement and energy that never seemed to cease. He explained how he'd learned to navigate the busy streets, the intricate systems of transportation that moved people and goods with remarkable efficiency. The gnomes, accustomed to the quiet rhythm of the garden, were amazed by the human world's frenetic pace, yet also intrigued by its complexity.

As Barnaby showed photograph after photograph, the gnomes' awe and wonder grew. They learned about strange and wonderful creatures, incredible landscapes, and the diverse cultures of the human world. Barnaby, in turn, was reminded of the simple joys and profound beauty of his own little corner of the world, the garden he called home.

Each photo sparked a new story, a fresh anecdote, filled with humor, excitement, and a touch of the extraordinary. He described navigating treacherous mountain passes, the thrilling chase of a mischievous monkey through a bamboo forest, the astonishing sight of a thousand fireflies lighting up a dark cave, and the serene beauty of a hidden waterfall cascading into a crystal-clear pool. He shared moments of both triumph and challenge, detailing the difficulties he faced and the lessons he learned along the way.

Grumbles, surprisingly, was particularly engaged. He peppered Barnaby with questions about the practical aspects of his journey – the best way to pack a backpack, how to navigate unfamiliar terrain, and the most effective methods for avoiding dangerous animals. His questions, though delivered in his characteristic gruff manner, were a testament to his hidden admiration for Barnaby's resourcefulness and resilience.

Willow, ever the dreamer, was fascinated by the exotic plants and flowers Barnaby had encountered. She pestered him with questions about their scents, their colors, and their unique properties. Thistle, ever the pragmatist, wanted to know about the logistical challenges of traveling across such vast distances – the planning, the preparation, and the unexpected setbacks that invariably occurred.

As the evening deepened and the fireflies began their nightly dance, Barnaby's stories began to intertwine with the gnomes' own experiences, creating a rich tapestry of shared adventures and common ground. Pipkin recounted a daring rescue mission of a trapped field mouse, highlighting the resourcefulness and courage of the gnome community. Willow shared a tale of a particularly stubborn weed that had taken an entire week to finally remove, illustrating the challenges of maintaining the garden's delicate ecosystem. Thistle narrated a comical story about a misplaced acorn cup, which had resulted in a lively debate about the importance of accurate accounting in the gnome community. Grumbles, surprisingly, shared a sentimental story about a lost ladybug he had carefully helped find its way back to its colony. These interwoven narratives revealed a world teeming with life, where even the smallest of creatures played a significant role.

The moon, now high in the sky, cast a silvery glow upon the garden. The air was filled with the gentle rustling of leaves and the soft chirping of crickets. Barnaby, feeling a deep sense of contentment, carefully closed his album, the weight of his journey settling gently upon him. The evening's sharing of stories had not only entertained the gnomes but had also brought him closer to them, forging deeper bonds of friendship and strengthening his connection to the magical world he inhabited. The garden, once again, felt like home, a haven of peace and belonging, where the smallest of creatures and the most extraordinary of adventures came together in a perfect harmony. The echoes of their shared stories, the memories of laughter and wonder, would linger, whispering promises of many more adventures to come.

The air, still warm, hummed with anticipation. A low murmur of excitement rippled through the gnome community as they gathered around a clearing bathed in the silvery light of the moon. This was no ordinary gathering. It was a feast, a grand celebration in Barnaby's honor, recognizing his incredible journey and safe return.

Pipkin, ever the organizer, had orchestrated the event with meticulous care. The clearing was adorned with glowing mushrooms, their caps pulsating with a soft, ethereal light, illuminating the scene like miniature lanterns. Tiny tables, crafted from polished acorns and dewdrops, were laden with an astonishing array of delicacies. There were miniature pies filled with wild berries, their crusts delicately woven from spun spider silk. There were cakes made from honeydew and pollen, their surfaces decorated with intricate patterns of candied flower petals. Tiny skewers of grilled grubs, seasoned with rare herbs found only in the deepest parts of the Whispering Woods, were arranged artfully on miniature plates of polished leaves. Even Grumbles, usually a creature of simple tastes, seemed impressed by the culinary extravagance.

Barnaby himself was amazed. He had seen bustling marketplaces and grand banquets during his travels, but nothing compared to the sheer artistry and charm of this gnome feast. Each dish was a tiny masterpiece, an ode to the gnomes' creativity and their deep appreciation for the bounty of the garden.

Willow, her face beaming with pride, presented Barnaby with a small, exquisitely crafted cake. It was a miniature replica of the towering mountain he had climbed, its snowy peak dusted with powdered sugar. "This is for you, Barnaby," she chirped, her voice filled with warmth. "A small token of our gratitude for sharing your amazing adventures."

Thistle, ever the practical one, presented him with a meticulously crafted pouch, filled with tiny, dried herbs and spices. "These are rare ingredients," she explained, her voice carrying a hint of professional pride. "You might find them useful for future expeditions."

Grumbles, surprisingly, offered Barnaby a rather large, somewhat lopsided mushroom. "This is a…" he paused, struggling to find the right words, "a particularly potent specimen. Good for… focus." He mumbled something about its ability to enhance one's concentration, though Barnaby suspected the mushroom's potency might stem from its slightly unusual appearance.

Pipkin, after a brief, highly formal speech expressing the community's gratitude, led the gnomes in a spirited song of welcome. Their voices, high-pitched and melodious, blended together in a beautiful harmony, filling the clearing with a joyous sound.

The feast itself was a symphony of delicious tastes and textures. Barnaby sampled the berry pies, their sweetness bursting on his tongue; the honeydew cakes, light and airy; the grilled grubs, surprisingly succulent. He even bravely tried a small piece of Grumbles's mushroom, discovering that while not exactly delicious, it did seem to sharpen his senses.

As the gnomes ate, they shared their own stories, interweaving their tales with Barnaby's adventures. They talked about the challenges of maintaining their meticulously organized garden, the joys of discovering new and exotic plants, and the importance of community in overcoming obstacles. Barnaby listened, captivated by their perspectives, realizing that even in a world so different from his own, the essence of life—the challenges, the joys, the bonds of friendship—remained the same.

Willow described a recent encounter with a mischievous band of squirrels who had attempted to steal their precious acorn stash. Thistle recounted the meticulous planning that went into the annual gnome harvest festival, a task requiring precision and coordination on an impressive scale. Even Grumbles contributed a surprisingly tender anecdote about a particularly grumpy caterpillar he'd befriended.

Barnaby, in turn, shared more details of his journey, describing the strange and wonderful creatures he'd encountered, the breathtaking landscapes he'd explored, and the lessons he'd learned along the way. He spoke of the kindness of strangers, the beauty of unexpected friendships, and the importance of perseverance in the face of adversity. He spoke of the vastness of the world and the enduring power of small acts of kindness.

As the night deepened, the moon climbed higher, casting long shadows across the clearing. The fireflies, their lights twinkling like a million tiny stars, joined the gnome's celebrations with their own enchanting spectacle. The air was filled with laughter, the aroma of delicious food, and the sounds of happy voices.

The feast continued late into the night. Barnaby, surrounded by his new friends, felt an overwhelming sense of belonging and gratitude. He had travelled far and wide, encountered wonders and challenges beyond imagination, but in the end, it was the simple joys of friendship and community that truly mattered. He had found a home, not just in the garden, in the hearts of these small, remarkable creatures.

As the last of the food disappeared, and the moon began to dip towards the horizon, a sense of peaceful contentment settled over the clearing. The gnomes, their tiny bodies weary but hearts full, began to prepare for sleep. Barnaby, feeling a deep connection to these extraordinary beings, helped them clear away the remnants of the feast, their laughter echoing softly in the quiet garden.

The memory of the celebratory feast would remain etched in Barnaby's mind, a reminder of the extraordinary things that can happen when unlikely friends gather to celebrate life's simple joys. The echoes of laughter and the shared stories would linger long after the last of the fireflies had faded into the dawn. It was a night of celebration, a night of gratitude, and a night that solidified Barnaby's bond with the gnome community, forever linking his adventures to the heart of the garden he now truly considered home. The journey had changed him, but returning to the garden, surrounded by the warmth of his newfound friends, made him realize that the greatest treasures were not found in distant lands but in the quiet, loving embrace of community. The simple act of sharing a meal, a story, a laugh, had proven far more valuable than any treasure he had discovered on his epic journey. And as he finally drifted off to sleep, Barnaby knew that this was just the beginning of many more adventures, both grand and small, to be shared with his beloved garden friends. The quiet hum of the night was punctuated only by the soft chirping of crickets and the gentle rustle of leaves, a lullaby that promised endless possibilities and the comfort of belonging.

The next morning dawned bright and clear, bathing the garden in gentle hues of gold and rose. Barnaby awoke to the sweet scent of honeysuckle. He stretched languidly, a feeling of deep contentment washing over him. Gone were the anxieties of his journey, the uncertainties of the unknown. He was home. Home, not just in the literal sense of his little cottage nestled amongst the towering sunflowers, but in the heart of this quirky community he had unexpectedly found.

He looked around his room. It was small, simple, but perfectly suited to him. The walls were adorned with pressed flowers, carefully arranged in intricate patterns. A tiny window looked out onto the garden, framing a picture-perfect view of the dew-kissed blooms. Sunlight streamed through the window, illuminating dust motes dancing in the air, creating a magical atmosphere. He felt a deep sense of peace, a quiet joy that settled deep within his soul.

He rose and donned his simple, earth-toned clothes, feeling the familiar comfort of the fabric against his skin. Stepping out onto the porch, he was greeted by the sight of Willow tending her prize-winning roses, her nimble fingers delicately pruning a particularly stubborn bloom. The gentle sounds of the garden enveloped him – the buzzing of bees, the rustling of leaves, the soft cooing of a dove perched on a nearby branch.

"Good morning, Barnaby!" Willow chirped, her voice bright and cheerful. "Sleep well?"

"Better than I have in months," Barnaby replied, his voice filled with genuine warmth. "It's good to be home."

Willow smiled, her eyes crinkling at the corners. "We're all so glad to have you back," she said, gesturing towards the garden. "There's a whole lot that's happened while you were gone. The squabbling between the bees and the bumblebees has finally been resolved, mostly thanks to Pipkin's clever diplomacy. And Thistle has successfully cultivated a new variety of glowing mushroom; it's spectacular!"

Barnaby spent the morning reacquainting himself with the rhythms of garden life. He helped Willow water the thirsty plants, his hands finding a comfortable familiarity in the task. He joined Thistle in her greenhouse, marveling at the extraordinary collection of rare plants she had cultivated. He even helped Pipkin with his meticulous organization of the gnome tool shed, marveling at the perfect alignment of each tiny trowel and watering can.

In the afternoon, he explored the garden's hidden corners, rediscovering familiar paths and delightful surprises. He found a patch of wild strawberries, their tiny fruits bursting with sweetness. He discovered a family of hedgehogs, their tiny snouts twitching inquisitively. He even found a small, forgotten clearing where sunlight dappled through the leaves, forming a peaceful, serene spot.

The afternoon sun cast long shadows across the garden as Barnaby sat by the bubbling brook, watching the water ripple and dance. He allowed himself to simply be, to appreciate the peace and quiet, the beauty of his surroundings. He had seen grand palaces and mountains during his travels, but none of them had offered the same comfort and solace as this humble, unassuming garden.

That evening, the gnomes gathered for a less formal, more intimate gathering. There was no grand feast, but a simple potluck of garden-fresh vegetables and fruits. They sat around a crackling bonfire, sharing stories and laughter. Barnaby listened, captivated by their simple tales, the everyday joys and challenges of their lives.

He learned about the intricate dance of pollination and the unwavering resilience of the garden itself. He learned about the inner workings of their society, the way they worked together, supported each other, and celebrated life's small victories.

Grumbles, surprisingly, contributed several insightful comments about the subtle changes in the weather patterns and how those changes affected the growth of certain plants. It turned out that Grumbles' grumpiness was only a facade, masking a deep love and understanding of the natural world. Barnaby felt a warmth spread through him, a deep sense of belonging. He realized that he had found more than just a home; he had found a family.

Days turned into weeks, and weeks into months. Barnaby settled into a comfortable routine, finding joy in the simple pleasures of life. He helped the gnomes tend their garden, sharing his knowledge and skills with them. They, in turn, taught him about the delicate balance of nature, the fragile relationships between plants and animals, and the importance of community. He learned to identify different herbs and spices, to weave baskets from willow branches, and to recognize the songs of the birds. He was part of the natural pulse of the garden, an integral part of the community, a cherished member.

He continued to share stories of his travels, but now his tales were interwoven with the everyday occurrences of the garden. The stories served not just as entertainment but as valuable lessons, teaching everyone the importance of courage, kindness, and the enduring power of friendship. He'd even started recording his adventures in a beautifully illustrated journal, filled with detailed sketches and whimsical descriptions, which was eagerly passed from gnome to gnome.

His little cottage became a gathering place for the gnomes, a place where they could share stories, discuss plans, and simply enjoy each other's company. The garden stood as a symbol of their shared life, a mirror of their resilient community and their capacity to adapt, grow, and thrive together.

The days passed softly, woven with simple pleasures and peaceful satisfaction. The bustling city, with its clamorous streets and hurried pace, felt a lifetime away. Here, in the heart of the garden, time seemed to slow, to stretch and unwind like a lazy cat basking in the sun. He found pleasure in the most mundane tasks – the soothing rhythm of planting seeds, the satisfying crunch of fallen leaves underfoot, the earthy scent of freshly tilled soil. Even the seemingly endless chore of watering the multitude of plants became a meditative practice, a connection to the vibrant pulse of life within the garden.

He learned the names of each flower, each herb, each vegetable, and discovered their unique personalities, their individual needs and preferences. He marveled at the graceful dance of the pollinators – the busy bees, the lumbering bumblebees, the flitting butterflies – each playing a vital role in the garden's flourishing ecosystem. He spent hours observing the tiny creatures that inhabited the garden – the industrious ants, the scurrying spiders, the darting lizards – each demonstrated that even the smallest space could hold a universe of life, connection, and meaning.

He discovered a hidden talent for pruning, his hands guided by an instinct he hadn't known he possessed. He learned to identify the signs of disease and blight, and to apply remedies with a gentle touch. His knowledge, gained from his travels, was surprisingly well-suited to the needs of the garden, offering new perspectives and solutions to challenges the gnomes had been facing for years. He taught them about sustainable practices, about crop rotation and companion planting, helping them to maximize their yields while minimizing their environmental impact.

He shared his stories of distant lands, but his tales were now interwoven with the familiar sights and sounds of the garden. He described the towering mountains, the vast oceans, and the exotic creatures he had encountered, but always brought his narrative back to the comforting reality of his home, highlighting the unique beauty and value of his present surroundings. The gnomes listened intently, their faces alight with wonder and appreciation, their hearts filled with a quiet gratitude for the simple gifts of their own community.

He discovered that his travels hadn't taken him *away* from something precious, but had, in fact, brought him *back* to it. The experience had broadened his perspective, deepened his empathy, and allowed him to truly appreciate the treasures he already possessed. The grand palaces and bustling cities paled in comparison to the quiet beauty of his small cottage, the vibrant life of the garden, and the warmth of his unexpected family.

His relationship with the gnomes deepened with each passing day. He learned to appreciate their unique perspectives, their deep connection to the natural world, and their unwavering dedication to their community. He learned to understand their subtle communication, their unspoken language of gestures and glances, and their shared love for the garden they had created and nurtured together.

He even found himself enjoying Grumbles' company, discovering a surprisingly dry sense of humor beneath the grumpy exterior. He discovered that Grumbles, despite his gruff demeanor, possessed an encyclopedic knowledge of the garden, its history, and its inhabitants.

He learned to appreciate the rhythm of the seasons, the slow unfolding of the year, the cycle of growth and decay, and the continuous renewal of life. He watched as the summer blooms gave way to the rich hues of autumn, and then to the quiet slumber of winter. He observed the subtle changes in the garden, the ways in which it adapted and responded to the changing weather patterns. He found a profound sense of peace in witnessing the natural world's unyielding resilience and adaptability.

One evening, as he sat by the bubbling brook, a sense of gratitude washed over him. He felt an overwhelming appreciation for the simple things in life – the warmth of the sun on his skin, the cool water flowing over his hands, the sweet scent of honeysuckle in the air. He realized that true wealth wasn't measured in gold or jewels, but in the richness of relationships, the beauty of nature, and the simple joys of everyday life. The contentment he felt was deep, a quiet joy that settled within his soul.

He began to spend more time documenting the garden, keeping a detailed journal filled with sketches, observations, and stories. He carefully recorded the flowering cycles of each plant, the migratory patterns of the birds, and the life cycles of the insects. He learned to identify the different types of mushrooms, the various species of birds, and the unique personalities of each gnome.

He started sketching the gnomes themselves, capturing their individual quirks and personalities in his drawings. Pipkin, with his ever-present magnifying glass and his neatly organized tool shed. Willow, with her radiant smile and her gentle touch with the roses. Thistle, with her wild hair and her deep passion for rare plants. And even Grumbles, whose gruff exterior hid a warm heart and a surprising wealth of knowledge.

His journal became a treasured possession, each gnome contributing their own observations and adding their own personal touches. It became a living document, a chronicle of the garden's life, its growth, its challenges, and its triumphs. It underscored the importance of collaboration, and the power of friendship.

One crisp autumn evening, Barnaby sat with the gnomes around the bonfire. He felt a deep sense of belonging, a deep gratitude for the unexpected journey that had led him home.

Chapter 13:

The Mystery Unravels

The bonfire snapped and sparked, casting flickering light over the circle of gnomes, their faces alight with interest as Barnaby continued his story. He described the opulent mansion, its towering facade gleaming under the moonlight, and the strange contraptions scattered throughout the vast, labyrinthine halls. He recounted the bewildering series of events – the unexpected capture, the elaborate disguises, the seemingly endless corridors, and the peculiar obsession with cameras.

He spoke of the meals, surprisingly delicious and served with an almost theatrical flair, the hushed conversations he overheard, snippets of information that hinted at a grand, elaborate plan. He painted vivid pictures of the individuals who held him captive, their eccentric personalities shining through their unusual behavior. He described the meticulous care they took in setting up their elaborate shots, their obsessive attention to detail, and their almost maniacal dedication to capturing the perfect image. They weren't cruel; they were simply… different.

He described the leader, a woman with a shock of purple hair and eyes that sparkled with an infectious energy. She moved with a captivating grace, her every gesture precise and deliberate. He described her passion for photography, her encyclopedic knowledge of cameras, and her unwavering commitment to her art. He described her assistants, a colorful cast of characters with unique talents and quirky habits – a man who could build incredible sets from the most unlikely materials, a woman who could craft costumes out of anything and everything, and a silent, enigmatic figure who handled all the technical aspects with an almost supernatural efficiency.

He spoke of the elaborate sets they constructed, transforming rooms into fantastical landscapes, creating breathtaking illusions that blurred the lines between reality and fantasy. He described their intricate planning, their meticulous preparation, and their tireless efforts to capture the perfect shot. He spoke of the hours spent waiting, posing, and performing, each moment carefully orchestrated, each expression painstakingly crafted. It was a world of exquisite detail, where every element was considered, every detail carefully planned.

"And then," Barnaby said, his voice dropping to a whisper, "it all came together." He described the final scene, the culmination of their efforts, the moment when everything fell into place. He explained how they had captured him, not out of malice, but as the final, unexpected element in their masterpiece. They hadn't intended to keep him long; their grand plan was to create a truly memorable adventure, a unique experience that would later be revealed through their magnificent photography.

He described the climactic moment when the truth was revealed. The leader, with a triumphant flourish, unveiled the photographic prints. The images were breathtaking, capturing not just the events themselves, but also the emotions, the tension, and the humor of the adventure. The photographs depicted Barnaby's reactions, his expressions ranging from confusion and apprehension to amusement and eventual acceptance. The entire sequence was a story in pictures, a visual narrative of Barnaby's unexpected journey.

He described the leader's explanation, her fervent passion for capturing the essence of a moment, and her ability to transform ordinary events into extraordinary narratives. He learned that their chosen subject wasn't just a random person; they were incredibly selective. They had been observing him for months, studying his personality, his reactions, his potential to react in unexpected and visually stunning ways. He was the perfect, unknowing participant in their elaborate artistic endeavor.

Barnaby realized the intricate choreography of his capture. Every detail, from the initial encounter to the seemingly endless corridors, had been thoroughly planned, each element serving a specific purpose in their grand photographic narrative. The mysterious disguises, the elaborate sets, the seemingly endless twists and turns – it had all been part of the larger artwork they were creating.

The gnomes listened, captivated by the tale. Their initial concern gave way to astonishment, then to laughter. They could not believe the intricacy of the plot, the sheer audacity of the plan, the unique perspective of these eccentric photographers. They imagined the photographs, visualizing the grand narrative that Barnaby had unknowingly played a part in.

"So," Barnaby concluded, "I wasn't kidnapped. I was...a muse. A living, breathing element in a photographic epic." He chuckled, shaking his head in disbelief. "I've become a work of art!"

A wave of laughter rippled through the assembled gnomes. Thistle, usually so serious, giggled uncontrollably, clutching her side. Pipkin, ever practical, adjusted his spectacles, his mind clearly processing the intricate details of the story. Even Grumbles cracked a smile, a rare and precious event.

"Imagine the artistry!" exclaimed Willow, her eyes wide with wonder. "To capture such a story in a photograph! It must be magnificent."

"Indeed," added Pipkin, "a true masterpiece of photographic storytelling."

They exchanged delighted glances, their imaginations running wild with the possibilities of this new perspective. They were not just witnessing the conclusion of Barnaby's adventure; they were witnessing the beginning of a new understanding, a new appreciation for the unexpected beauty and intricacy of the world around them.

Barnaby, watching the gnomes, felt a deep sense of contentment. He had not only survived his unexpected journey, but he had learned a valuable lesson about perspective, about art, about the unexpected beauty that could be found in the most unusual of circumstances. He had been a participant in a unique work of art, and although it had started unexpectedly, it had ultimately enriched his life in ways he could never have imagined.

He continued to share details of the final reveal, the photographers' genuine enthusiasm, and their heartfelt apologies for the unexpected nature of their artistic project. They'd explained that they valued their art above all else, but that they'd never intended to cause any genuine harm or distress. Barnaby, upon reflection, realized that while the situation had been unorthodox, there was no malice behind it. Their passion for their art was undeniable.

The gnomes peppered him with questions. They wanted to know about the cameras used, the lighting techniques employed, and the meticulous detail that went into creating such a stunning visual narrative. Barnaby, happy to oblige, described the equipment in detail, the antique cameras, the specialized lenses, and the advanced lighting systems that created such dramatic effects. He explained how the photographers manipulated light and shadow to create mood and atmosphere, turning ordinary rooms into breathtaking landscapes.

He detailed the behind-the-scenes preparation, the hours of planning and execution that went into capturing each image. He described the photographers' creative vision, their ability to see beauty and meaning where others saw only the mundane. He spoke of their meticulous attention to detail, their commitment to their art, and their unwavering belief in their creative vision. He conveyed their infectious passion, their dedication, and their surprisingly kind and gentle nature behind the initially alarming facade.

He realized that the "kidnapping" was, in essence, a diligently planned piece of performance art. It was an immersive experience designed to capture authentic emotional responses, not an act of malevolence. Barnaby had been the central character in a living, breathing artwork, a carefully orchestrated performance that culminated in a stunning collection of photographs. He described the final unveiling of the pictures, the photographers' proud display of their masterpiece, and his own astonishment at the result.

While he spoke, the sky shifted, sunset pouring bold hues across the clouds. Yet the gnomes, fully absorbed in Barnaby's story, barely noticed the approaching night. They were captivated by the unexpected narrative, the tale of a journey that had turned into a unique artistic collaboration. It was a story that transcended the simple narrative of a kidnapping, becoming a profound meditation on art, creativity, and the unexpected beauty that could be found in the most unusual of circumstances. The tale of Barnaby's adventure would become a legendary story within the gnome community, a celebration of the unique artistry of the eccentric photographers who had turned his journey into a work of art. The story served as a reminder that life, like art, is full of surprises.

The firelight danced in the eyes of the assembled gnomes, their faces illuminated by the flames and the lingering glow of Barnaby's incredible story. A hush fell over the group as a chorus of tiny wings beat the air, a shimmering cloud of spirits descending upon them. These were no ordinary spirits; these were the spirits who had orchestrated Barnaby's entire adventure.

Their leader, a spirit no bigger than Barnaby's thumb, with wings the color of amethyst and hair like spun moonlight, floated gracefully towards the gnomes. "Greetings, friends," she chirped, her voice surprisingly strong for such a tiny creature. "We overheard your captivating tale and felt compelled to offer our own perspective."

The gnomes exchanged bewildered glances. Spirits were rarely seen, let alone involved in such human-sized affairs. Their involvement only deepened the already incredible mystery. Barnaby, himself, felt a prickle of excitement. This was a whole new layer to the already astonishing narrative.

"You see," the spirit leader continued, her voice a tinkling melody, "Barnaby's journey was not simply a random occurrence. It was, shall we say, a deliberately planned… experience." She paused for dramatic effect, her tiny body shimmering with an ethereal glow. The other spirits buzzed excitedly around her, their tiny forms a whirlwind of iridescent colors.

"We, the spirits of Whispering Glade," she announced, "have been observing Barnaby for some time. We admire his adventurous spirit, his unwavering kindness, and his remarkable capacity for surprise. He possesses a certain…

Je ne sais quoi… a quality that makes him perfectly suited for our… artistic endeavor."

A collective gasp escaped the gnomes. Artistic endeavor? The spirits' words hung in the air, heavy with implication.

"You must understand," explained another spirit, a tiny creature with emerald wings and a mischievous twinkle in its eye, "We spirits are not merely creatures of whimsy and delight. We are also artists of the unseen, the orchestrators of magical narratives. We weave stories into the fabric of reality, creating experiences that are both wondrous and enlightening."

"Barnaby's journey," the leader interjected, "was one such narrative. We chose not to harm him, but to inspire him. To challenge his perception of reality, to broaden his understanding of the world, and to help him appreciate the beauty and wonder that lies beyond the ordinary."

"But how?" Pipkin, ever the pragmatist, squeaked, adjusting his spectacles. "How did you manage to move him from place to place without him noticing? How did you create those illusions, those seemingly impossible situations?"

"Magic, of course," chirped the emerald-winged spirit with a giggle. "But not just any magic. We used a blend of illusions, enchantments, and a touch of… well, let's just call it 'creative transportation'."

The spirits then proceeded to explain their intricate plan, their voices weaving together in a delightful symphony of explanation. They described how they used subtle enchantments to guide Barnaby's steps, subtly influencing his decisions without him ever realizing their influence. They revealed how they created illusions, shimmering mirages and temporary enchantments to transform ordinary locations into breathtaking and fantastical landscapes. They showed how they used clever disguises and subtle manipulations of time and space to seamlessly move him between locations, making his journey appear both seamless and bewildering.

One spirit, with sapphire wings, described how they had enchanted the mansion's inhabitants, turning them into unwitting participants in their grand performance. The eccentric photographers, the strange contraptions, the endless corridors – all meticulously crafted to contribute to the larger narrative. The spirits even explained that the delicious meals were magically enhanced, each bite designed to delight and intrigue Barnaby's senses, keeping him energized and curious throughout his journey.

Another spirit, whose wings were the color of a sunset, explained how they had anticipated every potential obstacle, every conceivable reaction from Barnaby, preparing for every eventuality with extensive detail and magical foresight. Their enchantments were designed not to control him, but to guide and protect him, ensuring his safety and comfort throughout his extraordinary adventure.

Each detail, from the initial encounter to the final unveiling, had been carefully considered, each element serving a specific purpose in their artistic creation.

The spirits recounted how they had subtly manipulated events to create moments of humor, tension, and surprise, all designed to enhance the visual narrative captured by the photographers. They hadn't just captured images; they had captured emotions, turning a seemingly random series of events into a compelling and emotionally resonant visual story.

"We wanted Barnaby to experience something truly extraordinary," the leader explained, her voice filled with a passion that transcended her tiny size. "An experience that would challenge his perceptions, broaden his horizons, and leave an indelible mark on his soul."

A delicate thread of magic, memory, and gifted vision connected them in that moment. The gnomes, captivated by the sheer audacity of the plan, sat in stunned silence, absorbing the magnitude of the spirits' creative endeavor. Barnaby, who had once been hesitant, now felt nothing but awe. He realized he had taken part in something both rare and extraordinary. What he had first believed to be a kidnapping was, in truth, a meaningful journey, a tribute to creativity and art. It was a masterpiece coming to life. And he, unknowingly, had been the central figure. The realization filled him with wonder and gratitude that overwhelmed him. It was a night he would never forget. A night where an ordinary gnome learned that life, like art, could be extraordinary.

The amethyst-winged spirit, whose name Barnaby learned was Lumina, continued, her voice a delicate chime. "You see, Barnaby," she explained, "we spirits of Whispering Glade possess a peculiar fascination with… well, with journeys. Not just any journeys, mind you, but those filled with unexpected twists, surprising turns, and moments of pure, unadulterated wonder."

Barnaby, still reeling from the revelation that his entire ordeal had been an orchestrated artistic endeavor, found himself nodding slowly. The idea that his haphazard adventure was someone's carefully crafted masterpiece seemed absurd, yet the spirits' evident sincerity and detail of their explanation left him without much room for doubt.

"We are, at heart, chroniclers of adventure," Lumina said, a playful glint in her eye. "But not with quill and parchment. Oh no, our medium is far more… visual. We capture the essence of a journey, not through written words, but through the magic of photography."

She gestured towards a shimmering orb that materialized in the air, its surface swirling with iridescent colors. The orb pulsed gently, revealing a breathtaking panorama of landscapes – from snow-capped mountains to sun-drenched beaches, from enchanted forests to bustling cityscapes. The images shifted and changed, each one capturing a different facet of Barnaby's journey.

"These are not ordinary photographs," Lumina explained, her voice filled with pride. "Each image is imbued with a fragment of the journey's magic, capturing not just what Barnaby saw, but how he felt, what he experienced, and the unique essence of each moment."

The spirit whose wings resembled the colors of a sunset, floated closer. "We followed you, Barnaby," she chirped, her voice soft and melodious. "We witnessed your courage, and your remarkable ability to adapt to the most unexpected of circumstances. You navigated treacherous landscapes, encountered bizarre characters, and solved riddles that would baffle even the wisest of gnomes."

"Each photograph captures a key moment, a significant turning point in your adventure," Lumina added. "Beginning with the eccentric photographers you met, continuing through your bold mansion escape, then the curious encounter with the singing flowers, and ending with your celebrated return to the village – each frame tells a piece of the story."

Barnaby looked at the images again, this time seeing them with entirely new eyes. He recognized the snow-covered mountain where he'd encountered the snow leopards, the towering tree where he'd rested after his harrowing escape from the mansion, and the flower meadow where he'd discovered the mysterious singing plants.

"But… why me?" Barnaby finally found his voice, his words tinged with wonder and a touch of confusion. "Why did you choose me for this… this photographic masterpiece?"

"We chose you, Barnaby," Lumina answered with a warm smile, "because you possess something very rare: an insatiable curiosity, an unwavering spirit of adventure, and a heart filled with boundless kindness. You are, in our humble opinion, the perfect subject for a truly extraordinary photographic narrative."

They showed Barnaby how they had cleverly disguised themselves among the eccentric photographers, manipulating the events surrounding him without him even suspecting their presence. They explained how they had created those unusual photographic props – the oversized teacups, the giant magnifying glasses, the colossal pencils. They were all integral parts of their composition. Every detail, even the seemingly random encounters, was deliberately designed to add to their photographic story.

There was something deeply compelling about the spirit's passion. The way they spoke, so precise, so enthusiastic, so full of care, left Barnaby with a quiet sense of wonder. He saw it now. His journey hadn't been accidental. It had been crafted with intention, a reflection of the spirit's talent and imagination.

"And the photographs?" Willow asked, her voice filled with wonder. "What will become of them? Will they be displayed somewhere? Will they become a part of your collection?"

Lumina smiled, a playful gleam in her eyes "Oh, the photographs will have a life of their own," she said. "They will travel, flitting from place to place, viewed by others who will be as captivated by their beauty as we are. They will travel far and wide, becoming a kind of magical legend that will inspire others to embrace the spirit of adventure and discovery."

"They will remind people that sometimes, the most magical journeys are not the ones we plan, but the ones that find us."

Barnaby sat in quiet reflection, absorbing the weight of their explanation. He looked again at the shimmering orb, each photograph a vivid echo of his unexpected journey. He had been part of something extraordinary, a creation that went beyond mere adventure. It was a work of art born from imagination and shared vision. What he had experienced was not just travel but the magic of collaboration, bound together by a shared passion for discovery and carried forward by the smallest, most whimsical of beings.

The spirits, sensing the gnome's awe, continued sharing snippets of their travel experiences. They spoke of their adventures through clouds, where they learned the secrets of rainbow formation, their explorations of hidden waterfalls in enchanted forests where cheeky pixies guarded ancient secrets, and their travels on the backs of giant butterflies through fields of shimmering blossoms. Each story was more captivating than the last, revealing the spirits' deep connection to their world and their insatiable curiosity.

Barnaby, enchanted by their tales, found himself sharing his own experiences of travel. He recounted his visits to nearby villages, his expeditions into the nearby forest, and his explorations of the winding river that ran close to his village. He spoke of his joy at discovering new plants, animals, and landscapes, mirroring the spirits' passion for discovery.

As the night deepened and the fire began to dwindle, a sense of camaraderie grew between Barnaby and the spirits. They shared a mutual appreciation for the wonder and beauty of the world around them.

Barnaby realized that his journey wasn't just a series of strange events, but a unique experience that fostered an unexpected friendship. The spirits, fellow travelers, fellow adventurers, and fellow artists, sharing a common passion for the journey itself and the art of capturing its magic. He knew this was a friendship he would cherish forever, a friendship born from a shared love of travel and discovery. The amethyst-winged spirit, Lumina, smiled, her eyes twinkling like distant stars. "Your journey, Barnaby," she began, her voice a gentle whisper carried on the evening breeze, "wasn't random at all. It was… curated. A carefully crafted experience, designed to reveal to you the boundless wonders of the world, and perhaps, even more importantly, the boundless wonders within yourself."

"We are, as I mentioned, chroniclers of adventure, but our methods are… unconventional."

"You see," Lumina continued, "we observed you, Barnaby. We saw your curiosity, your willingness to embrace the unknown, your inherent kindness. These qualities, we felt, made you the perfect subject for our next photographic narrative."

Barnaby thought back to the seemingly insignificant moments of his journey – the kindness he'd shown to the grumpy old badger, the help he'd offered the lost rabbit, the empathy he'd felt for the lonely singing flowers. He'd simply acted on instinct, never imagining these actions would be part of a larger, more profound design.

As the night wore on, Barnaby realized the spirits were not just skilled photographers; they were gifted storytellers, weaving their tales with a natural charm and captivating imagery. He found himself sharing his own stories of adventure – the time he'd climbed the tallest tree in his village, his exploration of the winding river that ran through his town, and his encounters with the diverse wildlife of his community.

He learned about their rigorous selection process for their "subjects." They weren't just looking for adventurous souls; they sought individuals with kindness, empathy, and a profound respect for the natural world. Barnaby, they explained, possessed all these qualities in abundance. His journey hadn't been a test, but a celebration of these very attributes.

They revealed that their photographic narratives were more than just beautiful pictures; they were designed to inspire others. Each photograph captured not only the visual aspects of a moment but also the emotions, the experiences, and the unique essence of the adventure. These photographs, they explained, would travel the world, shared through whispered legends and word-of-mouth, inspiring others to embrace the spirit of adventure and to appreciate the magic hidden in the ordinary.

As dawn broke, Barnaby felt grateful. What started in fear became something remarkable, an experience unlike any other. He discovered the wonders around him and within himself, understanding the quiet strength of kindness, the power of empathy, and the joy of friendship born in a strange, beautiful adventure.

He had spent the night listening to the spirits' enchanting tales, stories that danced between reality and fantasy, blurring the lines between what was possible and what was merely imagined. He'd heard of their thrilling escapades – a daring rescue of a baby griffin from a storm-tossed mountain peak, a secret mission to retrieve a stolen moonbeam from a grumpy goblin king, and a thrilling chase across a field of giant sunflowers with a mischievous troupe of giggling pixies. Each story was more fantastical than the last, each more captivating than the one before.

But it wasn't just the stories that connected Barnaby to these tiny beings. It was their love of adventure, kindness, and zest for life that created a bond as if it had always been there. Their connection went beyond appearances, size, or magic they lacked. What truly united them was shared wonder and curiosity in their hearts.

The spirits entrusted him with a small bag– a gift, they insisted, filled with miniature acorns, shimmering pebbles, and a feather from a phoenix (a particularly impressive feather, Lumina assured him, mentioning that it glowed faintly in the sunlight), a surge of contentment washed over him.

"We'll miss you, Barnaby," Lumina said, her voice soft but filled with genuine warmth. "Your spirit of adventure has brightened the glade."

Iris, ever the practical one, added, "And your photographs will be legendary! We'll send them to you, of course. And maybe… just maybe… we could collaborate on a future project?"

"I'd love that," he replied, his voice brimming with enthusiasm. "I've learned so much from you. Your creativity, your dedication to your art… it's inspiring." He thought of the intricate miniature sets they'd created, the skillful manipulation of light and shadow, and the delicate costumes they'd fashioned for their subjects. He realized he had witnessed a mastery of art that was both breathtaking and humbling.

They exchanged promises to stay in touch, creating a unique system of communication that involved leaving messages inside hollowed-out acorns carried on the wind. Barnaby, feeling both a heavy heart and a light spirit, said his farewells. As he turned for one last look, he took in their small faces and bright eyes, and noticed how the glade seemed to hum with life around them. He wished to say something grand, something poetic, but all that came was a quiet "Thank you."

The spirits gave a knowing nod. That was all that mattered.

Barnaby's tale spread like wildfire throughout the village, transforming from a fanciful adventure into a local legend. People began to notice the beauty in the ordinary, appreciating the subtle magic in the world around them. Children, inspired by his tale, began to look at the world with fresh eyes, seeking adventure in the most unlikely of places. They embarked on their own miniature explorations, creating their own stories and adventures in the backyard, the nearby woods, and even in their own homes.

The impact of Barnaby's adventure extended far beyond his immediate circle. His story traveled, carried on the wind, reaching other villages, towns, and even cities. It sparked a wave of creativity and imagination, inspiring people to embrace their own unique adventures and to seek wonder in the unexpected. Artists, writers, and musicians were inspired to create works celebrating the magic of nature, the power of friendship, and the joy of embracing the unexpected.

He continued to correspond with the spirits, their messages carried on the wind, their shared laughter echoing across the expanse. He knew that their friendship was a unique and valuable gift, a bond created through an extraordinary adventure that would always influence his life. He never forgot the lesson he learned: that sometimes, the greatest discoveries are not found in faraway lands or exotic places, but in the heart of an unexpected friendship that transforms both the giver and the receiver.

Years later, Barnaby would recount his adventure, not as a fantastical tale to be doubted, but as a testament to the magic hidden in the ordinary and the importance of believing in the unexpected. His story would become a treasured legend, shared from one voice to another, a quiet reminder that even the most unusual beginnings can spark remarkable friendships, unforgettable adventures, and a sometimes awkward, yet profoundly human, insight into oneself and the world around us. He would go on to use his experiences to inspire others, encouraging them to embrace their inner child, to discover adventure in the mundane, and to value the extraordinary connections that enrich other people's lives. And every time he looked at the sky, particularly when the clouds assembled just so, he'd remember his friends, the spirits of Whispering Glade, always watching, always waiting for their next collaboration.

Their friendship, like the images captured in their magnificent photographs, vivid and clear, a testament to the power of friendship forged in the heart of an extraordinary, meticulously planned adventure.

The adventure itself had ended, but the journey of discovery, both within himself and within the world around him, had only just begun.

Appendix

This appendix contains a selection of Barnaby's photographs from his adventure in Whispering Glade. Unfortunately, due to the technical difficulties of reproducing miniature spirit photography, these images are represented here as descriptions. Imagine, if you will…

Image 1: A close-up of a sleeping baby griffin nestled amongst giant puffballs, illuminated by the soft glow of fireflies.

Image 2: A panoramic view of the goblin king's castle, its turrets shimmering under a stolen moonbeam, surrounded by a swirling vortex of mischievous pixies.

Image 3: A captivating portrait of Lumina, perched atop a giant sunflower, her eyes twinkling with mischief and starlight.

Image 4: A dramatic action shot of Iris rescuing a lost firefly from a spider's web, her tiny hands moving with amazing dexterity.

Further photographic adventures with the spirits of Whispering Glade are anticipated and will, hopefully, appear in future volumes.

Spirits: Tiny, winged creatures inhabiting Whispering Glade, known for their artistic talents and adventurous spirits.

Whispering Glade: A magical meadow where spirits reside, teeming with fantastical flora and fauna.

Lumina: A particularly creative and enthusiastic spirit, known for her photographic skills.

Iris: A practical and resourceful spirit, always ready for an adventure.

Goblin King: A grumpy, yet ultimately fair, ruler of the nearby goblin kingdom, with a penchant for collecting moonbeams.

www.ingramcontent.com/pod-product-compliance
Lightning Source LLC
Chambersburg PA
CBHW072104300726
48975CB00003B/701